Y0-CCS-537

Previously published Worldwide Mystery titles by
L. C. HAYDEN

WHY CASEY HAD TO DIE
WHEN DEATH INTERVENES

WHEN THE PAST
HAUNTS YOU

L. C. HAYDEN

WORLDWIDE®

TORONTO • NEW YORK • LONDON
AMSTERDAM • PARIS • SYDNEY • HAMBURG
STOCKHOLM • ATHENS • TOKYO • MILAN
MADRID • WARSAW • BUDAPEST • AUCKLAND

If you purchased this book without a cover you should be aware that this book is stolen property. It was reported as "unsold and destroyed" to the publisher, and neither the author nor the publisher has received any payment for this "stripped book."

One of life's greatest pleasures
comes from building memories with true friends.
Thank you for the wonderful times we've shared.
To
Bobbye and Howard Johnson
With Love
and to the memory of
Mike Hoover
January 24, 1947–May 23, 2010

Recycling programs
for this product may
not exist in your area.

WHEN THE PAST HAUNTS YOU

A Worldwide Mystery/August 2014

First published by CreateSpace.

ISBN-13: 978-0-373-26908-2

Copyright © 2012 by L. C. Hayden

All rights reserved. No part of this book may be reproduced or transmitted in any form or by any means, electronic or mechanical, including photocopying, recording or by any information storage and retrieval system, without permission in writing from the publisher. For information please contact the author.

This is a work of fiction. Names, characters, places and incidents are either the product of the author's imagination or are used fictitiously, and any resemblance to actual persons, living or dead, business establishments, events or locales is entirely coincidental.

® and TM are trademarks of Harlequin Enterprises Limited. Trademarks indicated with ® are registered in the United States Patent and Trademark Office, the Canadian Intellectual Property Office and in other countries.

Printed in U.S.A.

Acknowledgments

A group of dedicated, hardworking folks exist behind every book. Thanks to everyone who had something to do with the production of this book. Also, a special thanks to Joe and Linda Randig, who answered my questions about Pennsylvania and who took it on their own to provide me with a lot of the information and pictures I needed about the state.

Lots of kudos goes to the people who honored me by allowing me to use their names. Joe Randig, Ellen Biebesheimer, Mike Hoover and Carol Babel: I salute you and thank you from the bottom of my heart.

Other folks who are behind the scenes include the manuscript's first readers. I am very thankful to all those of you who read, critiqued and edited the manuscript. The book is so much better because of you.

Last, but not least, a million thanks goes to all my readers. Without you, I wouldn't have a reason to write. I appreciate your support and loyalty. I couldn't make it without you—and so to you, this book is also dedicated.

Drop by my website at www.lchayden.com. Book club readers, for your convenience, I've placed a group of questions there that you can use to discuss *When the Past Haunts You.* Sign up at my website to receive my newsletter and friend me on Facebook. Look for L.C. Hayden.

As always, a very special thanks to my husband, Richard Hayden, who supports me by driving me everywhere, creating and maintaining my website, and always being there for me. Thank you, hon, for being you.

ONE

CAROL BRONSON SAT ramrod straight on the sofa waiting for her husband. Soon as he opened the front door to their motor home, she stood, her eyes, tiny slits on her face.

Under normal circumstances, at this point, Carol would place her left hand on her hip, wiggle her extended right hand index finger, and scold him. But not today.

That, more than anything, forced a gasp to escape from Harry Bronson's mouth. He took a small step forward. "Carol, sweetheart, what…"

"Have we ever kept any secrets from each other?"

A frown formed on Bronson's forehead. "No, of course—"

"Think before you answer."

When he worked for the Dallas Police Department, before he'd been forced to retire, he worked cases that placed him in mortal danger. He'd tell Carol not to worry, all was well. A small, white lie he knew she didn't swallow.

Since then, almost two years later, he hadn't kept anything from her. Unless… He reached in his pocket and felt the cell. Still there.

"I'm waiting," Carol said. "Is there anything you want to tell me?"

Bronson crossed his arms. "No."

"Then I'll start. Your sister called."

Carol spoke in a calm voice, but as far as Bronson was concerned, she might as well have shouted. He took a deep breath. "I don't have a sister." He swept past Carol, heading toward the bedroom. That was the main problem about traveling in a motor home. No space for privacy.

"Harry Bronson, you get back here."

Bronson stopped but didn't turn around.

"We've been married thirty-one years and in all that time, you never mentioned a sister."

Bronson felt her arms wrap around him. He wanted to turn around, face her, tell her the ugly truth, but he couldn't bring himself to do it.

"Why didn't you tell me about her?" She rested her forehead on the middle of his broad back.

Bronson squirmed, forcing Carol to release him. He turned to face her. "Last thing she told me was that she wanted nothin' to do with me or Mom or Dad. She made that decision, she should stick to it." He headed toward the door leading outside. "Now, if you'll excuse me, I'd like some time alone." He gently opened the door and let himself out.

THE SUN BEGAN to set, blanketing the South Dakota woods with a rich, warm glow. Bronson sat outside his camper, staring at the sunset. He could hear the laughter of children coming from the neighboring camp spots. Somewhere in the distance, a bird chirped and an airplane roared by.

The sun descended behind the mountain and the wind blew, bringing a cool breeze that penetrated his light jacket. Still he sat, unmoving, like a statue. Slowly, one by one, the lights in the neighborhood campgrounds dimmed and faded. Quiet time had arrived.

Bronson could no longer see the trees as darkness concealed them. He thought he detected some movement to his right. A deer, perhaps. Carol would love to watch the animal. He made no attempt to call her. He sighed when he saw the light in their bedroom go off.

He waited ten minutes. Half-an-hour. An hour. When

the chill penetrated his bones, he finally stood and headed inside. Carol had gone to bed, and he hoped, to sleep. He didn't feel like talking.

He lay down next to her, listening to her steady breathing.

"Do you feel better?" Carol asked.

Not asleep. Damn. "Maybe, a little."

"Sometime—not now—you'll need to tell me about Lorraine."

Lorraine. Hearing her name seemed surreal. He sat up.

"All those calls you've been receiving—the ones you told me came from telemarketers— that was Lorraine trying to reach you."

Bronson nodded, and then realized in the darkness she might not see him. "Yes."

"She's in trouble, she said. She needs her big brother."

NOT EVEN SEVEN o'clock and Bronson's cell buzzed. No need to look at the caller I.D. Every morning for the past eight days, a bit before 7:00, Lorraine called. Same as always, except that this time, he planned to answer.

He dug around for the phone and looked at his wife still sleeping. The cell in his hands stopped buzzing. He pressed one, got voice mail. He had eight messages. "Harry, hi. It's me, Lorraine. Bet it's a shock hearing from me after all these years. Call me. Please."

Delete.

Message two: "Hi. I'm getting desperate. You haven't returned my call. I really need to talk to you."

Delete.

Message three: "Please don't ignore my calls. I know I did lots of things wrong. But I've changed. Please call me. As soon as you can."

Delete.

Message four: "Big Bro? Pick up. Please, please pick up."
Bronson's trained detective ear recognized the sense of urgency. He hesitated and then deleted the message.

Message five: "Why haven't you called? I can't go on like this, alone. I need you. I'm waiting by the phone." Heart-wrenching sobs broke up the message.

Drama Queen. She'd always been a drama queen. He erased the other three messages, unheard. He sat at the edge of the bed, his hand playing with the cell, his mind bombarded by the memories he hoped he had forgotten.

Lorraine.

Only fourteen and already a drunk.

Lorraine.

High on pot and Lord knows what else.

Dad, with his weak heart, begging her to stop. Lorraine threw her head back, laughed, and blew smoke toward Dad's face.

Bronson stood and headed for the living room area. He bit his tongue—a habit he had developed when he didn't want to curse—and found his sister's number on the missed calls function. He pressed the call key.

Lorraine immediately picked up. "Oh God, Big Bro, you called. I need you."

"What do you want?"

A pause. "After all these years, those are your first words to me?"

"What do you want?" Bronson repeated. He tried to force the anger and the bitterness out, but like thick syrup, his resentment smothered his intentions.

"I want you to come."

"I can't."

"Please. I got involved in—" Another pause. "Please, I'm afraid. They're going to kill me. Please come."

"Tell me what's wrong."

"I can't."

"Then I can't help you."

"You've got to. I'll tell you when you get here. I don't want to say anything over the phone. I'm afraid it's bugged. You need to come."

"Where are you?"

"Whittle City, Pennsylvania, near Pittsburgh."

Clear on the other side of the United States. "Not sure I can get over there."

"Please."

"I'm in South Dakota."

"South Dakota? What are you doing there? Thought you were a detective for the Dallas Police Department."

How the hell did she know that? Worse, how had she gotten hold of his and Carol's cell numbers? "I'm retired. Carol, my wife—but I guess you know that since you talked to her. Anyway, we got a motor home."

"Retired?"

Did Bronson recognize a note of regret in his sister's voice? "Yes, retired."

"But you can still… You've got contacts, right?"

"What do you want?"

"I want you to come. Please. I don't have anyone else to turn to."

"You should have thought about that before you killed Dad and Mom." He hung up.

TWO

CAROL STOOD, ARMS crossed, leaning against the refrigerator. "That was Lorraine, I suppose."

Bronson nodded.

"What did she want?"

"She wants me to come."

"Are you?"

"Am I what?"

Carol rolled her eyes. "Are you going to go?"

"No."

"Why not?"

"Too far. She's in Pennsylvania. Too expensive."

Much to Bronson's surprise, Carol turned, opened the refrigerator door, and took out three eggs. "Omelets, okay?"

"I'm not hungry. Make one omelet and I'll take a small part."

"Fine with me." She began to chop an onion. "Onions and ham?"

Bronson knew she would add some vegetable. Always after him to eat healthy. He'd be one step ahead of her. "Might as well throw in some tomatoes, spinach, and any other healthy junk."

"That's an excellent suggestion. I'll do that."

Damn. He should have known better. She tricked him into agreeing on the healthy junk.

"Donna called," Carol said.

Bronson cast a glance at the picture of their daughters. Carol couldn't have possibly been more than eight in that picture. Now, she was a grown, married woman. Where did time go?

"She have anything important to say?"

"She's having problems and she needs her father."

Bronson sat up straighter. When it came to his daughters, he'd turn every stone in the world to help them. "What kind of problems?"

Carol shrugged as she sliced a tomato. "Doesn't matter. We can't afford to go see her."

"Of course we can. Remember we set up a savings account which we promised not to touch? The money there is tagged for Family Emergency only."

Carol smiled.

Bronson threw himself back onto the couch. He knew he'd been outsmarted—again.

"Donna didn't call, did she?"

Carol's smile widened. "No, she didn't." She took out the vegetable oil. "Soon as breakfast is over, we'll withdraw the money to cover one air ticket to Pittsburgh."

Damn.

BRONSON FLEW INTO the Pittsburgh International Airport even though Whittle City had a small airport. In the long run, it'd be cheaper to rent a car and drive to Whittle City, located less than fifty miles north of Pittsburgh.

Once the plane had landed, Bronson stared at the cell as though it would grow fangs. He hesitated a moment before punching in Lorraine's number. "I'm here," Bronson said when she answered on the first ring.

"Thank you, Big Brother, for coming."

Early in childhood, she started calling him Big Brother. Bronson never figured out if that was because he had always been taller and bulkier than the rest of their friends, or because he was two years older than she. "Yeah," he said in reference to her thanks. Sure, he was glad to be there. So much, in fact, he wished he was somewhere else. He wished he didn't have to talk to her. He wished he could forgive her. He wished. "Now what?"

"Meet me at the entrance of Glacier Valley Covered Bridge." The bridge located at Glacier Valley State Park ranked as the number one spot in the geologists' and photographers' must-see places. The picturesque 2,546 acres state park which had been formed by glaciers provided spectacular year-round views from sunrise to sunset. As kids, Bronson and Lorraine had loved that place. They even preferred it above Disneyland.

Bronson lowered his head and rubbed his eyebrows as though fending off a headache.

"Why there?"

"Because, Big Bro, I desperately need something I can hold on to. You and I—we had some great times there."

Indeed they had. Bronson remembered both of them racing each other along the two-mile loop trail that began on either side of the covered bridge. They giggled and made up imaginary scenarios as they followed the trail, a delightful walk along Sliding Rock Creek. But that was their past. He was no longer Big Bro. "Dad and Mom were there, too. They're the ones who introduced us to the place."

A long silence followed at the other end. Bronson thought he heard a sob. "I miss them, too. I wish I hadn't…" Another pause. "Can't change the past, no matter how much I want to." A long-drawn out sob followed.

Bronson kicked the floor. She'd been a kid then. Only fourteen. Get past it, but dammit, she had been old enough to know better. "How long will it take me to get to the bridge? I'm at the Pittsburgh airport."

"It's about a forty-minute drive if you take 79 North."

"See you in an hour."

"I'll be waiting."

To SAY THAT the drive to the state park was scenic would be an understatement. The centuries old forests stood majestically, giving way only to the occasional stream or creek. But for Bronson, one tree blended into the other until it all became a blur. He checked his watch and pushed down on the gas pedal.

Bronson felt his heart skip a beat as he saw the approaching Glacier Valley State Park exit. He slowed down, took the 488 ramp, and half-cursed Carol for forcing him to come. The park lay minutes away. Much to his surprise, the closer he got, the happier he felt. The park had brought back the magic of childhood.

All his early memories came rushing back like tidal waves that cleansed away the resentment. Bronson found himself looking forward to seeing his sister. Would he recognize her? After all, he hadn't seen her since their parents' funerals. He'd been only sixteen, she fourteen. Would their meeting be awkward? What will their first words be?

Bronson smiled as he recalled his sister's nickname for him. Some bullies had been picking on her while other school children watched. Bronson stepped forward and said, "Tough guys like you, picking on a girl. What does that tell me? You're a bunch of sissies." They turned on him, giving him a black eye and several bruises before the teachers broke up the fight.

Lorraine hugged Bronson before the coach had a chance to drag him to the office for fighting. "Thank you," she whispered in his ear. "You're my big brother, my protector, my Big Bro."

Big Bro.

So long ago. So much had happened since then. Bronson turned off the engine and for a second, hesitated before he opened the door and stepped out.

Lorraine. His complete opposite. He, a barrel of a man, even as a boy. She, small and delicate like a porcelain doll.

Her pert nose and inquisitive blue eyes set off by girlishly long lashes. Yeah, it would be good to see her.

Thank you, Carol. Somehow you always know what I want, even if I don't. He hastened his step, his gaze alert for her presence. He could feel his silly grin plastered on his face.

"Over here."

He looked down the covered bridge. She stood at its opposite end. He saw her smile accompanied by a trembling lip.

"Lorraine."

Each stood at opposite ends of the bridge, staring at one another.

Lorraine took a baby step forward. Bronson did likewise. Then she galloped toward him, her arms spread apart in anticipation of the hug. Bronson opened his arms, welcoming her.

A shot rang out.

Lorraine's eyes widened, but she continued to run.

"Get down!" Bronson broke into a trot, heading toward his sister. She collapsed into his arms and all energy seemed to drain away from her.

Bronson felt something familiar in his hands, something warm and sticky. Her blood screamed out at him. "Lorraine, no!" He looked up, hoping to catch a glimpse of the shooter.

"Don't leave me!" Her extended arm reached out to him.

He dropped to the ground and cradled her. Tears rolled down his cheeks. He dialed 911 and gave the location.

"Why didn't you come sooner? Why did you ignore my calls? I needed you, Big Bro." She began to shake. "I'm… so cold."

In the far distance, Bronson heard the wailing of an approaching siren, probably the park ranger. Bronson's head jerked up.

"The note…side of the bridge…remember…" She struggled to breathe.

Bronson remembered. As kids they noticed that the right hand side of the bridge had two signs. The left had none. Although they knew better, they pretended that the unmarked side of the bridge felt left out. To make it up to the bridge, they scribbled notes and placed them on the ledge at the foot of the bridge on the left-hand side. They held contests—Mom and Dad usually served as the judges—to see who posted the most original note. Strange she would bring that up now. "Shh. Don't talk. The ambulance is on its way. I can hear it." *Just hold on.*

"Too late…I'm afraid…what I did…back then. Will I… be punished now?"

Bronson cradled and rocked her. "No, of course not. You were a kid. Now hush, conserve your energy. They're almost here."

"Too late."

"Don't say that." Tears welled in Bronson's eyes. "You're going to be okay. You hear me? We're going to make up for all the lost time. You're going to be okay." *God, please don't let her die. Not like this, not now.*

She raised a trembling hand toward Bronson's face. "Don't leave me." She took a deep breath. "Don't leave me." She closed her eyes.

Bronson let out a heart-wrenching groan.

THREE

HEAD PARK RANGER Eric McLaughlin turned off the siren and slowed down as he approached the scene. He spotted a parked Chevy Cruze, a silver sedan just like the one he desired. He stared at the vehicle, then all around it. He detected no movements.

Still, he pulled his gun, stepped out of the ranger truck, and walked around the Cruze, looking inside. Nothing unusual. He looked up and got a clear view of the inside of the bridge.

A lone figure, kneeling on the floor, rocked back and forth cradling a woman's body. McLaughlin's first thought told him to make the man stand up. Put his hands up. He could be the killer. Instinct told him the man was as much a victim as the woman he cradled.

From the looks of it, the man wasn't going anywhere. McLaughlin decided to leave him alone and let the troopers take care of him. Instead, McLaughlin would focus on securing the crime scene. He hoped he'd do it right. He never thought he'd actually have to use the skills he'd learned in police training workshops.

To his left, a group of loud tourists headed his way. McLaughlin stopped them. "The bridge and mill are temporarily closed. Sorry for the inconvenience."

The tourists grumbled but turned back. McLaughlin let out a sigh of relief when he heard a siren approaching.

Minutes later, uniformed troopers arrived. McLaughlin filled them in on the little he knew. They called in the plain clothes and less than half-an-hour later, a tall woman in her indeterminate forties with an athletic body stepped out of the Ford Bronco she drove. She paused by the car, her gaze scanning the area.

McLaughlin headed down the hill toward the parking lot. "I'm Head Ranger Eric McLaughlin." He offered the trooper his hand.

She accepted it. "Ivy Cannady. What do we have?"

McLaughlin indicated the covered bridge with a nod. "A single male figure halfway through the bridge cradling a woman's body."

"She's dead?"

McLaughlin gasped. He had only assumed. "I didn't ask."

Cannady's eyes widened.

"But I briefly checked the area." McLaughlin quickly spat out the words. "Apparently, we're alone."

Behind them the squealing of tires announced another car's arrival. Two more troopers stepped out.

Cannady signaled for them to hurry up. "Hunsicker, cover me from the other side of the bridge." She pulled her gun. "Swanson, scan the area for anything you can find. Seems the shooter came from that direction." She pointed to the opposite end of the bridge. "McLaughlin, you follow me."

As silently as possible so as not to startle the man, Cannady and McLaughlin entered the bridge and worked their way toward the man and the woman. She watched as Hunsicker made his way in from the opposite end of the bridge.

Holding her .40 caliber semi-automatic Glock at the ready, Cannady used her authoritative voice. "My name is Cannady. We're here to help you. Don't make any sudden moves."

Bronson turned to face her, but held onto Lorraine's

body. "She said, 'Don't leave me,' but she's the one who left me. She's gone."

"Can you tell us who she is?"

Bronson leaned down and kissed Lorraine's forehead. "My sister. Lorraine. Lorraine Bronson." He gently set her down. "I'm a retired Dallas police detective. I'm going to reach for my I.D. in my back pocket." He placed one hand up and using slow movements, he retrieved his wallet and opened it.

Cannady looked at the I.D. "Detective Bronson." She bent down and felt for a pulse in Lorraine's neck. Failing to find one, she stood. "Tell me what happened."

Bronson told her and then stepped back. An ambulance arrived followed by the medical examiner. Troopers swarmed the area, each focusing on their own task. Cannady found Lorraine's I.D.—probably her driver's license— in her pants pocket.

Bronson thought about asking Cannady if he could see it, but his legs refused to obey. Part of him told him he should be involved, but the other part—the one that was the most dominant—forced him to remain aloof as though he was detached, wasn't part of the scene. His eyes recorded the activities but his mind wouldn't register them. Still he stood, watching the coroner and the photographer, and all the other people hustle around his sister's body.

Cannady noticed him and approached. "You don't have to hang around. We're almost through anyway."

Bronson nodded.

"Before you leave, I have to know where you'll be staying."

"My ex-partner's ex-wife lives in Pittsburgh. I'll crash there for a couple of days."

"Pittsburgh is a mighty big city."

Bronson retrieved his pocket notebook, tore off a sheet,

scribbled down Ellen Biebersheimer's address and phone number and then on second thought, added his cell number. He handed Cannady the paper.

Cannady looked at it, folded it, and put it in her pants pocket. "Thanks for adding your contact information, but I hope I won't have to use it to remind you to come to headquarters. I'll be expecting your visit, tomorrow at the latest. I may have some additional questions that need to be answered."

Bronson nodded.

"One more thing," Cannady said.

Bronson waited for her to finish.

"I want you to follow me to the barracks and give me a formal statement."

"Can do." Bronson took one last look at the bridge and at his sister's body, now covered with a sheet. He stuffed his hands in his pockets and headed for the Cruze.

From the far distance, a solitary figure made sure he didn't miss any of the goings on. He rubbed his chin as he saw the ranger's arrival and then the trooper's, followed by various other troopers driving in their official Ford Crown Victorias or other unmarked vehicles. Within seconds, the area swarmed with police activity. He always enjoyed watching them move like busy little ants doing their best to piece together the puzzle.

A puzzle they would never put together, for he alone held the key pieces.

He rubbed his chin harder and faster as he focused on the lone trooper. Soon, the trooper would find the area where he had hidden, and why not? Only a moron wouldn't be able to follow the trail he left behind. He had broken enough twigs and as if that wasn't enough, he had also cleared a path that would lead them to the right place.

The trooper must have noticed some of the broken twigs as he bent down and studied the ground. He immediately followed it to the hiding area about one-hundred yards from the bridge. The trooper stood for a few seconds analyzing the ground. He looked down and retrieved a plastic bag from his pocket. Using the bag, he picked up something and sealed the bag.

Most likely the trooper had found the cartridge. Good. The viewer rubbed his chin and nodded with approval. Amazing how easily some people could be fooled.

His gut told him to get the hell out before the troopers decided to expand the search. Still, he stood, rubbing his chin.

FOUR

ELLEN STARED AT the untouched now cold cup of coffee. Bronson sat slumped at the far edge of her couch, playing with the rim of the coffee cup.

"Don't you like my coffee?" Ellen asked.

"Hm."

"I've never known you not to drink coffee. Even while Mike was still courting me—way before he became your partner—I remember you always with a cup of coffee in your hands."

Bronson continued to stroke the rim of the cup. If he heard her, he didn't show it.

"Carol's coming?" Ellen asked.

No answer.

"Bronson."

Bronson looked up. He blinked his eyes rapidly and shook his head. "What?" He frowned.

"You called Carol. Is she coming?"

He nodded. "She's driving the camper. It'll be days before she gets here."

Ellen leaned forward and wrapped her hands around his. "I've never seen you like this before. I'm calling Mike."

Bronson didn't respond, and Ellen wasn't sure if he heard. Ellen stood up, stared at Bronson, and headed for the phone.

"HEY, BUDDY, WAKE UP."

Bronson opened one eye. The alarm clock read 2:59. The

sun brightly shining through the window told him he'd slept most of the day away. Already the afternoon and still he wore his pajamas. No matter. Nothing mattered. He rolled over and covered his face with the blanket.

"You're not getting off that easy." Mike pulled away the bed sheets. "Get up."

"I'm tired."

"Of what? Being in bed all day? What you should be tired of is feeling sorry for yourself. Now get up."

Bronson sat up, swung his legs down, and stared into his ex-partner's intense watermelon green eyes. As always, his solid white hair and impeccably ironed shirt made him look more like an executive instead of a police detective. "What are you doing here?"

"Ellen called me."

"She's your ex. Ex's don't call each other."

"You know better than that."

"Yeah. I know." Bronson ran his hands through his hair. "But it doesn't make sense. Nothin' makes sense. Why didn't I come when she first called? She'd be alive now. It's my fault she's dead."

It took Mike a few seconds to realize Bronson had switched from Ellen to Lorraine. "Stop right there." Mike sat down beside him. "You didn't pull the trigger. Some S.O.B. did. Tell me you know that."

"I could have helped her, but I chose not to." Bronson buried his head in his hands.

"Tell me you know this isn't your fault."

Bronson lowered his hands and pivoted his head toward Mike. "Her last words to me—"

"Bronson, don't do this."

"—'Don't leave me.'" He let out an empty laugh. "I did just that. I left her alone, and now she's dead. Don't tell me I didn't kill her."

Mike wrapped his arm around Bronson's shoulder and squeezed. Bronson remained rigid. Mike looked at the bedroom entry way and saw Ellen leaning against the door frame, her arms crossed and tears running down her cheeks. Using his eyes, Mike indicated Bronson.

She nodded and stepped forward.

Mike once again squeezed Bronson's shoulder, stood, and walked out.

Ellen reached down and wrapped her hands around Bronson's. He squinted and the lines between his eyes pulled into a little frown. "'Don't leave me,' she said."

"I know." She knelt down so their faces were at eye-level. "I'm not Carol, but I'm here for you."

"I know." He buried his face in her shoulder.

She held him tight.

WHEN BRONSON FINALLY got himself together enough to get out of the bedroom, he found Mike and Ellen sitting on the couch, their arms wrapped around each other. Ellen's forehead looked like that of an older woman's, but other than that, her soft features still held their beauty. Bronson smiled. "Hey, Mike, you're a fool. You shouldn't have let her go."

"She walked out on me, but she knows I'll take her back anytime. No questions asked." He spoke to Bronson but stared into Ellen's eyes.

Ellen's facial features tightened. "I can't be a policeman's wife. You know that. I don't know how Carol does it."

"Being a policeman is all I know how to do," Mike said.

Ellen nodded and looked down.

"Hey, buddies, thanks for being there for me. Sorry about being such a pain in the ass." Bronson cleared his throat. "Excuse my French."

"No problem." Mike squeezed Ellen's shoulder. She looked up at him and gave him a small smile.

"It is a problem or at least a huge inconvenience." Bronson sat on the recliner across from them. "Detectives can't just walk away from their cases very easily."

"Thing is, the captain has been after me to take some vacation time. Never had reason to. Now I do."

Bronson nodded. "How long are you here for?"

"I've got thirty-three days coming. As long as I don't exceed that, I'll be fine."

"I'm okay now. You don't have to babysit me anymore."

"Don't flatter yourself. I'm here to see Ellen. In fact, I've been thinking," Mike said, looking up at Bronson. "Why don't you call Carol, find out where she is, and the three of us drive out to meet her? Then we'll do the tourist bit."

"Can't. I've got a funeral to arrange and attend. Besides, there's a loose criminal out there, and I promised Lorraine, I'd find him."

Mike shot up to his feet. "Bronson, you can't. You're too close. Let the police do their work. Besides, you're no longer a policeman."

"But you are."

"Yeah, in Dallas. I have no jurisdiction here."

"Then we'll do this as private citizens."

"Bronson—"

"'Don't leave me,' she said." Bronson glared at Mike. "I'm never going to leave her again."

FIVE

BRONSON TOSSED MIKE the rental car keys. "You drive."

"Some things don't ever change." Mike half-smiled and shook his head. "You remembered the procedure. I drive and you carry the keys."

Bronson half-smiled. Mike never liked to carry anything in his pocket. "Guess you're right. Some things don't ever change."

They reached the Cruze and got in. "Which way?"

Bronson gave him instructions on how to get to Glacier Valley Covered Bridge. Mike started the engine and pulled off. They rode in silence, Bronson often squirming, unable to find a comfortable position. He rubbed his eyes, looked out the window, and shifted positions once again.

Mike gave him a sideways glance. "What's on your mind?"

"I shouldn't have dragged you into this. You've got your career to think of. I screwed mine. I can't ask you to do the same. I can handle this myself. No hurt feelings."

"Once a partner, always a partner. You can count on me." Mike nodded once.

Bronson nodded and less than an hour later, Mike took the 488 ramp that led them to the state park. "You sure you want to do this?"

Bronson eyed him.

"Okay, then." He parked the car. "Here we go."

Bronson stepped out. He stood on the unpaved parking lot, glaring at the covered bridge. Without further hesitation, he headed toward it, past the picnic area and the children's playground area. Minutes later, he found himself staring at the inside of the bridge. He could almost see Lorraine running toward him.

Don't leave me.

A smile on her face. Her arms wide opened.

Don't leave me.

A shot rang out.

Don't leave me.

Bronson's breathing came out fast and shallow.

"You okay, buddy?"

Bronson nodded.

"You're shaking."

"A chill. I got a chill, that's all." He swallowed hard and turned away from the bridge.

"Lorraine died in my arms. You knew that?"

Mike nodded.

"As kids we wrote notes and put them on the side of the bridge. As she lay in my arms, she mentioned that. I thought she was relivin' a childhood memory. Now I'm thinkin', she must have known she would be killed, so she left me a note. That's why we're here."

Mike's gaze drifted toward the bridge. "Show me."

Bronson led him to the bridge's left-hand side, stepped over the guardrail, and held onto the bridge for support.

Mike gasped. "Hey, what do you think you're doing? Fifty feet below you, that's Sliding Rock. Ellen told me that creek claims several lives each year."

"Then make sure I don't fall."

Mike threw his arms up, ran to Bronson's side, and firmly gripped his arm. Bronson leaned down. "There's a rock over there." He pointed to a smooth, almost flat rock, two feet away from him.

Mike looked at the area. "There are thousands of rocks over there."

"Not like this one." Bronson pushed it over, exposing a business card. Bronson picked it up.

SIX

MIKE HELD ONTO Bronson's arm as he stepped over the guardrail and back onto safe ground. "Geez, Bronson, what were you thinking? Did you and your sister really leave notes back there?"

Bronson looked down at the raging stream and small ledge he had stood on. "Yeah, we did."

"Your parents knew this?"

"Heck no. If they had, they would have killed—" He paused and swallowed a big breath. "—us both. They knew we wrote the notes, but they had no idea where we hid them."

Mike nodded and pointed to Bronson's hand. "What's that?"

"It's a business card for a restaurant called Devono's Steak House. It's in Pittsburgh. Ever heard of it?"

Mike shook his head. "I thought Ellen and I had visited every restaurant in Pittsburgh. Apparently not. Want me to call her, see if she's heard of it?"

"Sounds like a plan."

Mike whipped out his cell and punched in a number and then pressed another button. "I put it on speaker mode in case you wanted to ask her something."

On the fourth ring, Ellen picked up. "Hey, You Hunk, are you ready to come home now? I'm waiting."

Mike's face reddened. He gave Bronson his back and placed the phone close to his mouth. In a low voice he said, "You know I'm always ready and hungry for you—"

"Then—"

"But you're on speaker phone." He pivoted so he once again faced Bronson.

"Oops, but I'm sure we didn't shock Bronson. Did we?"

Bronson smiled. "Shockin' me would be next to impossible. I need to know if you've heard of a place called Devono's Steak House?"

"Wow, I'm the one who's shocked now. Yeah, I've heard of it. Everyone here in Pittsburgh is familiar with it. It's an up-scale place with fancy prices and food guaranteed to entice the senses."

"Why haven't we been there?" Mike asked.

"Because city gossip claims that it's a front for a high society prostitution ring. No matter how good the food is and how fancy the place is, I don't care to support places like that."

Bronson flipped the card and read the name someone had scribbled on the back. "Ever heard of Matthew Devono?"

"Again, based on gossip, he started out as a pimp, but he moved up the ladder fast. He now owns the place."

"Would you be willin' to compromise your ethics and accompany me for some fantastic food?"

"Is Mike going?"

Bronson eyed Mike. He nodded. "He certainly is."

"Then count me in. No way am I allowing him to go there without me, single or not."

"It's a date, then," Bronson said.

Mike walked away and talked to Ellen for a few minutes longer. When he disconnected, he returned to Bronson's side. "You're thinking Lorraine wrote that name on the back of the card in case something happened to her."

Bronson considered the possibility. He should report his finding to the trooper. What's her name—Cannady? He'd do that, soon as he was sure of the facts. "Exactly what I was thinkin', but I also realize that I don't know if that's her handwritin'. I know nothin' about my sister." He turned and headed back to the car.

SEVEN

ELLEN CALLED IN a couple of favors and got reservations for three at Devono's Steak House. However, earliest she could get was nine. Bronson and Carol always made it a point to eat by six. "This way you go to bed with an empty stomach, and you keep the pounds off," Bronson could hear Carol's warning even though she was still over a thousand miles away.

Bronson smiled at the memory. He wished he could hear it again, in person.

"Now what?" Mike sat on the recliner across from Bronson.

Ellen entered the living room carrying a tray. She set a glass of ice tea on the end table beside Mike and handed Bronson a steaming cup of coffee. "Don't tell Carol on me, but I actually put in three heaping spoonfuls of sugar and lots of milk. This is a onetime deal so you better enjoy it."

"You bet I will." He reached for the cup and took a swig. Ahh, perfect.

"We've got eight hours to kill before dinner," Mike said, kicking off his shoes and leaning back on the couch. "We can sit back and relax."

"Not me," Bronson stood up. "I've got an appointment to keep."

"With who?" Mike asked.

Bronson bent down and picked up his cup of coffee. "With Trooper Ivy Cannady. She's in charge of Lorraine's case."

Mike reached for his shoes. "Okay, let's go."

Bronson waved his opened right hand. "You and Ellen need some time alone. I can handle this on my own."

Mike eyed Ellen and a big grin spread across his lips.

LIKE MANY OF Southern Pennsylvania's small towns, Whittle City's history dated back to the oil and steel industries that once reigned in the area. Located in the center of town on Main Street, an old stone building served as the barracks for Troop G. Its façade made the edifice look old, but its inside filled with computers, fax and Xerox machines, informed Bronson this was no backward community.

Soon as Bronson stepped into the barracks, he approached the glass barrier. The trooper on the other side asked, "May I help you?"

Before Bronson could answer, Cannady headed toward the front. "Let him in."

The trooper buzzed him in, and Bronson stepped through the barrier.

The trooper offered him her hand. "Detective Bronson, thanks for coming."

"You asked me to come. Here I am."

"You must have a sense for perfect timing."

Bronson flashed a blank look.

"We just received the warrant to search your sister's house. Want to come?"

"Yes, of course." Bronson eyed the two plain clothes troopers standing by Cannady's desk. He assumed they would accompany them to Lorraine's house. "By the way, you can drop the *detective* part. I'm retired."

"I remember." Cannady headed back to her desk. "You showed me your retirement badge at the bridge."

Bronson nodded but had no recollection of doing so.

"This is Trooper Hunsicker." She indicated the smaller of the two and then pointed to the other man. "And Trooper

Swanson. You met them at the crime scene. They'll come
with us to search Lorraine's house."

Bronson nodded and felt amazed about how little he remembered about the day his sister died. He shook hands
with each of the troopers. "I'm ready if you are."

Cannady nodded and led them out.

Bronson followed them in his rental as they drove
through the narrow streets of Whittle City, out toward the
edge of town. Ten minutes later, they came to a stop in
front of a two-story colonial style white house sitting on a
couple of acres. The house itself had two huge wings that
tripled the size of the original structure. A fountain at the
entryway gave the mansion a touch of elegance.

Bronson swallowed hard. Her house spoke of wealth.
How did she earn the money required to buy and main-
tain such a monstrosity? He parked beside Cannady's Ford
and got out.

"This is it? Her house?"

Swanson smirked. "You really didn't know your sister,
did you? Where were you?"

Don't leave me.

Bronson looked away, hating the tears that glistened in
his eyes. "In Dallas, workin'."

Swanson opened his mouth to speak, but Cannady
wrapped her hand around Swanson's arm. "Let him be."

Swanson shrugged her grip off and stepped toward the
house. Bronson, face cast downward, followed behind.

Don't leave me.

EIGHT

Bronson found that what intrigued him the most about the search didn't stem from what they found but what they failed to find. Not a single utility bill or records of payments. No mortgage bills either. Or car payments. Based on the entries of her checkbook, she only bought enough groceries a month to feed her for less than a week. All of these bills had to have been paid, but how? By whom?

To add to the mystery of the sterile environment, they failed to locate an address book or even a list of phone numbers and addresses.

A search of the closet revealed a wardrobe filled with designer clothes. The few costume necklaces shared space with finer pieces of jewelry. The medicine cabinet revealed Lorraine had to have been in perfect health, except for an occasional cold.

Her appointment book told them she volunteered several hours a week at the local Daniel Jenkins School for Boys. Bronson wrote the name down and made a mental note to Google it at Ellen's house.

The only picture displayed on top of the mantle or any other place showed three boys playing football. The school served as a background.

The two messages on the answering machine came from Claudine, an employee at the school, asking Lorraine to call back.

As with most everyone, Lorraine's computer was pass code protected and Cannady packed it up and took it with her. When and if they found something, she promised, they would notify him. Bronson would then have to claim the computer, if he wanted it back. He planned to do that.

As Cannady, Swanson, and Hunsicker were ready to leave, Cannady said, "You can stay here if you want. We're through with our search. We're going to talk to the neighbors and call it a day. If we find something, we'll let you know. You do the same."

Bronson guaranteed her he would and walked them to the door. He thought about leaving but decided to wander from room to room, absorbing every detail, getting a feel for the house. Now that he had the keys, he'd come back when he had the time to fully devote his energy to this project.

Before locking the house, he gave it one last, long glance. *Who are you? Who's Lorraine Bronson?* He didn't know. If the house held any secrets, he promised Lorraine he'd find them. He gently closed the door and headed toward the rental.

Halfway back to Ellen's house, a brightly lit baseball field attracted Bronson's attention. The teams consisted of junior high age boys. The game itself didn't hold Bronson's interest. The stands, packed with cheering parents, relatives, and friends, captivated him. He pulled over and parked so that he could watch the game. But his eyes strayed to the stands.

As a boy, he and Dad had often been part of the spectators. Bonding time, Dad used to say. The two grew closer while Lorraine grew apart from them—and not just Dad, but Mom as well. Each time Lorraine drank, the chasm between Lorraine and the rest of the family widened, an irreparable crack meant to lead to oblivion.

The week before Bronson's sixteenth birthday, Dad promised him a spectacular surprise. Bronson knew that no matter what Dad had planned, he'd be happy and if not, he'd pretend to be thrilled. Lately, Dad's heart condition had deteriorated to the point that Bronson would wake up at night, his body drenched with sweat. The more Lorraine drank, the less Dad wanted to live.

The day before his sixteenth birthday, Bronson lay in bed trying not to listen to the screaming match going on in the living room.

"You will not take me out of school and make me go to some stupid private school." Lorraine's high-pitched voice grated on Bronson's nerves, like fingernails scratching a blackboard. "I won't go. My friends are at Lincoln High."

"Your friends are a bunch of losers." Dad's loud voice cracked and Bronson sat up in bed, his heart beating wildly in his chest.

His mother tried to force Dad to relax. "You're getting too agitated. Think about your condition." Her smooth voice, interwoven with nervous threads, failed to cover her concern. Bronson swung his legs over the bed, ready to bolt toward the living room.

"Calm down? Me, calm down? She's the one who needs to calm down." Dad's angry voice penetrated the walls, and something in his tone worried Bronson.

Bronson heard a *thump*, followed by his mother's scream. He bolted to the living room but wished he hadn't. He absorbed each vivid detail with a frightening clarity that would follow him the rest of his life. Dad, on the floor, clutching his chest. Mom, bent over him, her body protecting his.

"M-mom? D-dad?" Bronson took a step forward.

Mom looked up, tears streaming down her cheeks. "He's…he's having a…heart attack. Help him."

Fourteen year old Lorraine ran out of the room and Bronson dialed 911. As soon as he hung up, he rushed back to his father's side.

With a trembling hand, Bronson's father reached out for his son. "Bring me...the signed...card."

Bronson, unable to move, clutched his father's hand.

"He wants the card," Mom said. "Go get it."

Bronson knew exactly which card he was referring to. His father had often told him the story of how he and his father had attended a game at Yankee Stadium. The game had been the thrill of both his father's and his grandfather's lives, until the game was over. Then the Big Event—as they called it—happened. They met Mickey Mantle and he signed the baseball trading card. Bronson's father always carried it with him as a kid. Now, years later, it stood framed on his father's desk where everyone could easily see it.

"Go," his mother said.

Bronson jumped up and headed for his father's desk. He reached for the framed card, and then realized it was gone—and so was Lorraine.

Bronson dragged his feet as he headed back to his father's side. How could he possibly tell him Lorraine had taken it? Bronson knelt down by his father's side.

"The card, boy...where's...the card?"

Bronson wrapped his hand around his father's trembling hand. "You want to give me the card for my birthday. That's my surprise, right?" Tears formed in his eyes, and he wiped them away. "Tomorrow's my birthday. I want you to give it to me tomorrow. Right now, just get well.

Please, Dad, I need you."

"Get the card." Dad had trouble breathing and could hardly get the words out. "Do as I say."

"Dad—" Bronson looked away.

"Why won't you bring him his card?" Mom held her trembling hands close to her lips.

Bronson looked down.

"No!" Dad tightened his facial features. "You can't bring me the card, can you? It's gone." He did his best to look around the room. His lips began to quiver. "So is Lorraine."

"Dad, it's okay. I'll get it back."

Bronson's father's eyes went blank. "It's too late." He took a deep breath and closed his eyes.

Two weeks later, Mom died of a broken heart. Bronson saw his sister at the funerals but he never talked to her, and he never saw her after that—until the bridge. He spent the rest of his teenage years moving from one foster home to another, hating Lorraine for destroying the family.

A thunderous cheer jolted Bronson back to the present. Apparently, one of the team players had scored a home run and the crowd came to its feet, cheering him.

Good thing they had something to cheer about.

Bronson covered his eyes. He refused to give in to the tears but they came anyway.

NINE

TOURISTS AS WELL as residents enjoyed the charming, old-world traditions found in Pittsburgh's South Side. Located in its heart, Devono's Steak House exuded the same atmosphere of the area it served. Shimmering white tablecloths covered each table. The gold-rimmed china accompanied by gold-plated silverware and crystal glasses promised a succulent meal. Clearly, much too fancy for Bronson's taste which, according to him, a juicy hamburger and a steaming cup of coffee would satisfy.

Upon entering the restaurant, the maitre d' immediately ushered Mike, Ellen, and Bronson to a table near the back. The head waiter, wearing a tuxedo, reached for the neatly folded napkin resting on top of the stacked dinner plates in front of Ellen. He unfolded it by giving it a quick shake and placed it on Ellen's lap. Then he did the same for Mike.

Bronson quickly reached for his napkin, placed it on his lap, and flashed the waiter a smile. The waiter smiled back. "Your server will be Mario. In the meantime, I'll get your drinks."

Ellen ordered a glass of wine, Mike a beer, and Bronson a cup of coffee.

Soon as the head waiter left, another waiter stepped forward. Bronson read his name tag: Mario Serafin. While Mario recited the day's specials with the enthusiasm of an actor uttering the world's greatest lines, Bronson reached for his wallet and took out a fifty-dollar bill.

When Mario finished delivering the choices, he asked, "Any questions?"

Bronson placed his open palm on top of the bill and pushed it toward the waiter. "I have one. Do you know Matthew Devono?"

Mario's eyebrows knitted. "Of course, sir. He's the owner of this fine restaurant and as such, he makes sure he personally knows each of his employees. May I ask why you want to know that, sir?"

"I'd like an introduction." Bronson gave the fifty another small push.

Mario eyed the money but didn't reach for it. "I'm afraid that's impossible. Mr. Devono isn't here today."

"That's a shame because I wanted to talk to him tonight. But you will give him my message?" Bronson moved his hand, exposing half of the bill.

"I will do my best, sir, but he'll want to know who was inquiring about him."

"Tell him I'm Lorraine Bronson's brother."

Mario nodded as though familiar with the name. "And the nature of the visit?"

"Tell him I received Lorraine's message." Bronson removed his hand from the bill.

"Very well." Mario took a step forward. "I'll make sure to tell Mr. Devono about you." He looked down at the fifty, and then at the man he only knew as Lorraine's brother. Bronson nodded once and the waiter pocketed the money. "I'll give you fine folks time to check out the menu."

Bronson watched him as he disappeared behind the wooden swinging doors.

Mike leaned forward. "A fifty? Bronson, really? Retired cops don't make that much unless there's something you're not telling me. Carol's going to kill you."

"What happens in Pittsburgh stays in Pittsburgh."

Bronson buried his face in the menu as guilt consumed him. What was it about Lorraine that harbored secrets? The prices in the menu jumped at him and he thought maybe the seventeen-dollar tureen of soup should be his entire meal.

Much to Bronson's surprise, the soup not only teased his taste buds but also satisfied his hunger. Bronson hadn't realized that tureens came in such large sizes. When they finished, Mario approached as the busboy emptied the table of the dirty dishes.

Mario handed Mike and Ellen each a dessert menu. "Mr. Devono told me to tell you that tonight the three of you are his special guests."

Damn, Bronson thought. Was it too late to order the steak and lobster Mike had enjoyed?

Ellen had said that her prime rib was the best she'd ever had. Double damn.

"While your friends enjoy their dessert, Mr. Devono would like to speak to you, sir. If you will follow me, please."

No dessert either. Well, bummer, but this would be a lot better. Bronson removed his napkin from his lap, stood, and followed Mario through the swinging wooden doors.

Soon as he stepped in and the doors closed behind him, someone's fist landed on his stomach.

Good thing all he had was soup.

TEN

TWO MEN, ONE at each side, held Bronson up as Mario delivered the second punch. "We're going to release you, but you're not to pull any cute shit. Is that understood?"

Bronson straightened up, trying to breathe normally. "I understand perfectly well." The wind had been knocked out of him and he had trouble speaking. "But I want to know why."

"Mr. Devono told me to tell you the first punch was from Lorraine. The second from him."

Bronson started to speak, but Mario waved him off. "If you're ready, sir, Mr. Devono is waiting to see you."

Bronson forced himself to stand up straight and follow Mario up the stairs.

Devono's office, located on the back side of the second floor, didn't seem large from the outside. But once he entered, it told him a different story. Its mahogany floors blended with the light-colored wooden furniture, giving the room a feeling of opulence. A tall, lean cocoa-cream colored man with salt and pepper shaded hair greeted Bronson. "Mario tells me you're Lorraine's brother."

"And you must be the rude host who owns this joint."

"This joint? I'd hardly call it that. *This joint* clears over half a million dollars in profit each year, and that figure continues to climb." He indicated the leather couch next to his desk.

"I'm impressed." Bronson sat down.

"Funny, but you don't look impressed." Devono headed toward the bar. "Not that I care. Want something to drink?"

"What guarantee do I have you won't poison it?"

"It's not my style. If I wanted you dead, you'd be dead by now." He smiled, revealing a row of perfect white teeth. "Once again, what do you care to drink?"

"I was enjoying a nice cup of coffee downstairs. It's probably cold by now."

"How do you take it?"

"Three spoons of sugar—" An image of Carol scolding him flashed in his mind. "Make that two heapin' spoons of sugar and plenty of milk."

Devono nodded at one of the two bodyguards stationed like tin soldiers by the door. The one to the right nodded and left. Mario remained standing rigidly at the edge of Devono's desk.

Devono sat on the couch facing Bronson, a coffee table separating them. "Lorraine may have been your biological sister, but I was more of a brother to her than you ever were."

Don't leave me. Bronson swallowed hard and cast his glance downward. "That may be true, but now I'd like to learn as much about Lorraine as I can."

"Why, Mr. Bronson? She's already dead. Why would you want to get to know her now?"

"Because she was murdered. She died in my arms. I want to find her killer and bring her justice."

Devono remained quiet for a moment. When he spoke, his voice was soft, yet firm. "To honor her, I'll co-operate, but know I'm doing this for her and nothing for you. Frankly, Mr. Bronson, you disgust me."

Which was perfectly fine with Bronson. At this point in his life, he disgusted himself. No matter what Mike said,

Bronson had allowed his sister to die. He should have come earlier. Then he might have been able to prevent her death.

Don't leave me.

"What can you tell me about her?"

Devono leaned back. "I met her when she was still a kid. She arrived in downtown Pittsburgh by bus, a frightened, lonely child, barely fourteen. Made her way all the way from Dallas to Pittsburgh. That's a heck of a distance for a kid to travel by herself. I always wondered what brought her here."

The bridge. The damn covered bridge. The one good memory she had of family life. Bronson should have known about its lure, although at sixteen, Bronson hadn't cared. "You knew she was underage. What did you do?"

"I fed her and cleaned her up. I gave her the love you failed to provide."

Bronson tightened his fists. "You're a pimp."

Devono threw his head back and widely smiled. "I see you did your homework. I'm impressed."

Bronson leaned forward. "You son of a bitch. You took an innocent fourteen-year-old and—"

"—kept her safe, which is a lot more than I can say about you."

The coffee arrived and the bodyguard set it down on the coffee table. He returned to his post by the door. It took all of Bronson's will to ignore the drink.

"Your sister—even at fourteen—had a special quality about her. So I didn't send her to the streets to turn cheap tricks. Instead, I taught her the finer points of society. I showed her how to look like a twelve-year-old but act like twenty-one. She learned fast."

Bronson shot to his feet but even before he could fully stand up, the bodyguards saddled him and pushed him back down.

"One more outburst like that, Mr. Bronson, and our meeting is over. Is that understood?"

Bronson shrugged off the bodyguards who still held onto his shoulders. He slumped down on the couch.

Devono snapped his fingers and pointed to the bar. Immediately, Mario headed toward it and began mixing a drink. "Now, where was I?" Devono's gaze locked on Bronson's. "Oh yes, I was telling you how I managed to turn your sister into my highest paid escort."

Mario set the drink down in front of Devono who picked it up and half-emptied it. "She had this special quality that appealed to high-ranking police officers, politicians, businessmen, millionaires, even movie stars. She could play the role of a twelve-year-old for those who liked that or be a glamorous twenty-odd-year-old, all within the same day." Mario finished his drink and signaled for Mario to prepare another.

Mario picked up the empty glass and set out to mix another.

"I only offered her services to the good politicians, the good lawyers—"

"Those are oxymorons."

Devono flashed him a blank look. "What?"

Bronson waved him off. "You were sayin'?"

"Over the years, she made me lots of money, and I rewarded her very well. Then one day shortly after she had turned nineteen, Mark Willington III entered her life."

The name quickly captured Bronson's attention. He recognized it as being that of the man who the press had nicknamed Mr. Steel. Willington represented what early Pittsburgh stood for. His mill remained one of the few that still thrived, making him one of the country's wealthiest men.

Mario handed Devono the second drink. Devono set

the beverage down without sipping it. "At first Mr. Steel requested her on a monthly basis. Then every two weeks, then he increased it to weekly. If I offered him someone else's services, he'd refuse. Only one he wanted was Lorraine. Then he started asking for her on a daily basis. Then one day, the requests stopped. By the end of the second week, I assumed we'd never hear from him again. On the third week, he stopped by and landed the bomb on me. He would pay me half-a-million dollars each year. The police would never bother my establishment, and in return, Lorraine would move in with him." He reached for his drink. "I had no choice. I lost Lorraine that day but she'd come and visit occasionally. She was, after all, my little sister." He took a sip. "You might not know this—it's been kept a secret—but Mr. Steel is on his deathbed. It's an end of an era. If I were you, I'd talk to him as soon as possible."

THE MAN SITTING four tables away from Bronson's carefully noted the time Bronson followed Mario through the wooden swinging doors. He also recorded the time he returned. He'd been gone exactly twenty-six minutes. Plenty of time to gather a lot of information. He wished he'd been able to bug Devono's office, but it was too late for that.

No matter. He knew exactly what Devono would tell Bronson. He rubbed his chin as he watched Bronson and the other two people walk out of the restaurant.

ELEVEN

THE GOOGLE SEARCH showed Bronson that the Daniel Jenkins School for Boys had been named after the congressman who had donated a vast amount of money to build the facility. Since it first opened its doors a decade ago, Jenkins Sr. was its greatest benefactor.

And now he's a presidential hopeful, Bronson thought. This looks good on his resume.

During the school's early history, its faculty prided themselves in housing troubled boys and turning them into productive young men. Testimonial after testimonial attested to this. Now it educated the nation's elite.

Bronson closed the computer window and leaned back in the chair. "Thanks for the use of your computer."

Ellen put down the book she was reading. "You're welcome. Did you learn anything?"

"That it used to be a school for troubled boys."

"I could have told you that."

"That somewhere along the line, it stopped admitting troubled boys and now only educates the country's cream of the crop."

"I could have told you that too."

"That Congressman Daniel Jenkins is the school's main financial contributor."

Ellen looked at him and raised her eyebrows and twisted her lips. "That too."

Bronson opened his hands, placed them in front of him, and waved them. "What can I say? Some people have to learn the hard way." He turned off the computer. "Why do you think Lorraine volunteered her time there?"

Ellen stood up and headed toward Bronson. She placed her hand on his shoulder and squeezed. "Maybe she felt bad about her childhood so she reached out to those boys, hoping to prevent them from making the same mistakes she did."

Bronson sighed. "Yeah, maybe so. Makes sense." He moved the mouse next to the computer so it wouldn't fall and stood up. "I'm going to call Carol, and then I'll hit the sack. Good night."

BITS AND PIECES of Lorraine's life plagued Bronson's dreams. He found himself sitting up in the bed more often than lying on it. By six in the morning, eagerness to get the day started forced him to get up. He shaved and showered. By 6:30, he was downstairs, playing with the coffee maker, cursing himself for not asking Ellen where she kept the coffee and filters.

"Far top right hand side cabinet."

Bronson pivoted and saw Mike leaning against the door frame.

"Why are you up so early?" Bronson reached for the can of coffee.

"I've always been an early riser. Feel I'm wasting the day if I stay in bed." He grabbed two coffee mugs and handed one to Bronson. "Ellen's still asleep."

Bronson turned on the coffee maker. "Think the two of you will ever hook up again?"

"I plan to follow your example and retire while I'm still young. When I do that, she'll take me back for sure."

"Retire, you? When will this be?"

"Soon. Real soon."

The coffee finished dripping and Bronson poured Mike

and himself each a cup. Mike blew into the coffee and sat down at the dinette table. "What's today's agenda?"

"I'm payin' Mr. Steel a visit."

"Mr. Steel?" Mike's eyebrows furrowed. "Oh yeah, you mean Mark Wellington, alias Mr. Steel because that's how he built the family fortune."

"Right."

"Need some company?"

"I can always use your company, but I think we can use our time more wisely if you head to the congressman's school for boys. Find out what Lorraine did over there, whom she was close to, anything along those lines." Bronson poured what he thought was the equivalent of two, maybe three, teaspoons of sugar and added cream. "You know the routine." Bronson half emptied the mug with one swig. "I better call Trooper Cannady and fill her in on what we've learned and what we're planning to do."

"Think she'll tell you to back off?"

"Nah. I think she welcomes the help as long as we keep her informed."

NOT ONLY DID Cannady not get upset, she embraced the idea. "I've already talked to Mr. Steel, but he was tight lipped. Didn't give us a damn thing to go on. Maybe you'll have better luck. Just keep me posted."

Bronson promised her he would and disconnected. Soon as he finished his coffee, he headed out. The drive back to Pittsburgh gave him plenty of time to think about Lorraine. He was now remembering the good times and pushing aside the bad ones. Less than an hour later, he slowed down as he executed a left onto Wellington Ave. Two blocks down, he found Mr. Steel's residence, the address and name embossed on the stone pillars by the gate.

He pressed the intercom button located on the outside

of the locked wrought iron gate. From there, the driveway curved and disappeared into a cluster of trees that hid the mansion from the public's view.

"May I help you?" came a male voice behind the inter-com box.

"I'm here to see Mr. Mark Wellington III."

"I'm sorry, sir, but Mr. Wellington isn't taking any visi-tors."

"Tell him I'm Lorraine's brother."

"Just a minute, please."

A cool chill infiltrated Bronson's car and he wished he could roll up the window but didn't want to take a chance on missing the answer. He waited and wrapped his arms around himself.

He waited some more.

Damn, looked like he'd have to find another way to meet Mr. Wellington. Just as he was about to back up, the gates rolled open. Bronson didn't wait for instructions. He drove in.

The three-story mansion loomed before him and awed him with its splendor. Bronson wondered how much time Lorraine had actually spent there. He parked and rang the doorbell. A pair of dark oak doors opened and a middle-aged man stepped aside. "Mr. Bronson, I assume."

Bronson nodded and entered the large vestibule that con-sisted of high ceilings and museum-quality Biedermeier furniture.

"Mr. Wellington will see you in the music room." He turned and Bronson followed him. They walked past the magnificent art collection that hung on the walls and the seemingly comfortable, richly upholstered couches.

The butler reached for a door to his right. "Mr. Wel-lington hasn't been feeling too well lately. Please don't upset him."

"It's not my intention to." Bronson stepped in and the butler closed the door behind him. A distinguished looking man in his seventies sat in a wheelchair by a grand piano. He wore a white shirt and a silver necktie along with a matching silver colored silk robe. A music themed blanket covered his lower torso.

"You look very much like I pictured you." The millionaire rolled his wheelchair toward Bronson and offered him his hand. "Lorraine spoke often of you."

Don't leave me. Bronson closed his eyes. In all these years, he hadn't once thought of his sister.

"Care for something to drink?"

Coffee. But he was such a jerk he didn't deserve the drink. "No, thank you."

"My condolences to you."

"Thank you, and my condolences to you. I understand you loved my sister."

The old man let out a small laugh. "That, I did. Still do." He pointed to the plush couch. "Please make yourself comfortable."

Bronson sat.

"I'm twenty-six years older than your sister. My own children, some older than Lorraine, called me a dirty old man. But the thing was, Lorraine made me feel young. She liked me for who I am, not what I am."

Bronson's eyebrows furrowed. "Liked you?"

"Yes, *liked*, not *loved*." He sighed. "She never pretended otherwise. Thing is, she was in love with someone else. Never told me who and I never asked. But I accepted her choice. We were together a lot, and she made me laugh, made me feel good about myself. She never asked for anything. I'm the one who willingly gave her all the creature comforts she had."

"You bought her the house she lived in, and you paid the utilities and all the other bills."

Wellington nodded.

"And in return, what did you get?"

"The pleasure of her company. Nothing more. Nothing less."

Bronson digested the information. "What can you tell me about the man she loved?"

Wellington wet his lips and looked away. "Not much."

"How do you know he even existed?"

"I could tell. I knew Lorraine probably better than anyone else. I could tell when she was thinking about him, which was most of the time."

"And that didn't upset you? Make you jealous, perhaps?"

Wellington rolled his chair away from Bronson and planted himself in front of the window. The view revealed an Olympic-size pool with life-size statues of Greek women emptying their vases into the pool. Further on out, tennis courts sat, empty and desolate. "You want to know if I was jealous." A long pause followed. "Yes, it's only natural, but I didn't act on those feelings. I didn't get to be Mr. Steel by giving in to impulses." His fingers played with the folds of the blanket. He remained quiet.

Bronson let the minutes pass before he got up and stood facing the same window Wellington did. "Beautiful view out there."

"Yes."

"Did my sister swim in that pool?"

"Occasionally. She preferred this room. She loved her music. She even made me this blanket." He stroked the blanket, which was decorated with musical notes and symbols. He raised it up so that it covered him from his waist down.

"Nice blanket."

"It is."

What else didn't he know about his sister? "She played the piano?"

"Like a pro."

Silence reigned and Bronson felt comfortable with that. He watched Wellington's fingers as he continued to quickly fold and unfold the edge of his blanket. "Now tell me what you've been avoiding telling me."

Wellington's lips formed a thin line. "You've only been here less than an hour, and you can already read me. Just like Lorraine." He turned and stared at the piano. "Just like Lorraine," he repeated. He looked up at Bronson. "She left me, you know, one time, for almost a year. That really hurt, not so much that she walked out, but that she wouldn't come to me in her time of need."

"Where did she go?"

"She didn't say, and I didn't ask."

Exactly what Bronson thought he was going to answer. "But you knew anyway. You made it a point to find out."

Wellington covered his eyes. Slowly, he nodded. "She had a baby."

Bronson gasped.

"Unfortunately, not mine," Wellington continued. "Prior to her walking out, she spent a lot of her time with Matthew Devono, her ex-pimp. Then one day she and Mario Serafin took off and vanished from the face of the earth."

Bronson's eyebrows moved infinitesimally. "Mario Serafin?" His voice came out as a coarse murmur.

"I assume you know him."

"The waiter at the restaurant?"

"Don't let that fool you. Serafin is Devono's right-hand man, but he waits tables occasionally so that Devono can give him a glorified, but legal, paycheck."

"You think Serafin's the father?"

"I didn't say that. I'm simply giving you the facts as I know them. She and Serafin took off together and when she came back, there was no baby, only that hollow, empty look that lasted for months."

"What became of the child?"

"If the baby ever existed, I couldn't tell you its whereabouts."

"How old would that baby be now?"

"A teenager, I suppose." Wellington rubbed the bridge of his nose. "All I know is that Lorraine's love for…for that man never diminished. But she came back to me, and I was satisfied."

Bronson, like a sponge absorbing water, took in the room's contents. The grand piano, now silent. An electric guitar, a violin, music sheets on each of the stands, plush furniture, a chandelier. All the money in the world couldn't buy Wellington what he wanted the most, Lorraine's love. "Thank you for being honest with me."

"I'll have my secretary cut you a check for thirty-thousand dollars."

"What for?"

"Lorraine told me you were a cop."

Something else Lorraine knew about him. How?

Wellington continued, "A great cop, at that. I'm hiring you to find her killer."

"I'm retired now, and I don't have a private eye license."

"But you have the will and determination to bring the bastard to justice."

"And I promise you I will."

"Then take the money for business expenses."

"I'm not sure I can do that."

"Then I will send you a VISA card. You can charge your meals, your gasoline—anything you want. To solve a case like this, you're going to need a lot of money."

Bronson took one last look at the room his sister loved and headed out.

"One more thing," Wellington said. Bronson stopped but didn't turn around.

"You remind me a lot of your sister. Your attitude, your mannerisms—those also belonged to Lorraine."

Bronson closed his eyes and swallowed hard. "Thanks for seein' me." The more he learned about his sister, the less he knew her.

Don't leave me.

TWELVE

BRONSON SAT IN the Chevy Cruze, trying to conjure a mental image of Lorraine. Tough on the outside, soft on the inside, and full of contradictions. *You remind me a lot of your sister.* Bronson shook his head as though trying to clear the image. He reached for the ignition key and drove away.

He needed to go back to his sister's house. He stopped at the stop sign, the house now several blocks away. He adjusted the rearview mirror and spotted a maroon-red Aston Martin more than a block behind.

Surely, while searching Lorraine's house, the troopers and he missed something that at the time didn't seem important. If he took his time, emptied every drawer...

He looked at the rearview mirror once again. The classic sports car had sped up and was approaching fast. Bronson changed lanes. So did the Aston Martin. A coincidence? Bronson didn't believe in them. He executed a right and so did the maroon-red car.

Bronson sped up, made a sharp right, and pulled in behind some parked cars. He let the engine run. Seconds later, the Aston Martin turned, the squeaking tires announcing its urgency. The car sped past Bronson's parked Cruze and then slowed down as though looking for him.

Bronson pulled out into the traffic lane and soon caught up with the pursuer. Half a block later, the sports car driver tapped the brake pedal several times in quick successions before turning on the right hand signal.

Bronson got the message. He was to follow the car into the strip mall's parking lot.

Bronson executed a right and placed his car so that it faced the classic car. With the engine still running, Bronson waited for the driver to get out. He scooted down into the seat, enabling him to see and at the same time making himself a small target.

The Aston Martin's door slowly opened and a woman in her early forties stepped out. She wore high heel shoes and a bright blue dress that revealed every curve she had and those she didn't.

Not your typical pursuer, but experience had taught Bronson not to trust anyone. Bronson opened the door to his car. "Step away from the car and put your hands up."

The woman hesitated for a moment and then did as told. "I'm Amanda Wellington. You just talked to my dad."

"What do you want?"

"I need to talk to you. I mean you no harm."

The parking lot swarmed with people, and cars constantly flew by on the busy street. Odds were in his favor. No one in their right mind would shoot with so many witnesses around. He turned off the engine and stepped out. "Put your hands down. Sorry about that. I had no way of knowing." Except for the Aston Martin. He left that part out.

Amanda lowered her arms. "We need to talk. Is there a place we can do that instead of this damn parking lot?"

Bronson scanned the strip mall's buildings. One read "Lisa's Place: Coffee and Pastries." What luck.

THIRTEEN

THE MAN RUBBED his chin as he sat waiting for his boss to finish with the meeting. Although several other people also waited—some longer than he had—he knew he'd be next. He'd done this hundreds of times before. So why was he a bundle of nerves this time? He rubbed his chin faster.

The woman sitting across from him looked at him and squinted, her eyebrows slightly arched downward. By rubbing his chin he had attracted her attention, making himself stand out in a room filled with people.

Definitely not a good idea. He placed his hand under his leg and forced himself to relax.

The door opened and his boss along with two men, both dressed in suits, stepped out. As they shook hands, the boss glanced at him and indicated the office.

The man raised his hand to rub his chin, remembered not to, stood up, and waited for his boss to step in before he did.

The boss waved goodbye at the two men and turned to the small crowd of people waiting their turn. "Thank you for coming. I hope you gave my secretary your name. As always, I'll be seeing you in the order you arrived." The boss reached for the doorknob and smiled. "This won't take long."

The man rubbed his chin as he closed the door behind them.

The boss turned to the man who stood at attention toward the entryway, walked around the desk, and sat down. "Relax, will ya?" A small pause followed. "So what's up?"

"I did as you told me. I checked up on Bronson."

"Yeah, and?"

"His reputation as a stubborn detective follows him. He won't rest until he solves his cases. He was one of Dallas' best."

"Are you saying he's going to be a problem?"

He nodded.

"Then take care of him."

"It's not that easy." The man rubbed his chin, saw the irritation in the boss' eyes, and stopped. "First Lorraine, then her brother. Too much of a coincidence. The troopers won't swallow that."

"Couldn't a car accident take care of our little problem?"

"I'll use that as a last resort."

The boss leaned forward. "What do you have in mind?"

"My plan will eliminate Bronson, but to do so, my idea requires your full co-operation."

The boss inhaled deeply while the eyes drilled the man who sat on the other side of the huge desk. "Tell me about it."

FOURTEEN

A TWINGE OF pride swelled within Bronson. Carol was no-where around and he had put only one-and-a-half spoon-fuls of sugar in his coffee. Too bad Carol was so far away and couldn't share his triumph. Too bad because he missed her.

Too bad about so many other things.

He forced his mind to clear and focus on the woman sitting across from him. Somewhere a rich cosmetic surgeon had given her the teen-like skin that she'd wear for the rest of her life, or at least until his services were needed again. Narrow eyes offset her tight skin and filled the air with a sense of exotic beauty. Her eyes missed little but did a great job of luring in those around her. Her pinkie finger elevated as she stirred her latte or whatever fancy coffee she had bought. Cancel that. No such thing as fancy coffee existed. "So you wanted to talk to me." Bronson sipped his plain, not-so-sweet, almond-brown coffee.

"Yes, Mr. Bronson, I do."

"You can drop the mister. Most everyone calls me Bronson."

She cleared her throat and shifted positions. "I suppose you can call me Amanda."

I'll call you Mandy and knock the socks off your pretty panty-hosed legs. Bronson stirred his coffee even though he had already done that. He raised his cup, smelled its sweet aroma, and took a sip. "Ms. Amanda." He emphasized the *Ms.* part. "What can I do for you?"

"Ever hear of François La Carcé?"

Sounded like a stuffy name. "Can't say I have."

"He's an up and coming artist who lives in an artist community in a remote part of France. He's a recluse and devotes all of his time to art which is his only passion."

That explained the name. "I wish him luck."

"Which he doesn't need, especially from a commoner like you. His income per month is way above what you would ever hope to make in a year. It's already in the high five-figure amount."

"Must be nice for him." *Or at least this commoner thinks so.*

A young couple, she with long black hair that cascaded past her waist and he with a mop of curly blond hair, sat at the table next to them. Amanda frowned and turned her back to them. She shouldn't have bothered. They were too engrossed in each other. Amanda said, "Sweet, dear François did a painting for us as an heirloom. He gave it to my father. I'm sure we could sell it right now for a cool million dollars. Imagine if we keep it as an investment for a few more years."

"Imagine."

Amanda's lips formed a tight line across her face and as unlikely as it seemed, her eyes narrowed even further. "Your sister stole the painting from us."

Bronson put on his best poker face that had fooled people many times. He reached for his coffee, slowly sipped it, and set the cup down. "And you can prove this."

"Mr. Bronson, I want my painting back."

Bronson's left brow shot up. "Don't you mean your father's painting?"

Amanda stood up with such abruptness that her chair would have fallen had Bronson not caught it. "You have twenty-four hours to hand me that painting."

"Before what?"

Amanda glared at him and stormed out of the café.

THE WOMAN WITH the long, black hair who sat at the table behind the one that Bronson and Amanda had occupied moved away from the man she had been kissing. She watched as Bronson headed out. "Should we follow him?"

The blond headed man shook his head. "We'll be too obvious. If Bronson's got any brains, and based on all of our reports, he has more than his share—he's bound to make us."

The black haired beauty frowned. "We can't just let him drive away. He's going to lead us to the painting."

The blond man swept the tip of her nose with his index finger and winked. "I'm not stupid. I have no intention of losing him. My brother can follow him and report his whereabouts. We'll take it from there."

She reached for her cell and made the call.

FIFTEEN

BRONSON SAT IN the Cruze, his lips a tight line, his un-blinking eyes focused straight ahead, his mind not registering any images. His hands formed fists, then opened, then formed fists once again.

Lorraine. A common thief.

No. She had changed. He had to believe that. She had outgrown her wild youth. He reached for his cell and punched in some numbers. He heard the phone ring, then: "Wellington Residence."

"Mr. Wellington, please."

"I'm sorry, sir, but—"

"Tell him Bronson is calling. He'll want to talk to me."

"Just a minute, sir."

Bronson waited an eternity before he heard someone pick up the phone. "Bronson? Wellington here. Does this mean you've decided to accept my offer? What have you got?"

"A question."

A small pause followed. "Okay. Go ahead."

"What can you tell me about François La Carcé?"

"He's a very talented painter, so I funded him some money to set up his studio. In return, he created a breath-taking sea storm painting called *Mother Nature's Anger.* He gave it to me as a thank you gift. Why do you ask?"

"Where's the paintin' now?"

"I imagine it's hanging somewhere in Lorraine's house. Why?"

"Why would Lorraine have the paintin'?"

"I gave it to her."

Bronson let out the air he didn't know he held. "You gave her the paintin'?"

"That's what I said. Why are you asking this? Has it been stolen?"

"I have no idea. I'm on my way to her house." Bronson started the car and blended with the traffic. "Last time I was there, I didn't see it, but I wasn't lookin'."

"What's so important about the painting, and this time answer my question."

"Amanda cornered me after I left your house."

Wellington sighed. "Oh, Mandy." A slight pause followed. "Let me guess. She wants the painting back."

"She does."

"Don't give it to her. It belonged to Lorraine, and I suppose it now belongs to you or whomever she left it to in her will."

"She had a will?"

"That, I wouldn't know."

A car cut in front of Bronson and he had to stamp on the brakes. Inside, he cursed the driver. Outside, he forced civility in his tone. "Thank you for the information."

"It didn't come without a price tag."

"Meanin'?"

"When you get to her house, I want to know if you find the painting." His voice sounded far away. Bronson guessed he was worn out.

"I'll let you know." Bronson disconnected and concentrated on his driving. He was within a mile of reaching his sister's home when a snappy tune played on his cell. Bronson checked the caller I.D. The Steel Man himself. "Mr. Wellington, what can I do for you?"

"I don't know if this is helpful or even if it's relevant."

"What's that?"

"About six months ago, I took Lorraine out to eat. We bumped into the family lawyer. When I introduced them, I got the distinct feeling they had already met. Maybe she did leave a will."

"What's the lawyer's name?"

"Sam Glass."

"Got contact information?" Bronson pulled over, reached for his shirt pocket, retrieved the small spiral notebook, and the pen.

Wellington gave him the number and Bronson wrote it down.

"One more thing," Wellington said.

Bronson checked the side and the rearview mirrors before pulling back into traffic. "What's that?"

"If the painting was stolen, could that have been the reason Lorraine was killed?"

"That's not a very likely scenario, but at this point, I can't rule anythin' out."

Wellington gasped. "That means I'm the reason she's dead."

"No, you're not responsible. Had it been a simple theft, why would the killer follow her to the bridge when all he had to do was break into her house and take the paintin'? There's got to be something more than just the burglary."

"I feel better." Bronson could almost see Wellington smile. "Thank you, Mr. Bronson." He hung up.

The light turned red and Bronson stopped. His fingers drummed the steering wheel as he waited for the light to turn green. What he had told Wellington was the truth, but what he hadn't said was that the painting could easily have led to his sister's death.

If the painting had been stolen from his sister's house,

Lorraine might have known who took it. Killing her would guarantee that the villain's I.D. remained a secret.

Bronson thoughts drifted back to Amanda.

SIXTEEN

NOTHING COULD POSSIBLY go wrong today. The signs all around the curly blond haired man guaranteed his success. The sky the color of blue-tinted glass assured him that things would go his way. He had followed Bronson from a safe distance, confident in his knowledge Bronson would never know. The fool had led him to Lorraine's house, so now here he sat two doors down, watching the mansion.

Quite a nice pad, he had to admit. Two stories, plenty of windows peeking at him like creature eyes in the forest. The long columns at the entryway gave it a flair of once being a strictly colonial architecture type house. But now that two wings, one at each side, had been added, the new design blended its former architecture with the contemporary look. The end result pleased his eye, and more than tripled the living area. He shrugged. More places to search.

Not his problem. The quiet neighborhood told the curly blond haired man he had done right. Way he saw it, Bronson would either walk out with the painting or leave it behind. If he carried the painting with him, he would clobber Bronson and relieve him of his burden. If Bronson decided to leave the painting in the house, he'd wait until Bronson drove off before letting himself in.

Either way, the painting was his—theirs. He scrunched down on the seat, making himself almost impossible to spot. While he waited, he called his twin and the Raven. He wanted to share the good news with them.

COULD BE A COINCIDENCE, but Bronson had long ago stopped believing in them. He remembered that the last time he was at his sister's house, he had watched Cannady and the other troopers search the premises. In the library, Cannady had opened the desk's top right hand drawer, revealing a nice looking pair of binoculars.

Bronson headed for the library and quickly retrieved them. As he went up the stairs, he took two at a time. The front guest bedroom had a perfect view of the street below him. He could look out, but no one would be able to look in. But just to make sure, he'd hide behind the curtains. He peeked out, exposing as little of himself as possible.

Just as he thought. A solitary figure sat behind the green Toyota Camry LE, the same car that had followed him from Lisa's Place. Its driver had parked it across the street, two doors down. Maybe the car and its driver belonged there. Maybe it didn't. Either way, he'd contact Cannady. She would want to check on that.

Bronson adjusted the binoculars so that the license plate clearly showed. He jotted down the information. He moved the binoculars up trying to identify the figure in the car. No such luck. He couldn't get a clear view because the man sat low in the seat. As far as Bronson could tell, he was alone.

He retrieved his cell, called Cannady, and told her about Amanda, the painting, and the car that followed him.

SEVENTEEN

EXACTLY EIGHTEEN MINUTES had passed since Bronson began his search. How fricking long does it take to grab a painting and walk out? The curly blond haired man squirmed in the car seat and tried to make himself comfortable. It didn't work. He wished he could get out and walk some of the cricks out. He hated sitting in the car doing nothing but watching.

His cell buzzed. "Hey, twin, what gives?"

"You've got to get out of there. The troopers are coming."

The twin sat up, his hand reaching for the ignition key. "How do you know?" He held on to the key ring but didn't start the engine.

"My twin radar told me to warn you."

Maybe because his twin had been born minutes before him, he assumed the role of leader. As such, his older brother had saved him on several occasions. "How do you know they're heading this way?"

"Soon as I got the feeling, I zoomed in on your cell and got your whereabouts. Me and the Raven drove down and parked by the public pool, a safe distance from you. We're several miles away. Didn't want to blow your cover in case I'm wrong. We'd been here less than five minutes when two trooper cars sped past me going in your direction which made me think they're probably heading your way."

"Thanks for the warning."

"What are you going to do?"

"I've got to cover my tracks so I'm going to pay the neighbor a visit, then get out of here."

"Act fast."

"Will do." He pocketed the car keys as he watched each window, wondering which one Bronson stood behind. No matter how hard he tried, he couldn't see Bronson. Hiding that way and not letting him in on the fact that he knew he was being followed, took a lot of skill. He had underestimated Bronson. He'd never do that again.

He bit his lip. The signs had betrayed him. He'd have to be more careful. Make sure he read the signs correctly. He reached for the car door handle and stepped out. He hesitated a few minutes before heading toward the house located beside the parked Toyota. He hoped to hell Bronson was watching right now, but he had no way of knowing.

He rang the doorbell, not sure what he'd say when someone opened the door. He waited the appropriate amount of time before ringing again. No one was home. Good. That saved him the trouble of trying to figure out what to say.

He headed back to the Toyota, forcing himself to take normal steps. Let Bronson think he was just a casual caller waiting for his friends to show up. Just for good measure, as he walked back to the Camry, he pretended to make a call. He placed his cell on his cheek and moved his lips as though talking.

He reached the safety of the car. His heart could stop pounding now. Bronson better thank his lucky stars. He had won this time, but not ever again.

AFTER BRONSON FINISHED talking to Cannady, he walked from room to room memorizing every detail. In his search, he found neither the picture nor any signs that a painting had once adorned any of the walls.

He glanced out the window and saw the same car parked in the same place. He hoped Cannady would hurry.

Turning away from the window, Bronson concentrated on his search. He had counted five desks scattered throughout the mansion: two in the study, one in the den, one in the library, and one more in her bedroom. The most likely desk to hide any information should be the one in her bedroom. He'd start there.

Bronson looked under the desk and saw nothing unusual. He opened its top drawer and emptied it of its contents, mostly pens, pencils, ruler, scissors, and notepads. Before setting each paper aside, he thumbed through each one, making sure he didn't miss anything. He felt the empty drawer for a false bottom. No such luck.

He moved on to the second drawer and did the same. Then the third drawer and finally the last drawer. By the time he finished, he knew nothing more about Lorraine than he had before.

One desk down and four to go. But first, he'd check on the car.

Still there.

Although Bronson didn't expect to find anything, he nevertheless examined the desk in the study with the same amount of detail he had devoted to the first.

Again, nothing, zip, zero.

He glanced out the window. Nothing changed.

He worked on the third desk. Same results. His watch told him Cannady should be arriving any minute now. He stood by the window and watched.

Seconds later, the driver opened the car door and stepped out.

Bronson stood straighter, watching. Waiting. After a small hesitation, the blond man strolled up the walkway leading to the house where he had parked the car.

Watching from the second story window made it hard to notice details, but Bronson did his best to memorize as much as possible. First and most important, he focused the binoculars on the man. Blond, curly hair, possibly average height, average weight. Dressed casually, blue jeans, blue T-shirt. Nothing unusual about him, or at least nothing visible from Bronson's limited view.

He watched the man ring the doorbell, wait, ring it again. Taking his time, the man headed back to his car as he talked on the cell. He reached his car and drove away.

Maybe coincidences did exist. Seems he had been waiting for the folks across the street after all. He called Cannady and reported the latest development.

She listened quietly, then said, "I checked on the license plate you gave me. It's assigned to a Hertz-Rent-a-Car company. Paperwork from them shows the driver is a man named Frederick Parson. The driver license picture that Hertz faxed to the barracks shows him to be a twenty-six year old blond headed man, just as you reported. He has no record. So I tend to agree with you. We're barking up the wrong tree."

As they talked, Bronson headed for the desk on the den. "Yep, should know better. Nothin' ever comes this easy."

"Don't get discouraged. We'll find the killer."

"Won't rest 'till we do." An awkward pause followed, which Bronson noted.

Cannady cleared her throat. "What are you doing at Lorraine's house?"

"Givin' it a thorough search."

"You will remember to report anything you find." A statement, not a question.

"Naturally."

"Then I'm turning back. I can be more productive at the barracks." Cannady disconnected.

Bronson finished searching the desks. Although he hadn't expected to find anything, he still felt disappointed at the failure. He flopped down on the couch, frowned, and rubbed his eyes.

He stood up, glanced down at the couch, and removed the cushions. Nothing, but what had he expected to find? The painting? A note scribbled to him? He placed the cushions back on the couch and sat down.

Each nook and cranny offered the possibility of discovery. If only he knew what to look for, he could narrow his search.

He had already given up on the idea of finding the painting within the premises, but it had to be somewhere. Assuming he found the painting, would that lead him to the killer? Unfortunately, he had no way of knowing and at this point, the painting was the only loose thread he had. He would follow it. Somewhere in this house, Lorraine had left him a hint. Every instinct told him that. All he needed to do was find it.

If he were Lorraine, where would he hide the clue? As kids, Bronson remembered playing a form of hide and seek. Instead of hiding themselves, they would hide an object. Bronson quickly learned that Lorraine would always hide the item among her favorite toys.

Her favorite toys. Now replaced by music.

He sprang off the couch and headed for the room located to his left. He stood at its door, absorbing every detail. A grand piano majestically occupied the middle of the room. A bookshelf held books, all relating to composers' lives or similar topics. An opened violin case, with its bow resting on top of the instrument, lay below a stand. Did she play the violin too? He groaned as he realized how little he still knew of Lorraine.

Bronson's eyes drifted toward the sheets of music resting

in their proper place above the piano, waiting to be played. Mozart's bust to his left seemed to smile as it absorbed the beautiful notes that once filled this room.

Without the musical scores, the room would be void of sound. They were an essential part of the room, her passion. Here, if any place, is where Lorraine would leave him a message. He carefully removed each sheet, looking for any handwritten marks. Other than an occasional scribbled fortissimo or pianissimo, he found none.

What he did find was a business card. He picked it up. On the upper right hand corner a still life painting added a sense of glamour to the card. The center of the card read Larry S. Miller, Artist. An address, phone number, and website at the bottom completed the information. Bronson pocketed the card.

An artist's card. A missing painting.

Interesting.

EIGHTEEN

Soon as Bronson hit the freeway heading back to Ellen's house, he used the Bluetooth to call Wellington. His personal caretaker informed Bronson he didn't feel well and was asleep. However, he expected an update on the painting soon as he woke up.

"Tell him the paintin' wasn't at her house, which may or may not mean anything. I have a lead to follow."

"Very well, sir, I will relay the message."

"One more thing," Bronson added.

"Yes?"

"Tell him I hope he feels better."

"He won't. At this stage, all we can do is keep him comfortable."

"I know," Bronson said, "but tell him anyway."

"Will do."

They disconnected and Bronson called Carol. They talked until Bronson pulled into Ellen's driveway.

"Give Mike and Ellen a big hug for me. Tell them I really appreciate them taking care of you," Carol said. "As for you, I'm sending you a big, slurpy kiss."

Bronson smiled. What had he done to deserve such a great woman? "I love you." He put the cell away and turned off the engine.

Mike greeted him at the door. "Hey."

"Hey yourself."

"Just got home myself, less than five minutes ago."

Bronson unlaced and removed his boots and collapsed onto the couch. "Tell me about your day."

"The Daniel Jenkins School for Boys is a huge facility that rests on several well-kept acres. The buildings are immaculate and all the boys, ranging from six to eighteen, wear uniforms. The latest, most up-to-date technology occupies not only their living quarters, but also their classrooms. This is the school for rich boys, as it takes a bundle to have your child enrolled there, but they can almost guarantee that when your child graduates, he will be a productive member of our society. They have the testimonials to confirm this."

Bronson stretched out on the couch and half raised his left brow.

"Just giving you background information," Mike said. "Never know when it comes in handy."

Bronson continued to stare at him.

"Okay, now to the stuff you really want to hear." He took a deep breath and spoke as though reciting a dissertation.

"Lorraine devoted several hours every day—including most Saturdays and Sundays—to the school. Most of the kids highly regarded her. Those that didn't, say she had her favorites, three in particular."

Bronson recalled the only picture that Lorraine displayed in her house, three boys playing football.

"She taught music."

No surprise there.

"Her closest and only friend at the school, a woman named Claudine Ramirez says the school would have hired her as a teacher, but she wasn't certified so they couldn't. But she was so good with the kids and she knew her subject so well, they kept her as a volunteer."

"Did Claudine tell you anything about Lorraine that could help you?"

"Unfortunately, no. Even though she was the one whom Lorraine talked to the most, Lorraine wasn't very communicative. Kept to herself most of the time."

A loner—that's the Lorraine, Bronson remembered. Somehow it seemed to reassure him. "Did you talk to the three boys?"

"I'm supposed to go back tomorrow. Seems the kids haven't been notified of her death. The administration wanted to be reassured that the deceased was indeed their beloved music teacher before making an official announcement. Later on today, they will call a mandatory assembly for all students, faculty, and staff. That's where they'll inform everyone about her death. Counselors will be on standby today and tomorrow morning. I'll be there in the afternoon."

"Thanks, buddy."

"Don't mention it. You'd do the same for me."

"You don't have a sister."

"That you know of."

Bronson half-smiled. He had done an excellent job of keeping that secret all to himself. "Anythin' else?"

"Yeah, just my personal observation. Her so-called only friend at the school, Claudine, didn't seem to be distressed. She gave me the impression of being more nervous than upset. I got the feeling that there was something she wasn't—or couldn't—tell me."

NINETEEN

ALL NIGHT LONG, Bronson tossed and turned. Bits and pieces of unformed thoughts attacked his dreams. The painting. Bronson rolled over so he'd lay on his right side.

Carol driving across the country by herself. He went back to lying on his left side.

Mr. Steel. The pimp. Bronson rolled to his back.

Lorraine's mansion, huge but void of any personal touches, as if she hadn't really lived there. Bronson rolled on his side, again. He wished he could find a comfortable position.

The baby. Oh God, the baby. His nephew. Niece? Lorraine's child. How could a mother give up her own baby? Or did this child even exist?

Bronson sat up, his body drenched with sweat. The alarm clock's digital numbers read 5:16. The sun hadn't even made its presence known, but still he'd get up. He dragged himself out of bed and headed for the computer.

Two hours later, Bronson continued to pound on the keys. He half-jumped when someone placed his hand on his shoulder.

"Sorry I startled you," Mike said. "I've been calling your name, but you were too focused to hear me. What gives?"

"I Googled Larry S. Miller."

"Who's that?"

"A local artist. I found his business card buried between my sister's music sheets."

Mike headed for the kitchen. "He must be somebody really interesting to make you forget your morning coffee."

Bronson's eyebrows shot up as he glanced at the empty space normally occupied by the cup of coffee. "Guess I got too busy."

Mike opened the cabinet door and retrieved two cups. "What makes this guy so fascinating?"

"Lorraine's painting is missing, and I found an artist's card hidden in my sister's sheets of music. His website's motto is "You Want It Painted, I Will Paint It.' I think I need to pay him a visit."

The room filled with the tempting aroma of coffee. Mike poured two cups. "I tend to agree with you. The missing painting and the artist's card call for a visit."

Bronson nodded and remained quiet.

Mike folded his arms, leaned against the door frame, and waited for Bronson to finish.

"That's not all I Googled."

Mike returned to the kitchen and picked up the sugar bowl, a spoon, and the cup of coffee already light with milk. He handed them to Bronson. "Tell me about it."

Bronson lowered his head and let out a long breath. "I'm checking on my nephew or my niece. Lorraine's kid."

"And?"

"I checked for a Bronson baby born in the last twenty to ten years to a Lorraine Bronson. No matches. I also checked death certificates. I began with Pittsburgh and gradually increased the search area. I'm all out of options and I'm empty-handed." Bronson poured the sugar in his coffee and stirred.

"Birth and death certificates could bear the father's last name."

"I know." Bronson shut down the computer. "Mr. Steel heavily hinted that Mario Serafin may have been the father."

"Serafin?"

"The pimp's right-hand man."

Mike cocked his head as though trying to remember. "Oh, the waiter, you mean, the one at Devono's Steak House?"

"That's the one, except the waiter part is a cover. He's really Devono's personal guard. Do you remember anything unusual about him?"

"Can't say I do. He seemed like an ordinary, but darn good, waiter."

"I'll pay him a visit."

"Want me to tag along?"

"No need. I know in the afternoon you're visiting the boys' school again, but your morning is free."

"Uh oh." Mike set his cup of coffee in the sink. "Why do I have a feeling that my morning schedule just got full?"

"If you can tear yourself away from Ellen, I thought maybe you could pay Mr. Steel's lawyer a visit. I wrote his name in my pocket notebook and that's in the bedroom. I'll get you the information in a few minutes."

"Okay, but tell me again why I want to visit this lawyer."

"Mr. Wellington, alias Mr. Steel, says that he took Lorraine out to eat and they bumped into the lawyer. When Wellington introduced them, he felt like Lorraine already knew him although neither of them ever mentioned the incident again. I thought maybe you could go see if he knows anything about the baby, and while you're there, you might as well check to see if Lorraine left a will."

"I can do that, but I don't know if it'll do any good. First thing the lawyer is going to do is quote me the lawyer-client-confidentiality clause. But maybe under the circumstances, he'll be willing to talk. Ellen is pretty good at getting people to reveal information. Think I'll take her with me. We can have lunch somewhere before it's time to

visit the boys' school." He headed toward Ellen's bedroom,
let himself in, and closed the door behind him.

Bronson remained in the den, drinking his coffee. The
baby. How old was this child now? Where was this kid?
Oh, Lorraine. I should have been here for you.
Don't leave me.

TWENTY

As far as Mario Serafin was concerned, the only disadvantage to living outside Pittsburgh's city limits was the long drive he had to make every day, especially on days like today. Already past eleven at night and Mario was barely pulling into his driveway. He looked forward to a fast shower and flopping down on the bed. He felt tired, and he would sleep well tonight.

All that changed as soon as he opened the door. A tingling sensation began at the base of his neck and worked its way down his spine. Beware, it said.

He pulled his gun and stepped in.

He checked the living room.

Nothing.

The kitchen and laundry room.

Same results.

The bedrooms and bathrooms came next.

He put the gun away. He had felt so sure something had changed, a detail he hadn't noticed but would change his life forever.

Only three minutes past eight in the morning and someone banged on his front door. Mario trotted toward the large living room window, drew the curtains open, and saw Bronson. What the hell?

He opened the door. "What do you want?"

"I need to talk to you. Can I come in?"

Mario frowned. He hadn't slept well and his disposition

was on the short fuse mode. "You're here. You might as well come in." He moved to the side allowing Bronson to step in. "How the hell did you know where I live?"

"I talked to Devono earlier today. He gave me your address."

Mario's lips trembled as he bit his tongue. Devono had no right to give his address to anyone. It wasn't like him to do so. Why was Bronson the exception? No matter. Soon as Bronson walked out, he'd let his boss know exactly how he felt. "You had to have given Devono some information in exchange for my address."

"I did." Bronson sat down even though he hadn't been asked to.

Mario waited for Bronson to continue but when he didn't, Mario opened his hands and said, "And what was that?" He flopped down on the couch facing Bronson.

"I told him what I had found out about you and Lorraine and the baby."

Mario stopped breathing. He forced his breaths to come at even intervals. "What baby?"

"Don't play me the fool."

Mario leaned back on the recliner. "I'm not saying I know anything about a baby. I'm curious, that's all. What have you heard?"

"I know Lorraine was pregnant and you and my sister took off. When she came back, she was no longer pregnant and there was no baby."

Mario bolted to his feet. "What are you trying to insinuate? That I got rid of the kid? I had nothing to do with that. Lorraine was the one who—" A movement outside his window caught his eye. He looked again, but no one was there. Probably just the large elder tree's shadow moving in the wind.

"You were sayin'?"

Mario's gaze drifted back to Bronson. "What?"

"You said 'Lorraine was the one who.' Then you stopped. Who, what?" Bronson's eyes narrowed. "Are you the baby's father?"

Mario had a split second to glance at Bronson before a shot rang out. The bullet traveled through the window, and lead fragments and broken glass lodged themselves in Mario's brain.

He tumbled down, dead before he hit the ground.

TWENTY-ONE

EARLIER THAT DAY, Devono hung up the phone with a slam. Bronson had verified what he always feared. Mario was Lorraine's baby's father. The news shouldn't have come as a shock. After all, deep down he had known, but he hadn't wanted to believe it. When the suspicions surfaced, he'd pushed them aside.

Mario wouldn't betray him.

Mario knew how he felt.

Mario would be faithful.

Devono slammed his fist on the desk. Drops of his morning coffee jumped out of the cup. Devono grabbed a tissue and using broad, jerky movements, he wiped at the mess.

Such betrayals called for a harsh punishment. His men needed to learn this lesson. No matter who was involved, Devono wouldn't tolerate such actions. Mario, his favorite, wouldn't be the exception. No one would be. That's the message his men would receive.

Devono lowered his head and rubbed his eyes. His hand lingered above the phone handle. He clenched his fist, picked up the phone, and made the call.

LIGHT BARS PULSED, flashing through Mario's living room window. Pieces of shards of glass lay scattered on the floor. Radios squawked and troopers moved around the house, each with his own task.

Bronson had seen this same scene hundreds of times

before, but this one unnerved him. Too soon after Lorraine's death.

Bronson shook himself and forced himself to remain calm, help Cannady any way he could.

Cannady finished talking to Hunsicker. He nodded and headed out the door. She turned to Bronson. "That about wraps it up. You're sure you didn't see anything? Is there something else you'd like to tell us?"

Bronson shook his head. "I wish I had seen something. I ran outside hopin' to catch the sniper. No such luck."

"What were you thinking? You ran out with no gun?"

Instinct had taken over. He hadn't thought through what he would do once outside. "This thing with my sister. It's taken a toll on me. I'm not thinking straight."

"Ivy!"

Cannady looked toward the bedroom where Swanson had called her. "Yeah?" She spoke over her shoulder.

"You've got to see what I found."

Bronson and Cannady exchanged looks and both headed toward the bedroom.

"Under the bed," Swanson said. "More like under the springs."

Cannady got on her knees and looked. "Well, I'll be."

"What?" Bronson asked.

"There's a rifle under there."

Bronson stood perfectly still. "A rifle?" A rifle had ended his sister's life.

Cannady stood up. "I didn't tell you, but Swanson found the ejected cartridge at the scene of the crime. We'll test for a match."

"Will you notify me, either way?"

Cannady nodded. "I'll need a formal statement from you, again."

"I'll drop by the station." He started to walk away.

"One more thing."

Bronson stopped and turned.

"This is the second time we have to do this."

"Do what?"

"Meet under circumstances like these. Try not to make it a habit."

"I'll try, but there's no guarantees."

Cannady's lips formed a shape of a smile. "Get out of here."

TWENTY-TWO

BRONSON HAD WANTED to pay the "I Will Paint Anything" artist a visit today, but it was already late in the afternoon. He knew Ellen had prepared pot roast—her specialty—for dinner. She was gracious enough to allow him to stay with her. After all of her hard work in the kitchen, he wasn't about to let her down by not showing up.

Bronson drove at a steady sixty-miles an hour, the speed limit, and figured that at that speed, he would be getting to Ellen's around four. That would give him plenty of time to relax before Ellen served dinner. Minutes later, he spotted his exit ramp. He was closer to Ellen's than he thought. He followed the beige Ford Ranger down the exit ramp. Three cars behind him also took the same exit.

Trivia. Why did he always fill his mind with such trivia? He knew exactly why. He didn't want to think about Mario Serafin's death. Had he caused it by telling Devono that Serafin might be Lorraine's baby's father? Cannady said she would follow up on that, but both she and Bronson knew that would lead them nowhere. Devono would know how to cover his tracks.

The Ranger in front of him slowed down, forcing Bronson to step on the brake. Good thing he wasn't speeding. Otherwise, he would have rear-ended him.

The rifle. Why had Serafin hid the rifle under the bed? Would Cannady be able to prove that was the rifle used to kill his sister? Bronson grasped the steering wheel so tight that his knuckles turned red.

If Serafin was the killer, Bronson regretted that he never got the chance to punch him.

The Ranger in front of him slowed down even more, now going too slow for Bronson's comfort. He checked the side mirror. A white Focus on the left hung back just enough not to allow Bronson to change lanes.

Bronson thought about honking, but what good would that do? An off-green Altima behind Bronson pulled in to Bronson's right, creating its own lane. Bronson cursed the driver's stupidity. He slowed down, wanting to give the Altima the opportunity to get in front of him.

Instead, the Altima to his right and the Focus to his left increased their speed so that all three cars were lined up and all doing the same speed. Bronson glanced at the rear-view mirror. A red Civic tailgated him, preventing Bronson from backing up or slowing down.

A trap. A beautifully, carefully executed trap and Bronson had fallen for it. The Ranger stopped, forcing Bronson to do the same. The cars beside him, as well as the one behind him, followed suit.

Bronson visually inventoried the car but failed to find anything that could help him. He picked up the cell and called Cannady. The Altima driver raised a gun and pointed it at Bronson. He signaled for Bronson to put the phone down.

Bronson lowered the cell, but didn't disconnect. Without bending down, he used one foot to kick the boot off the other, ready to use it as a weapon.

Bronson watched as the Ranger's door opened and a man he'd never seen stepped out of the truck and headed his way.

TWENTY-THREE

As soon as Mike stepped inside the house, the aroma of a freshly cooked meal greeted his nostrils. When Ellen set her mind to it, she could create one heck of a good meal. Mike headed for the kitchen where he found Ellen chopping an apple. He wrapped his arms around her waist. "How's my favorite gal?"

She smiled. "Glad you're home."

"Why? Because you want me to help you with dinner?"

Ellen's smile widened. "Hm, that's not a bad idea." She handed him some bananas. "Cut these for me, please? I'm making a fruit salad."

Mike nodded, washed his hands, took out a plate, and got to work. "Did you know that the Daniel Jenkins School for Boys is no longer just for troubled boys?"

"I did, but tell me about it."

"Seems the school holds such high standards that influential folks are enrolling their kids there. Guess who their number one celebrity kid is?"

Ellen swept the apple slices into the salad bowl. "I'm not at all familiar with any of the celebrity kids so you've got me on that one."

"Congressman Daniel Jenkins' own kid. He's a big shot in the school. Lorraine was under orders to pay special attention to him and his buddies."

"That figures. The ultra rich always get the special attention. Everyone should get equal treatment."

"You're as right as right can be." Mike leaned over and gave her a kiss. "That's for being so thoughtful."

"If I get a kiss for being thoughtful, I can be a lot more thoughtful than that."

"Sweetheart, I'll kiss you any time. All you've got to do is choose me."

Ellen's gaze slipped away from Mike. She mixed the salad ingredients. "What's the congressman's kid like?"

Mike frowned and took a deep breath. "Don't know. Didn't get to talk to him. Seems he and all the other kids took the news very hard and were in no condition to talk."

THE MEN IN the three cars surrounding Bronson stood outside their cars. The Altima driver had put away his gun but Bronson had no doubts that the other hoods, like the Altima driver, carried.

Bronson memorized the Ranger's license plate. Barely moving his lips, he said, "License plate of beige Ranger CLQ 478, Pennsylvania plate. Man approaching: average height, black hair with Army-style cut, light complexion. About 150 pounds. Wearing jeans, blue pullover shirt." Bronson hoped the troopers at the other end of the cell could hear him. He gave the location. "I'm at the Whittle Exit off the highway. Need help."

The man stood in front of Bronson's car for a fraction of a second before heading toward the driver's side.

Bronson lowered his hands and without bending down, reached for his boot.

"You know you can't escape," the man said once he stood by Bronson's side of the car. "Lower your window. I don't want to scream."

"I'll have to turn on the engine to do that."

The man nodded.

Bronson turned the key and pushed the button down. He lowered the window two inches down and stopped.

The man leaned down and spoke through the partially opened window. "Mandy Wellington sent us as your friendly painting committee. We're here to remind you that your twenty-four hours to hand us that painting is past. Where is it?"

"Ran into some unexpected trouble. I haven't had time to locate it."

"That's a flimsy excuse, Mr. Bronson. But due to our generosity, we'll give you twelve more hours. Then we'll come back. If you don't have the painting by then, we won't be as nice next time we meet."

TWENTY-FOUR

BRONSON SAT STILL, watching the painting committee drive away. He put his boots back on as he grabbed the cell resting on the front passenger seat. All of this time, it had been on speaker mode and he hoped Cannady had heard the conversation. "Is anybody there?"

Silence.

Shiiit.

Bronson thought about disconnecting but then decided to add, "Hello? This is Bronson. They left."

"Thank God you're okay." Bronson recognized Cannady's voice. "You are okay, aren't you?"

"I'm fine, just pissed off. Wish I had my side arm."

"As often and as easily as trouble follows you, I'm glad you don't have one."

"I'd only use it to get out of trouble."

"Yeah? I'm not sure that's how it'd work out." A small pause followed. "I've got a visual."

Bronson glanced at his side view mirror. He could see two trooper cars heading toward him. "Sorry to have dragged you out here for nothing. They're gone."

"Wasn't a complete waste. We ran that license plate you gave us. Its owners reported it stolen two days ago."

"Naturally."

"At least now we know the make and model of the car."

"Bet you that if they haven't yet, they'll ditch that plate real fast."

"Unfortunately, you're probably right."

The lead trooper, Cannady's car, pulled in behind Bronson's parked Cruze. The other vehicle sped past Bronson. Bronson waved at the trooper, hung up, and pocketed the cell. He stepped out, leaned against the car, and watched Cannady walk toward him. "Again, my apologies for wasting your time."

"Our job is to serve and protect. You needed us. We came. It's all part of doing our duty. Where are you headed?"

"Ellen's making dinner tonight. I promised her I'd be in time to enjoy her efforts. Why did you ask?"

"I didn't want you to get any stupid ideas like paying Amanda Wellington a visit. They more than hinted that she sent those hoods to threaten you. Even though she probably sent them after you, I want to remind you that we're the troopers, not you. We will follow up. You're to stay away from Ms. Wellington. Is that clear?"

"Perfectly clear." Bronson meant what he said. He would stay away from Amanda. Instead, he would pay the "I Will Paint Anything" artist a visit. Bronson realized he had never mentioned the artist to Cannady. He should, he knew, but he'd do so after the visit. "Anything else?"

"Yeah. Have a good dinner."

He planned to, after he'd talked to the artist.

Cannady walked away and Bronson drove off. Guilt consumed him. He had promised Ellen to be there for dinner but now he was planning to pay the artist a visit. If he did, he might not make it in time for dinner. He called Mike and told him what had happened. "What do you advise?"

"This is strictly selfish advice, but if you don't make it for dinner," Mike said, "Ellen will have another reason for hating the job. Come over, have dinner, then we'll both pay the artist a visit. On the way over there, I'll even fill you in on my day at the school and at the lawyer's. Just no business talk during dinner."

Bronson agreed.

THE LARGE SIGN predominantly displayed at the entrance read: Sam Glass, Attorney at Law. Inside, a blend of oak furniture offset the Aubusson rug that shimmered on the dark tile. Glass waited until his secretary—in fact, until after everyone—had left before making the call.

The phone rang three times before Miller picked up. "I Will Paint Anything for You. What's your pleasure today?"

"Cut the sales pitch. This is Sam Glass. We may have a problem."

The artist waited for the lawyer to explain. When he didn't, Miller said, "What kind of problem?"

"Mike Hoover was here this morning."

"Never heard of him."

"He's a Dallas detective and Harry Bronson's ex-partner. Bronson was also a detective in Dallas but is now retired."

"Bronson?"

"Yeah, as in Lorraine Bronson's brother."

"What did Hoover want?"

"Asked me what my connection with Lorraine was. Naturally, I played ignorant. I told him she was Wellington's special friend and Wellington has been my client for years, but other than that, I had no ties to her."

"Did he believe you?"

"Seems to. He asked me if I had prepared a will for her. I told him, truthfully, no. He thanked me and left."

"Then there's nothing to worry about."

"Hope you're right," the lawyer said. "Still, I wanted you to know. Maybe Bronson is trying to connect the dots."

"I'm an artist. You're a lawyer. What could possibly link us together?"

"The painting."

"Except no one knows what we've done."

"Lorraine knew and look where she ended up."

"That was her fault for butting in where she shouldn't have."

TWENTY-FIVE

BRONSON AND MIKE kept to their agreement. During dinner, neither mentioned anything relating to the ongoing investigation. Bronson knew Mike wanted to hear the details about his day, and he certainly felt eager to learn what Mike had found out about the school and the lawyer. But neither mentioned anything. Instead, they talked about mutual friends, the economy, Carol, and even the weather. After the main course, Ellen surprised them both with homemade apple pie.

The meal had been extremely satisfying, and Bronson wished he could kick back and watch T.V. Instead, both he and Mike helped clean the dishes. But even that, Bronson enjoyed. He liked seeing Ellen and Mike together, thrilled at their special relationship. Made him miss Carol more than ever.

"I've got some DVD's we can pop in and watch." Ellen opened a cabinet door revealing an extensive collection of movies.

Mike wrapped his arm around her. "Sorry, sweetheart, Bronson and I've got an errand to run."

Ellen smiled. "No problem. Maybe when you get back. In the meantime, I'll watch a girlie movie."

Mike kissed her goodbye and turned to Bronson. "Ready?"

"Ready." Bronson tossed Mike the car keys. "You drive."

"Glad to see some things never change."

"You boys be careful," Ellen said.

"It's nothing like that," Mike answered. "We're going to talk to an artist named Miller. See if he can lead us to the missing painting."

"With Bronson around, that could be a dangerous mission."

"Now you're beginning to sound like Carol." Bronson kissed her cheek.

"I'll take that as a compliment."

During the drive to Miller's house, Bronson told Mike about Serafin's murder and the incident involving the painting committee. Mike listened and asked several questions. Then he told Bronson about the school and his meeting with the lawyer.

"What's your gut reaction?" Bronson asked. "Do you believe him when he said he only knows of Lorraine but has never actually met her?"

Mike frowned. "Glass must be an excellent lawyer. I couldn't read him. On the surface, he seems to be what he claims, Wellington's personal lawyer, but if there's a connection to Lorraine, I couldn't tell you."

"Do you think it's worth pursuing?"

"No I don't, at least not at this point."

Bronson looked out the window. Some dirt bike enthusiasts enjoyed the rough trails the mountains provided. A car filled with kids pulled up to an empty picnic bench. A man with his camera captured one of the many breathtaking vistas. People everywhere, enjoying this mountain playground. One day, he too might be able to enjoy himself, but not now.

Bronson turned his attention back to his ex-partner. "Consider it dropped." He leaned his head back on the head rest. "What about the boys at the school? Do you think we should pursue that?"

"Yeah, definitely. If they're that upset, they must have

known Lorraine quite well. We might get some insight that can help us." Mike slowed down.

"I agree. Maybe we'll do that tomorrow."

"It's a deal."

Mike executed a left, taking them down a tree-lined street. All the trees had reached maturity and had probably been planted at the same time these houses had been built, sometime in the 1950's.

Mike parked the car in front of a gray wood shake, U-shaped home. Two large windows, both facing the front, gave little opportunity for Bronson and Mike to arrive unannounced. A single-car garage made up the left part of the U and therefore offered no windows, but also no protection for Bronson and Mike.

"Wish us luck." Bronson rang the doorbell and pocketed the car keys Mike handed him. Seconds sped by. Bronson was about to ring again when he heard the sounds of a bolt being unlocked.

A small, frail-looking man opened the door. "Yes?" A screen door separated him from Bronson and Mike.

"Are you Larry S. Miller?" Bronson took a step forward, reaching for the screen door handle, finding it locked.

"Who wants to know?" Miller asked.

"Mind if we come in for a minute? We need to talk."

"About?" A mixture of shock and fear crossed his face. "You must be Bronson." He simultaneously tried to slam the wooden door shut and pivot. He succeeded with neither. He stumbled, caught his balance and took off running, moving away from the front door.

"He's probably heading for the back door," Mike said. "I'll cut him off."

Bronson pushed the screen door until the flimsy lock gave in. He ran past the living room and into the dining room. Bronson saw that the door leading to the backyard was closed. He tried the door handle. The door was un-locked. He stepped into the backyard and looked over the wooden fence that screamed for repairs.

He saw Mike running down the alley. He shook his head and shrugged. He too had lost Miller.

Shiiit.

Where had the little prick gone? Bronson heard the neighborhood dogs bark. What had agitated them? He ran back inside the house, this time heading for the hallway. He opened the first door. The bedroom's window stood wide open, its curtains billowing out in the wind. As he climbed out the window, he called Mike on the cell. "He's heading south. I'm following the barking dogs."

When Bronson reached the sidewalk, he could see a fig-ure running down toward the end of the next block. Bron-son would have a hard time catching up with him.

Bronson got in the car, drove to the next block, and parked parallel to Miller. Not bothering to take the time to turn off the engine, Bronson threw the door open and bolted toward Miller.

By now the artist was half-a-block away, but he lost pre-cious seconds by often turning to see how far back Bron-son was.

Bronson increased his speed. His muscles protested, re-minding him he was no longer the youthful man he once had been. Bronson ignored his screaming muscles and vi-sualized catching his prey.

Bronson gained on Miller. When he was within touch-ing distance, Bronson tackled the artist with the determi-nation of a linebacker intent on winning. Both went down, Bronson on top of him.

It took Bronson a few seconds to regain his balance and breath. He knelt but hung on to Miller. Bronson turned him over and frisked him.

"Hey! Hey! What are you doing?"

"It's not what I'm doing. It's what you're going to do."

Mike arrived and helped Bronson and Miller stand up.

"W-what d-do you mean?" Wide-eyed Miller first eyed Bronson, then Mike, then Bronson again.

A middle-aged man with more muscles than brains stepped out of his house. He carried a broom. He took a couple of hesitant steps forward.

Bronson reached into his back pocket, took out his wallet, and opened it, revealing his retirement badge. He flashed it toward the good Samaritan. "This is official police business. This man is armed and dangerous. Get back inside."

The man did as he was told.

"Bronson, are you crazy?" Mike spoke loud enough so only Bronson and possibly Miller could hear.

"Crazy enough to beat the shit out of this asshole unless he starts talking."

TWENTY-SIX

THE CALL CAME just as Cannady was about to leave. She immediately picked up. "Did you get a match?"

"What? No 'Hi, Elaine. How are you? Thanks for moving heaven and earth to help me.'"

Cannady rolled her eyes. "Hi, Elaine. How are you? Fine? That's great. Me, too, I'm fine. How's the family? Good. Mine, too. Well, not really. I don't have a family. I live alone. Now that that's out of the way, can we get to the purpose of the call?"

"Yes."

Cannady immediately picked up on Elaine's curt answer. She closed her eyes and rubbed them. "I'm sorry. I really appreciate you going out of your way for me. I've gotten very little sleep in the past few days and it's catching up with me. Still, that's not an excuse for rudeness. I apologize."

"Apology is accepted, and I'm sorry, too. I shouldn't have barked at you."

"Apology is accepted." Both laughed. Cannady said, "Glad we're friends again."

"That we are and always will be."

Cannady smiled, straightened up, and returned to her business mode. "What've you got?"

"It's a match. The rifle you found under the bed was used to kill Lorraine Bronson."

Cannady formed a fist and gave the air a victory punch. "You're sure?"

"I'm as sure as day follows night."

Prior to his death, Cannady had interviewed the suspect. He had no way to verify his whereabouts at the time of Lorraine's death. He had known the deceased and claimed to have loved her.

"Did she love you?" Cannady had asked.

He bit his lip and looked away.

Love gone wrong—always a motive for murder.

Cannady made the thumbs up signal and smiled at Elaine. "That's great news. I'll notify Bronson." She turned, heading back to her desk. Mario Serafin killed Lorraine and someone killed him. Was there a connection? Had she actually solved Lorraine's murder?

BRONSON AND MIKE, each on either side of Miller, dragged him back to his house and dumped him on the couch.

Miller began blabbering even before Bronson and Mike released him. "I—I didn't do a-anything. P-please, don't hurt me." His lip quivered.

Bronson slammed his fist several times into the palm of his opened hand.

Miller whimpered.

Mike bent down, violating Miller's personal space. His face was barely three inches away from Miller's face. "Let me tell you how it goes. Me? I'm the good guy. I wouldn't hurt you. But my buddy here? He's got a real mean temper. He snaps and I can't control him." Mike backed off.

"I'm listenin'," Bronson said.

Miller wet his lips. His eyes narrowed and he looked ready to cry.

"My patience sure is wearin' down." Bronson took a step forward.

Miller covered his head with his arms. "Don't h-hit me. I—I don't know what to say."

"Begin with the paintin'."

"The...the painting?"

Bronson took another step toward Miller.

Miller once again cowered. "Okay, okay. It wasn't my idea. Lorraine came to me. I didn't ask her to come. I d-did nothing wrong."

Mike placed a reassuring hand on Miller's shoulder. "Take a deep breath."

Miller did. He kept his gaze glued on Bronson's face.

"Now begin at the beginning."

"All I know is Lorraine gets this La Carcé painting worth close to a million bucks. She tells me she's desperate for money so she wants to sell it. Problem is this guy she cares for gave her the painting and she didn't want to hurt his feelings."

Bronson rubbed the bridge of his nose. Why would Lorraine need money—especially such a large amount? Wellington would give her anything she asked for. "What was her plan?"

"She figured if she sold it, and he found out, he'd be pissed and hurt. So she asks me to paint the same picture. She hangs up the copy in her house and sells the original."

"Did she have a buyer?"

"Yeah. Sa—somebody arranged that for her. Don't know who."

"Do you have the painting?" Mike asked.

"Yeah, not here, though." He bit his lip. "I'm almost finished with the second copy."

Bronson glared at him. "You painted two copies?"

Miller gasped. "No, no." He waved his arms sporadically. "I meant first copy. The original is one. The duplicate is two. The second copy."

Bronson looked down the hallway. "You have a studio here?"

Miller nodded. "Last door, down the hallway."

The door to the studio was closed. "You're sure that when I search that room, I won't find the paintin'."

"N-no or yes. It's too valuable to keep here."

"Mind if we take a look?" Bronson asked.

"Go ahead, but you ain't gonna find it."

"Where is it, then?"

"I have another studio. No one knows about that one."

"Take us to it."

"No. That's my secret place. I will go there, tomorrow at ten. I'll get the picture and bring it to you. Meet me here at three."

TWENTY-SEVEN

A FEW MINUTES before seven in the morning, Bronson parked the Cruze four doors down from Miller's house. The early morning sun glinted like aluminum foil, and a gentle breeze blew, flicking a small branch against the car's windowpane.

Bronson reached for the large thermos filled with coffee the way he liked it. He poured himself a cup and returned the thermos to the passenger seat. He was early, he knew, but he didn't want to miss the chance to follow Miller to his other studio.

Mike had offered to come with him, but Bronson refused. He knew Mike hated surveillance work as much as he did. No use both being bored. Let him enjoy an intimate breakfast with Ellen.

An hour dragged by and still no activity from Miller. Bronson called Carol. She picked up on the second ring. "Hi, honey. I didn't wake you up, did I?"

"No, of course not. I'm anxious to get to you, so I've been on the road since six."

Bronson knew Carol liked to sleep at least until eight. "Be careful. Take lots of breaks."

Carol promised him she would and told him she'd see him tonight, maybe by seven. They talked for an hour longer, which made time fly. Bronson regretted having to say goodbye. The idea that they'd see each other tonight made the parting more bearable.

By nine, Bronson found himself squirming in the seat.

He felt tired and uncomfortable. He wished he had brought something to snack on. Cookies. Candies. Anything. He poured the last of the coffee and continued to watch.

A few minutes before ten, Miller walked out, got in his car, and pulled out of the driveway. Bronson turned the ignition key and followed him at a discreet distance.

Twenty minutes later, Miller pulled into a parking lot. Bronson parked across the street where he could watch the parking lot and its surrounding buildings. Miller lingered for a few minutes before heading for the building to his right, reaffirming Bronson's suspicions. The large sign in front of the building read Sam Glass, Attorney at Law. As Bronson stared at the sign something—a forgotten thought, a bud of an idea—formed in his mind.

Sam Glass, Attorney at Law, the sign read.

Bronson nodded. When he asked Miller if Lorraine already had a buyer, Miller had said, "Yeah. Sa—somebody arranged it. Don't know who." Bronson had thought Miller had stuttered as he often did when he was nervous. But he hadn't. Instead, he had made a mistake from which he quickly recovered.

Sa-somebody.

S…a…as in Sam.

Sam Glass.

Interesting.

ELLEN OPENED THE door wider and allowed Cannady in. "What can I do for you?" Ellen led her to the living room. She indicated the couch and both sat down.

"Actually, I'm here to see Bronson."

"I thought that's what you were going to say. I'm sorry, but he's not in."

Cannady squinted and her brows knit. "I was hoping he

was home. I have two bits of information I'd like to share with him."

"If it helps, you can tell me and I'll pass the information to Bronson, or you can reach him on his cell." Ellen had been cooking some bacon when the doorbell rang and she could still smell its enticing aroma. "Would you care for anything to drink or eat?"

"No, but thanks." Cannady waved her hand as she filled her lungs with air.

Ellen thought she was probably inhaling the flavor, wishing she could say yes.

"Or I can come back later," Cannady said.

Ellen nodded. "That, too."

"I've got his cell number, but when I have good news to deliver, I prefer to do so in person."

"Don't blame you there. One sees a trooper at the front door and immediately assumes it's bad news and most of the times, that's the case. Seldom do you get to deliver good news."

Cannady half smiled. "That's so true. Sounds like you speak from experience."

"My ex is a Dallas detective."

Cannady snapped her fingers. "That's right. Bronson told me that." She stood up. "I won't take anymore of your time. Sorry I interrupted your breakfast."

"You didn't. I'm still in the process of preparing it. Mike's taking a shower."

Cannady stood up. "Mike? Your ex?"

Ellen nodded.

"Isn't that awkward for you, him being here at your house?"

"After all these years, we're still very much in love. It's my fault we're not together. I don't know how to be a policeman's wife. Every time he'd go out, which of course was every day, I got sick from worrying. Couldn't live like that anymore."

"Unfortunately, that's a common happening. Don't blame yourself. It's normal." Cannady stood up. "I won't take anymore of your time. Tell Bronson that the medical examiner released his sister's body. If he lets me know which funeral home he chose, I can call them to pick up the body."

"I'll tell Bronson." Ellen also stood.

"The other thing I wanted to tell Bronson—the good news part—is that we caught Lorraine's killer."

"Mind if I ask? I know Bronson would like to know. Was it Mario Serafin?"

Cannady eyed her. "I guess Bronson has been filling you in."

Ellen half nodded and looked away.

"Tell Bronson that Serafin's rifle and the cartridge we found at the scene of the crime matched. Not only that, but he had the motive and the opportunity to kill Lorraine." Cannady headed toward the door and Ellen followed her. "If Bronson wants to discuss it, he knows how to reach me."

You bet he'll want to discuss it, Ellen thought.

TWENTY-EIGHT

THE SHADOWY WOODS stretched out on either side of the highway, casting a feeling of tranquility on the road. Bronson leaned back on the driver's seat as he headed toward the Daniel Jenkins School for Boys. He had thought of stopping by Ellen's and picking up Mike, but decided Mike could better spend his time with Ellen. Those two loved each other, yet spent their lives ripped apart by miles and stubbornness.

Bronson had also thought of asking Mike to take over the surveillance, see where Miller went after leaving the lawyer's office. But that wouldn't be important. Miller, who knew Lorraine, had gone to see Glass, giving birth to the possibility that Glass had lied and was also acquainted with Lorraine. The connection between the three was something Bronson planned to confront Miller about when they met today at three.

Bronson spotted the exit for the school. He slowed down and followed the signs that led him to a wooded park-like acreage that made up the famous institute. Several three story, red-brick buildings with multiple chimneys spread out, each building separated by the woods. A cluster of boys of various ages occupied most of the benches under the shade of the trees.

A large portico in front of one of the largest buildings drew attention to the place. Bronson assumed that had to be the Administration Building and headed that way. Kids were everywhere, but he wondered if the building would be open since this was Saturday. He hoped someone would be able to help him. He parked the car and headed for the building.

He lucked out. The edifice not only housed the administrative offices but also served as a recreation center. To his right, the sign painted on the door read Principal's Office. He opened the door and let himself in.

A woman with shoulder-length dark brown hair and a bit on the chubby side looked up across the pile of folders she was filing. "May I help you?" Her warm, inviting smile told Bronson this place catered to guests.

"I'm looking for Claudine Ramirez."

"That's me." The smile remained plastered on her face.

"I'm Harry Bronson."

The smile slipped away as she rushed to the other side of the counter. "Mr. Bronson, I'm so sorry about Lorraine."

Don't leave me. A chill covered Bronson. "Me, too."

"Would you care for a cup of coffee?" Claudine indicated the large coffee urn.

Would he care for a cup of coffee? Is the Pope Catholic? "That would be nice."

Claudine got busy pouring two cups. "I liked Lorraine. She was quiet, kept to herself mostly, but she was truly a beautiful person, inside and out."

Something Bronson never got to experience. "Thank you." He busied himself opening three packs of sugar and dumping them in the coffee.

"Your partner—Mike Hoover, that's his name, right?"

Not exactly his partner anymore, but Bronson liked the sound of that. He nodded.

"He was here yesterday," Claudine said. "He told me you'd be coming to talk to the boys."

"Yes, I'd appreciate it if you could arrange that."

"By all means, but I suggest you talk to each one

individually. They probably would be more open that way. Otherwise, they might be forced to put up a false bravado for their friends."

"Thank you, Ma'am, for the suggestion. I'd like to talk to all three. Which one do you suggest I talk to first?"

"The leader of the group. He was the closest to Lorraine and can probably address most of your concerns." She headed toward the main door. "I saw him playing one of the video games just a little while ago. I'll go get him. You can use the conference room for privacy." She pointed to the door to their left.

Bronson finished fixing his coffee. "Thank you. Can you tell me his name?"

Claudine froze on her way out. "I'm sorry. I thought you knew. It's Daniel Jenkins Jr., son of our congressman and our great benefactor."

TWENTY-NINE

THE DOOR OPENED and Daniel Jenkins Jr. stepped in. At first Bronson wasn't sure that the right person walked in. This seventeen-year-old looked more like a man than a teenager. Bronze-gold hair framed a square face with ice-blue eyes. Bronson had seen pictures of his father, had seen him on television, and junior didn't resemble him at all, except for those ice-blue eyes. Same as Dad's. But unlike Dad's medium bone structure, junior had a perfectly tanned, athletic body and a powerful build.

Daniel looked around the small room as though he had never seen it before. An oak table and six cushioned chairs occupied most of the room. "Mr. Bronson?"

Bronson nodded.

"I'm Daniel Jenkins Jr." He offered Bronson his hand. "I feel as if I know you."

Bronson accepted the handshake. "Why's that?"

"Lorraine spoke of you often."

Really? How could that be? "What did she say?"

Daniel shrugged. "Stuff about both of you as kids, how you were the best detective Dallas ever had, but that you're now retired. Not that it mattered, she said. You continued to get yourself into trouble."

Bronson tilted his head, like a dog at attention. "Did she say what kind of trouble?"

Daniel pulled out the chair closest to him and sat down. "She told me about the cases you've been involved in after you retired. She told me about the time your wife was kidnapped and you had to go on a geochaching expedition to get her back. Then there was the time when you got caught in the killer's den." He leaned back on the chair as though recalling Lorraine's words. "Everyone was petrified and prayed for your safety."

Bronson flopped down on the chair beside him and rubbed his forehead. What the hell? "Did she by any chance tell you how she knew all of that?"

Daniel's eyes widened. "I assumed you told her."

"Then you don't know."

"Know what?"

"Lorraine and I were estranged."

Daniel's eyebrows arched. "Estranged? As in not speaking to each other?"

Bronson nodded.

"Wow. That's heavy." Daniel sank back into the chair. "I told her I wanted to meet you. Each time she had an excuse for not inviting you."

"What can you tell me about her?"

"She's—was…" Daniel's voice broke and he cleared his throat. "…the most thoughtful, generous person alive. Sometimes I felt closer to her than to my own mother."

"Isn't that rather unusual?"

"No, not really. You know my dad—"

"Not personally."

Daniel half smiled. "You know of my dad."

Bronson nodded.

"He's always wanted to be President, even back then when I was a kid growing up. He was always attending some political function or doing a good deed and making sure he got plenty of coverage. Mom, of course, had to be by his side."

"What about you?"

Daniel raised his hand and swept the air. "We—my

brother, my sister and I—we were never neglected. Each one of us had our own separate nanny, someone who would devote one-hundred percent of her attention to each one of us. Mine was Lorraine."

A little grunt escaped Bronson as though he had suddenly lost all of his wind. That, he had never expected. "So you've known her—"

"Since I was a baby."

Question after question popped into Bronson's brain like a race car unable to stop. "So there must be a lot of pictures of her with you and your family."

"You bet. There's even some of her with Mom when she was pregnant with me. Mom was huge."

Bronson breathed easier. "I'd like to see those pictures."

"Sure, but I don't have them here. They're in my bedroom, back home." His eyes watered. "I wouldn't mind seeing them myself. Lots of good memories there."

Bronson reached out and squeezed his upper arm. "Thank you for bringing happiness to her life."

"It's really the other way around. She lit up a room with her smile." Daniel's shoulders started to shake and his tongue licked his lips. "When's the funeral?"

"The medical examiner hasn't released her remains yet. Soon as they do, I can make the arrangements."

Daniel's face became ashen. "If it's okay with you, I'd like to go."

Bronson nodded, "I'll personally come pick you up."

"That won't be necessary. I bet you, Dad and Mom, as well as my sister and brother, will want to be there too. We'll go as a family."

"I'm sure Lorraine would want you and your family to sit up front with me and my wife."

Daniel's lips trembled. "We'd like that."

"Did Lorraine ever tell you anything that might help me find her killer?"

Daniel hung his head. "About a month ago, she started acting very agitated. I asked her what was wrong. She said she had money problems. I told her my parents would help. She refused."

"Why did she need money?"

Daniel shrugged. "Dunno."

"Did she say or do anythin' else?"

Daniel shook his head.

"If you think of anythin'…" Bronson handed him his business card.

Daniel pocketed it without looking at it. "I'll let you know."

"One more thing."

Daniel looked up.

"She had an original François La Carcé paintin'. Do you know anythin' about that?"

Daniel shook his head. "No, sorry."

"Are you going to be all right?"

"I'm almost eighteen. I don't need my nanny anymore, but I wish to God, she hadn't been taken from me." He broke down and wept, his hand plastered to his face.

Bronson stood and bent down so they were eye-level. Daniel looked at him and they stared at each other for several seconds. Bronson reached out and hugged him. Both cried like babies.

THIRTY

BRONSON AND TIME played a race and the latter seemed to be winning. He had stayed longer at the school than he should have. Not that it mattered. In fact, it had been good for him. All of this time, he had carried the frustration, the guilt, and the anger associated with his sister's death. To safeguard himself, he had locked those emotions in his heart.

Today, with Daniel, he had released them so that now he could focus on the task at hand without carrying the extra baggage. He still felt the pain and the guilt, but hoped he could control them when they surfaced.

Bronson thought about the interview with the other two boys. They hadn't been as emotional and he had learned nothing new other than the fact that the two boys deeply loved her and respected her. As far as they were concerned, she was the best teacher around.

The car's digital display read 2:32. Less than half-an-hour to pick up Mike and get to Miller's by three. Maybe he should call Miller, let him know they'll be late. Bronson reached for his cell and stopped. Once he and Mike were on the road, he'd have a better idea of their arrival time.

Bronson stomped on the accelerator, and the Cruze shot forward, the tires squealing in protest. If he hurried, they might still make it on time. The scenery around him blended into one large blur.

Seventeen minutes later, he pulled into Ellen's driveway and honked. Both Mike and Ellen walked out. Now what? He stepped out of the car. "Ellen, what?"

"Cannady was here." She seemed breathless from fear or excitement, Bronson couldn't tell.

Bronson held his breath, bracing himself. "And?"

"They caught Lorraine's killer. They closed that part of the case."

"Who killed my sister?"

"Mario Serafin."

That son of a bitch. "She's sure?"

"He had no alibi, had the means and motivation, plus they matched the cartridge case to the rifle they found hidden under his bed. They're sure Serafin did it."

Bronson sighed and looked up toward the sky.

"I'm so sorry about Lorraine," Ellen said. "But it's over now. You can relax."

What about the alleged child and the painting? He needed answers to those questions.

Ellen placed her arm on Bronson's shoulder. "Cannady also said that the medical examiner has released Lorraine's body. They need to know which funeral home you've chosen."

"Carol will be here tonight at seven. We'll choose one then."

Ellen nodded, kissed Mike, hugged Bronson, and stepped away.

Bronson tossed Mike the keys. "You drive."

"What else is new?"

Soon as Mike pulled out of the driveway, Bronson called Miller. The answering machine came on after the fourth ring. "Miller? Bronson. We're running a bit late but we'll be there in about twenty minutes. It's now 2:53."

"Ouch!"

Bronson disconnected and looked at Mike. "Ouch?"

"This thing stabbed me." He handed Bronson a fingernail file, the old fashioned type with a sharp point.

Bronson squinted. "What are you doing with this?"

"It's Ellen's. She gave it to me to hold for her, and I forgot to give it back. Put it in the glove compartment, and I'll give it to her later on."

Bronson called Cannady as he put it away.

Cannady didn't bother with the niceties. She got right to the point. "It's over. You can bury your sister in peace and go on with your life."

"What was Serafin's motive?"

"He fathered Lorraine's child. He loved her but she toyed with his feelings. First Wellington, then Devono, then back to Wellington. Now that Wellington is on his deathbed, she spent a lot of time with him. Serafin's jealousy doubled. He snapped and killed her. Like most murders, this was a crime of passion."

Bronson shook his head. "The package is too neat. Somethin' missin'."

"What's that supposed to mean?"

"Let's assume that Serafin killed Lorraine. Who killed Serafin?"

"That's our business." Cannady's voice came out dry and forced. "Stay out of it. You're a retired cop and you have no jurisdiction here. This is Pennsylvania, not Texas, and I don't think I need to remind you that interfering with an ongoing investigation is a crime."

"It seems to me—"

"Drop it!"

The command came loud enough for Mike to hear through Bronson's cell. Bronson and Mike eyed each other.

Cannady continued, "You're no longer part of our investigation—not that there's one, as far as you're involved, and if we catch you harassing our citizens, I will personally prosecute. Is that clear?"

Shiiiit. "Perfectly clear."

"Which funeral home should the M.E. call?"

"My wife, Carol, will arrive today at seven. We'll make arrangements tonight or tomorrow. I will call in the information." Without saying goodbye, he hung up.

Mike's gaze temporarily left the road and landed on Bronson. "You okay, buddy?"

"Yeah." Bronson shifted positions. "No." He sat up straighter. "I don't know. I think somebody is putting the heat on her."

"Sounds like it." Mike nodded. "You don't think Serafin did it." A statement, not a question.

"Maybe he did. Maybe he didn't. For sure, he won't be able to defend himself. What bothers me is if he did it, who killed him and why?"

"Good question."

"Yep, and I'd also like to know if this paintin' is connected to my sister's death. And what of Lorraine's child?"

"Lots of unanswered questions."

"Yep, and if I'm going after answers, I need my gun."

"Don't go crazy on me."

"Carol arrives tonight."

"You've told me that." Mike slowed down as they neared Miller's house.

"That means the camper will also be here."

Mike located the house and parked in front of it. "I see where this is going. Bronson, you don't need—"

"But the gun's already there, and I can legally carry."

"True, but you shouldn't be doing anything that requires a gun." Mike turned off the engine and handed Bronson the keys. "Uh-oh."

"What?"

Mike indicated Miller's house. Its front door stood wide open.

"Shiiiit." Bronson frowned, then relaxed. "He's expectin' us. Maybe he left the door open for us."

"Let's hope so."

"Still, wish I had my gun," Bronson said.

They walked up the driveway and stood in front of the door.

The puddle of blood inside the house screamed for their attention.

THIRTY-ONE

THE MAN LOOKED at the menu for the fourth time. He had almost memorized the damn thing. He rubbed his chin as he waited for his boss to show up. Late, like always.

The waiter approached him. "Ready for your order, sir?"

The man dropped his hand from his chin. "Not yet. I'm waiting for someone."

The waiter nodded and turned his attention to a couple sitting by the window.

Twenty-seven minutes later, the boss walked in, nodded at his friend, and signaled for the waiter. They both reached the table at the same time. The waiter immediately took their order.

Once they were alone, the boss leaned forward. "What news do you have for me?"

"It's done. The troopers found the rifle under Serafin's bed. I made all the details fit. Cannady fell for it."

Their drinks arrived and the boss moved back while the waiter set them down. The boss picked up the wine glass and raised it in a toast. "Well done."

They clinked glasses and each sipped their drink. The man set his drink down and rubbed his chin. "I've done my part. Now do yours."

"And what's that?"

"Get the troopers to drop all investigations."

"One call will take care of that." The boss played with the rim of the glass. "What of Bronson? Do you think he'll continue on his own?"

"I hope he's smart enough to drop it."

"I hear he's stubborn and determined."

The man reached for his chin and pulled it. "He'll be a problem, then."

"A problem you can take care of?"

"It'll take a bit of doing, but yes."

BRONSON AND MIKE stared at the puddle of blood. "We better call Cannady," Mike said, reaching for his cell.

Bronson stopped him. "No, not yet. Let me go check it out first."

A puzzled look crossed Mike's eyes. "Why? This could be a murder scene. You can't go in and contaminate it."

"I'll be careful. I know what I'm doing." He took out a handkerchief and covered his hand.

"Damn it, Bronson, what are you doing?"

"You're forgetting that I heard Cannady's tone. We or rather just me—I'm not allowed to continue investigating anything, and I have a feeling neither does Cannady. She made it very clear that I'm to bury my sister and leave town." Bronson looked deep into Mike's eyes, hoping for understanding. "I need to do my sister justice. I let her down once. Never again."

Mike shook his head. "I can't talk you out of it."

"No one can." He paused for a few seconds. The silence hung between them like a rope around their necks. "All I'm going to do is check on Miller and erase my phone message. No use looking for the painting. I'm sure if it ever was here, it's gone now, so mainly, I'm just going to simplify things and erase that message."

Mike's eyes opened wider.

"Cannady will listen to them. She'll know we were coming to see him."

"You don't plan to tell her we were here or tell her what we know?"

"Not yet."

"Damn you, Bronson. This isn't right."

"I know that, but I have to follow this through and I know Cannady won't—or can't." He stepped in and turned. "You have a career to worry about. I don't. Go back to the car. You have nothing to do with this. I'm on my own from here on." Bronson turned and walked into the house.

THIRTY-TWO

"AND WHAT IF you're wrong?" The curly-haired blond man leaned forward so that his twin could hear him.

The other twin's gaze momentarily left the road and glanced at his brother through the rearview mirror. "Relax, will ya? We know how Bronson operates. He'll be at Miller's at 3:00, like he said he would." He looked at his watch. "He should already be there." He stepped on the accelerator.

The Raven, the beauty with long, black hair, sat on the front passenger seat. "I bet Bronson brings his partner with him. What's his name?"

"Hoover," the driver answered. "Mike Hoover, and it's his ex-partner."

The Raven waved her hand dismissing the topic. "Whatever."

The twin in the back ran his fingers through his hair. "Think that's going to make a difference?"

"None whatsoever," his brother assured him.

"Just to make sure we're all on the same note," the Raven said, "let's go over our plan one last time."

The twin in the back threw his weight against the seat. "Come on. It's such a simple plan. It doesn't need going over."

"I want to hear it aloud, make sure we all know our parts and that it flows smoothly."

The driver executed a left turn. He let out a long sigh. "About a block before Miller's house, we stop and let my brother out."

Without breaking stride, his twin continued, "I get down, walk to Miller's, and position myself behind the bushes just like we rehearsed."

"In the meantime," the driver continued, "I park the car in front of Miller's house where Bronson can see us."

"While Bronson's attention is glued on you," the twin in the back passenger seat said, "I come from the side and shoot him." He frowned. "We may have a glitch."

The Raven pivoted, wide-eyed. "What?"

"You mentioned Hoover might be there. What if he is?"

"Your job is to shoot. If Hoover gets in the way and ends up getting shot, then that's just the way it goes. Bronson will get the message either way. As far as I'm concerned, we have a perfect plan."

"Good, 'cuz we've reached our destination," the driver said. "Little Brother, this is where you get out."

"Little Brother?" He semi-smiled, shook his head, and opened the door. "You're only a few minutes older than me."

"That makes you my little brother. Now, get out and be careful."

He stepped out and watched his twin drive away. Taking a quick glance around to make sure no one was watching, he positioned himself behind the bushes where he had a clear view of Miller's house. Soon Bronson would step out, exposing himself to him.

THIRTY-THREE

MIKE SLAMMED HIS open hand against the steering wheel. In all the years he'd been working with Bronson, he had never seen him out of control. Sure, Bronson took needless chances and often played the wild card, but never like this. Bronson had gone over the edge.

As his best friend, his ex-partner—hell, as his almost brother, Mike should have never allowed Bronson to get involved in his sister's murder case. He knew better. Hell, Bronson knew better.

At least Carol would be arriving later on tonight. That should keep him occupied. Get him thinking about something else.

Through the rearview mirror, then through the side mirror, Mike saw a compact green car approach. He's driving slowly because he's almost home, Mike reasoned.

His thoughts turned back to Bronson. Carol will talk sense into him as only she can. By this time tomorrow, everything will be fine. Bronson will be his old self.

The green car—a Toyota Camry LE—why did that sound so familiar? Mike squinted, trying to clear his mind, trying to remember, his attention focused on the approaching vehicle.

The driver stopped and parked the car against the flow of traffic, parallel to Mike's car. A woman with long, black hair sat in the passenger seat and a blond-headed man in the driver's seat. Both stared at Miller's house.

Like a picture flashing in his mind, Mike remembered

Bronson telling him about a green Toyota Camry LE that had followed him and then disappeared before Cannady arrived. Now, here it was again.

Mike didn't like being sandwiched between the Camry and Miller's house. He scooted down and adjusted the rear-view mirror to watch the blond man and the black haired woman. Neither paid attention to him. They both focused past him toward Miller's house.

He had to warn Bronson.

AMAZING HOW A gun gave Bronson a false sense of security, something he currently lacked. Here he was entering a possible crime scene and for all Bronson knew, if Miller had been murdered, the killer could still be here, and Bronson had no gun. Fortunately for him, other than Miller's body, no one was home.

Bronson found the artist sprawled on the kitchen floor. Based on the trail of blood, the best Bronson could piece together was that Miller had been shot in the living room then he either dragged himself to the kitchen or the killer took him there. Why? He looked around the kitchen, opened all the cabinet drawers, and looked for something that didn't belong. Nothing stood out.

The back door lay only a few feet beyond Miller's reach. He had hoped to escape, but failed.

Bronson returned to the living room, spotted the phone, and the answering machine. Being careful not to step on the blood trail or puddle of blood, Bronson saw that Miller had three messages. One from his doctor reminding him of his appointment tomorrow morning, another from the owner of Art Supplies and More, wanting to know if he should include the oils as well as the acrylics with this month's order. The last message was from him. Bronson erased it.

His cell rang. Bronson checked caller I.D. Hoover. "I haven't even been here for five minutes. I'll be—"

"We've got company."

Bronson frowned and headed toward the front window. "I see it. Green Toyota Camry LE, same as the one that followed me before. Do you have a visual on the driver?"

"Blond curls, male. On the passenger side, female, long, black hair."

"I'm willin' to bet that the blond is the same person who followed me. Wonder what he wants?"

"Without a gun, I'm not about to ask them."

"Miller's dead. Think maybe the blond is the killer?" Bronson returned to the kitchen.

"Doesn't make sense. Why would he come back?"

"For the paintin'? I didn't see it anywhere. Maybe they didn't find it either. Maybe they think we have it." Bronson rummaged through the kitchen drawers, found two sharp knives, and pocketed them.

"I'm sure they see me." Mike looked at them directly as he spoke. "But they haven't made any moves. Still, I don't want you coming out of that house and exposing yourself."

"I could go out the back door."

"And I can stay here, making them think you're still inside."

"I don't like it, buddy. You're a sitting duck."

"Like I said, they haven't made a move. I'm okay."

"But as soon as you move, you'll become the target. I won't allow that. They want me, not you. I'm comin' out the front door."

"Bronson, no!"

Bronson disconnected, stepped out, crouched, and ran in a zigzag pattern.

A shot, coming from Bronson's left hand side, rang out.

THIRTY-FOUR

DEVONO SHOVED THE gun deeper into the soft flesh of Edward's chin. "I tell you, 'Mario needs to learn a lesson.' You say, 'Don't worry, boss. I'll take care of it.' I say, 'Okay.' You know I want Mario roughed up. I said nothing about killing him. *Capisce?*"

Edward's lips trembled, his eyes cast downward, trying to see the gun that at any minute could end his life. "I...I s-s-swear. I-I d-didn't d-do it."

"You didn't, eh?" Devono nodded as if in disbelief. His gaze shifted from Edward to the two bodyguards stationed at each side of the door leading to Devono's office. They shrugged.

Devono signaled the guards with a slight tilt of his head. The guards positioned themselves so that one stood by Edward's right side, and the other one by his left. They grabbed him under the arm pits and held him up.

Devono lowered the gun, stepped away, and sat behind his messy desk. He rested his head on the palms of his opened hands. "If you didn't do it, then please enlighten us as to why Mario is dead."

"S-some-body sh-shot h-him." Edward ran his tongue across his parched lips. "Wh-when I g-got to his h-house, I s-saw th-that th-the pl-place was surr-surrounded by po-police. Uh, troopers—I m-mean. Mario w-was al-already d-dead. I-I s-swear. Pl-please be-lieve m-me. I-I d-didn't k-kill him."

"So your story is that he was already dead when you got there."

Edward swallowed hard and nodded.

Devono picked up a pen and drummed his desk with its point. Each tap made Edward jump up. *Tap, tap, tap.* Then silence. *Tap, tap, tap.* Devono threw the pen down. It bounced twice, each time giving off a clatter that made Edward jerk. "Okay. So you're innocent. Now tell me why I shouldn't kill you."

"I h-have…a l-little girl. Sh-she's on-only fif-fifteen months old. Sh-she…needs her d-daddy."

Devono stood up with such abruptness that the chair under him rolled away, bumping against the wall. "Yeah? I had Lorraine, and now she's gone, but I still had Mario. Now Mario's gone. I feel like taking it out on someone. You're a handy target."

"No, please." Edward barely mouthed the words. "Pl-please." Tears gushed out of his eyes.

Devono walked around his desk and faced Edward. "I'm a fair man. I don't kill for pleasure."

Edward let out an audible sigh of relief.

"But I'm angry," Devono continued, "very, very angry, and when I get like this, I have to quench my thirst. There's only one way to do that." Devono pulled the gun and shot Edward between the eyes.

THIRTY-FIVE

BRONSON DROPPED TO the ground and squirmed his way to the car. No other shots followed. Mike had the engine running and the front passenger door opened. Bronson threw himself into the car, slammed the door shut, and Mike peeled out. The tires screeched in protest.

Bronson noted that sometime between the time he stepped outside and now, the Toyota had disappeared. Bronson leaned back on the seat. "That was an adventure."

"Is that what you call it?" Mike cast him a side glance. "Because I'd call it a suicide mission. What were you thinking?"

Bronson shook his head and looked out the window. "Not sure."

"You better start being sure. Put your head back on and from here on, think."

"Yes, Dad."

Mike eyed him speculatively and then smiled. "Dad?"

"You sounded just like him."

"And that's a good thing." Mike turned down the main street that would lead them to Ellen's. "While I'm still Dad, do you have any confessions I need to hear?"

Bronson reached into his pocket and felt the papers. "Would now be a good time to tell you that somehow Miller's checking account transaction register ended up in my pocket?"

Mike's eyes snapped shut for a second as his features

tightened like a fist. Through clenched teeth, he hissed. "Why would you do that?"

"Thought maybe we could see if he's made any monthly payments for rental space. If we find his other studio, we might find the paintin'."

"You still plan to pursue this, even after today?"

"I'm only seekin' the paintin', nothing else. Let the troopers find Miller's killer."

"Why is the painting so important?"

"It belonged to Lorraine. I'm just defendin' her right to keep it."

"I bet."

Bronson shrugged and looked away. "Reckon I better call the troopers and report Miller's murder."

"Reckon so."

Bronson unpocketed his cell and dialed the trooper's main line. "I'd like to report a homicide."

"Your name?" the trooper at the other end asked.

Bronson gave him the address and hung up.

Immediately, his cell buzzed. Bronson recognized the ring tone, *The Sea of Love*, his and Carol's song. "Sweetheart, are you here?" Bronson's smile stretched from ear to ear. He looked at his watch: 4:55. "You're early."

"Unfortunately, I'm late."

"What do you mean?"

"I'm at a repair shop. The camper broke down."

"Are you all right?"

"Yes, of course, but the mechanic said it was a special part and it'll take three to four days for it to arrive. Once it's here, they'll have the piece put in the camper in less than an hour and it will be good as new."

"Where will you be stayin'?"

"In the camper. I can use it as long as I dry camp. At

night, they'll lock me in their parking lot so I'll be more than safe."

"I can drive over and get you. Or be with you."

"No use, honey, but I appreciate it. You take care of things over there. When's the funeral?"

"Cannady said the M.E. released Lorraine's body yesterday. I still need to make the arrangements." Dang, he should have done that this morning.

They talked for a while longer. When they disconnected, Bronson told Mike about the camper and Carol not coming for several more days.

"Damn." Mike tapped the steering wheel.

Bronson was about to ask him what that was about but decided to let it go. Instead he asked, "Mind if we go to the funeral home close to Ellen's? I need to make the arrangements."

"No problem."

Quite on the contrary, Bronson thought. It presented a huge problem. His gun, locked away in the camper's overhead cabinet, would remain there for three or four more days—maybe even longer. He vowed he would never again get caught without his gun.

After supper, he'd pay Devono a visit. Bronson felt sure a slimeball like that could provide two, hard to trace guns. One for him, and one for Mike.

THIRTY-SIX

Bronson played with the VISA card Wellington had sent him. If he used it, he'd be indebted to him, but that wouldn't be so bad. The old man was dying. Without the money, Bronson couldn't purchase the guns. He opened his wallet and slipped the new card in.

He flopped down on the bed, took out Miller's checkbook register, and studied each entry. A pattern began to form. Once a month, on the third, an automatic withdrawal for five hundred and fifty dollars went to Fine Homes Realty Company. Bronson would be willing to bet that paid the rental for the studio. Tomorrow, he would pay them a visit.

The aroma of fresh baked bread along with the mixture of several spices, meat, and heaven knows what else drove Bronson out of the bedroom and into the kitchen. He kissed Ellen's cheek.

She set the salad bowl down. "What was that for?"

"For always making sure my hunger pains are taken care of." He helped Mike finish setting the table.

They sat down to a meal consisting of some type of chicken, mixed vegetables—not Bronson's favorite, but he ate them anyway. Carol would be proud of him—salad, and homemade biscuits. Bronson helped himself to another serving of chicken. "I was thinkin'."

"Oh, oh, that's always dangerous," both Mike and Ellen said in unison.

Bronson waited until both settled down. "Ellen, you're

always cookin', and I really appreciate your efforts. This is absolutely delicious."

"Thanks. I enjoy piddling around the kitchen."

"But not always, I'm sure. Everyone deserves a break."

By now, Mike was eyeing him suspiciously. "Where's this leading?"

"Thought maybe tomorrow afternoon, I'd drive into Pittsburgh. Catch a museum or two, the ones Carol would have no interest in. I'll also check on places to take Carol to once she arrives."

"Uh-huh." Mike's suspicious look continued.

Bronson ignored him, something he had learned to do a long time ago. "Thought maybe the two of you could take in a movie and have dinner some place nice."

"That sounds delicious, don't you think so?" Ellen's eyes sought out Mike's.

Mike let his eyes slip away from Bronson and met Ellen's. "I'd like that."

"Good. It's a date." Ellen served herself more vegetables.

"Besides doing the tourist bit, what else do you plan to do?" Mike asked.

"Miller made monthly payments to a realty company. Thought maybe that's for space rental. Thought maybe tomorrow mornin' we could go check it out. We'll be back by noon in plenty of time for you to keep your date with Ellen."

FINE HOMES REALTY COMPANY occupied the largest office space in the two block long strip mall. Mike parked almost in front of the company and tossed Bronson the car keys.

The only employee this early in the morning was an elderly lady. She looked at Bronson and Mike above the top of her wire rimmed glasses. "Can I help you, gentlemen?"

Bronson flashed her his retirement badge. Mike made no attempt to take out his Dallas one. Bronson glared at him. Mike ignored him, something he had learned to do a long time ago.

Bronson turned his attention to the Realtor. "We're here to talk to you about Larry Miller."

"It's true, then." She slammed the cabinet drawer shut. "He's dead?"

"I'm afraid so."

The Realtor shook her head. "That's really a shame. He was a harmless little man. Why would anyone want to harm him?"

"We're hopin' that by visitin' his studio, we can find an answer to that question."

"I see." It seemed obvious she didn't. "But how can I help?"

"We know your company rented him the space that he used as his studio. We'd like that address."

"Oh, sure, sure." She opened the middle cabinet drawer and thumbed through the folders.

She pulled one out. "Here it is." She handed Bronson the contract. "Anything else you need?"

"You wouldn't have a duplicate set of keys for Miller's studio, would you?" Bronson briefly skimmed the contract and jotted down the address.

"No, sorry, I don't."

Bronson handed the Realtor the contract. "Thank you, Ma'am."

"I'll make you a copy, if you wish."

"That won't be necessary. I wrote down the information I needed, but I do have one more request."

She nodded. "Go ahead."

"Miller pays you, and you in turn pay the owner the correct percentage of the rent. Who is that owner?"

The Realtor bit her lip and looked up at the ceiling as

though the answer lay there. "I'm really sorry. I don't know. That's Maggie's department. She's in charge of finances."

"No apology is needed, just tell me where I can find Maggie. I'd like to talk to her."

"She's not due to come in until one. I'd give you her cell number, but she's getting a divorce and her soon-to-be ex called her constantly. It drove her crazy, so she canceled the service. Then to top it all, she's living with a different friend or family member until she finds a permanent home. I have no way to contact her."

Bronson handed her his business card. "As soon as she gets in, tell her to look up that information and then call me."

"I will." She accepted the card.

Once back in the car, Mike sat in the driver's seat, tapping the steering wheel. "I suppose we're going to the studio."

"I suppose so."

"And how do you plan to get in?"

Bronson flashed him a smile. Mike rubbed his forehead.

THIRTY-SEVEN

THE ADDRESS THE Realtor gave Bronson and Mike led them to a row of small duplexes that looked more like rectangular boxes than homes. The painter must have had food on his mind when he painted the duplexes. The color and texture resembled slabs of pancakes.

Mike slowed down to where the car barely rolled. "That's it, isn't it?" He indicated one of the duplexes toward the middle of the row.

Bronson looked down at the address he had scribbled and up at the numbers painted above the door. "Yep." He reached for the car door handle.

Mike stopped the car and grabbed his arm. "You sure you want to do this?"

"Yep."

"We have a term for it."

"Yep."

"It's called Breaking and Entering."

"Yep."

"It's illegal."

"Yep."

"Think, Bronson."

Bronson removed his hand from the door handle and leaned back on the seat. Three seconds later, he again grabbed the handle. "Thought about it." He nodded once. "Yep, still want to do it." He opened the door and stepped out before Mike could stop him.

Before he slammed the door shut, he heard Mike say, "Shiiit."

Mike joined him on the sidewalk where Bronson waited for him.

"You can't use that expression, you know," Bronson said.

"Why not?"

"It's my expression."

"If you can break and enter, I can steal." Mike headed toward the door.

Bronson smiled and hurried to catch up.

Mike knocked on the door. Both waited. No answer. He knocked again.

Bronson looked at the doorknob. "Lookee here. It's one of those simple locks, the kind that belongs on the inside of the house, not the outside. Wonder if Miller knew his Cracker-Jack studio had no security." He took the new VISA card out of his wallet and snickered. If only Wellington knew. "This is the first time I'm using my new credit card." He wiggled the edge of the card against the sliding bolt. He then leaned closer to the door and listened, sliding the card gently in a north-south direction.

Mike rolled his eyes. "I can't believe I let you talk me into doing this."

Bronson heard the telltale click and the door swung open. "Success."

"Shit," Mike said as he stepped in.

"That's shiiit."

The one-room studio stunned Bronson. Off to his right, a kitchenette area contained a two burner stove, a microwave, an apartment-size refrigerator, and a single set of cabinets. Next to that, a closed door. Bronson assumed it led to a bathroom. Toward the back, facing Bronson, a couch covered with a pillow and blankets held the distinct honor of being the only piece of furniture in the place. An art stand in the middle of the room held a new canvas and two brushes, each a different thickness. A flat five-by-six foot piece of wood on top of bricks burst with various paint tubes and other art supplies.

Paintings of various sizes and shapes and in various stages of completion filled the rest of the room. Next to one of the piles that rested against the walls, a portfolio case large enough to hold the largest of paintings lay open.

"How are we ever going to find that painting?" Mike asked.

"Process of elimination, I guess. We'll have to look at each individually."

"Do we even know what we're looking for?"

"A storm at sea is all I know. If there's an ocean paintin' and the waters are calm, we'll eliminate it. We'll stack all the angry seas and take them to Wellington to identify."

Mike nodded. "That's about all we can do."

"Yep, so let's get to work. I'll start with this stack of paintings." Bronson indicated the pile next to the portfolio's right. "You start on that one." He pointed to the left of the portfolio.

"We'll work around until we meet or find the paintin', whichever comes first."

Two hours later, Bronson and Mike met. Bronson waited a few minutes for Mike to finish looking through his pile.

"That's that." Mike dusted the dust off his hands.

"Unbelievable. There's at least five hundred paintings here and not one of an angry sea."

"I think your estimate of the number of paintings is on the low side."

"Maybe so."

Mike stuck his thumb out and wiggled it in an up-and-down motion, pointing it toward the door. "Nothing left for us to do here. Let's hit the road."

"Not yet." Bronson took a step backwards and studied each stack of paintings.

"Now what?"

"Not sure, buddy." Bronson exhaled audibly. "Not sure."

Mike threw his arms up in the air. He flopped himself down on the couch.

For five minutes, Bronson studied the paintings. He walked around the room, carefully focusing on each pile. "I see it."

Mike perched tentatively on the edge of the couch. He looked at the paintings, then at Bronson, back to the paintings. "What?"

"Look at the frames."

The frames to the left of Bronson were the type found at discount stores. The ones to the right were ornate, obviously expensive.

"That's interesting." Mike stood up and bent down to look at the frames.

"What bothers me is that the cheap drawings have fancy frames. The better looking paintings have plain frames." Bronson and Mike eyed each other. Both nodded.

Bronson picked up the first of the fancy framed paintings, turned it over, and removed the back. Directly behind the displayed painting, Bronson found a different painting. On its backside, the provenance displayed the various museums and galleries where this piece had been displayed. Behind the original, three forgeries, complete with their fake provenance awaited to be sold.

Mike grabbed the fancy frame painting closest to him. Same results.

Half an hour later, they found the angry sea painting along with one finished forgery and another almost three-quarters complete.

THIRTY-EIGHT

BARBARA CULVERSON DREW back the curtains as she watched Bronson and Mike load a stack of paintings into their car. Her duplex, like Miller's, looked identical to all the others up and down the street. But hers, if anyone saw it, would stand out from the rest. Her room, instead of housing hundreds of paintings, harbored weapons. All sizes, all shapes, all forms. Her fortress, she called it.

Ever since she was a little girl when her father would take her hunting, she had developed a love for guns. She knew how to use each and she was precise. She never missed her target.

As a little girl, she enjoyed watching the animals die. The rush, knowing she had the power of life and death, gave her a thrill that grew stronger each day. By the time she became a teen, she'd shoot the animals only to wound them. She'd then approach them. Watching them die sent the adrenaline rushing through her veins. At first, she only watched the animal die, but she soon discovered the all thrilling pleasure of beating the defenseless animal.

Her father sat on the ground and watched his daughter. Tears welled in his eyes. "Barb, honey, this is wrong. I should have stopped you before. I'm sorry I didn't. You can't do this anymore."

The teen, whose facial features depicted the pureness of beauty, looked at him and flashed him a seductive, full teeth smile.

Her father looked down and shook his head. "I think it'd be better not to hunt anymore."

"No, Daddy, this is our special bonding time. You can't take this away from me."

Her father stood up and wrapped her in his arms. "We'll find other ways to bond. What you do to the animals, it's not, well, it's not nice. Not normal. You need help."

"Then help me, Daddy." The sixteen-year-old beauty winked flirtatiously at her father.

"You've always been my strength." She ran her hands up and down his arms.

He pushed her away. "Barb, what's the matter with you? I'm your father. This is wrong."

"Wrong, Daddy? How can it be wrong for me to love you more than any man out there?"

She smiled seductively.

Her father covered his eyes and rubbed them. He sniffled. "I'll take you to a doctor. Get you well, I promise."

Barb moved away and leaned against a tree. "That's it, then? No more hunting for us? No more special outings? Just me and a shrink?"

"You'll get well. You'll see." He cleared his throat. "We'll do things together, just not hunting." He held back sobs.

"Will I still be your little girl?"

"Always, honey. Always."

"Even if I do this?" She raised her gun and shot him, making sure to only wound him. She wanted to watch a human die. She waited. Two hours later, he died. She walked away.

The police had ruled the shooting as a hunting accident. Barbara—no longer Barb—had played the part of the grieving daughter to perfection.

Barbara smiled as she watched Bronson and Hoover

drive away. If she made the call, she knew what her orders would be, and that pleased her.

She drew the curtains shut and headed for the phone.

THIRTY-NINE

BRONSON INSISTED ON returning to Ellen's. Mike wanted to pursue their current leads. Somehow, Bronson would have to make Mike see it his way. "I promised Ellen I'd have you home in plenty of time for your date. We follow the paintin' trail, you won't make it."

"Ellen would understand." Mike stopped at a red light.

"Would she?" Bronson looked straight at Mike. "She'd say it was okay, but deep down, she'd resent the job even more. Do you really want that?"

Mike exhaled audibly. "Damn it, Bronson. Why do you have to be so logical about what I should do and so damn stupid about what *you're* doing?"

"I only see the logic behind it."

For the rest of the drive, they remained quiet. As Mike turned into Ellen's driveway, he looked at Bronson and shook his head.

Mike knew Bronson very well, in fact, too well. Bronson would have to play his cards with care. "What?"

"I'm worried about you. I'm afraid you're going to do something that proves you're bullheaded."

"Like what? Steal a piece from one of the museums I'm going to?"

"You're really going to the museum?"

"As promised. Two of them." Bronson opened the car door. "Now relax. You and Ellen have a great time. Hope you win her over, and by the time you're ready to leave, you're engaged."

"Engaged? Hell, we'll just move in together."

"Which is different from what you're doing now—how?"

"It'll be on a permanent basis."

"Gotcha." Bronson opened the car door, took out his cell, and showed it to Mike.

"Speaking of living together, I've got a call to make. I'll catch you inside."

Mike waived at him. "Tell Carol 'hi' for us."

"Will do." Bronson walked away.

He called Devono.

DEVONO LEANED BACK on his leather chair behind his desk. "You never cease to amaze me. Just like Lorraine. Two from the same pod. I want to hear again what you just requested. I want to make sure I heard right."

"I want two difficult to trace handguns."

"Two? You had just previously mentioned one." Devono's eyebrows arched. "Why two?"

"One's for me and the other one is for my partner."

"You do realize that if you accept even one of those guns, you'll be committing a felony."

"I am well aware of that."

"And still you want the guns?"

Devono raised his hands as if in surrender. "If you're that determined, I hope you find your guns, but you won't find them here." He put on an innocent face. "Whatever made you think I had guns that I could give you?"

Bronson perched at the end of his chair. "Cut the bullshit. I have no reason to set you up. I thought that, above all, you would want Lorraine's killer caught."

Devono's jaw dropped and his eyes widened. "Mario?"

"Yeah, the troopers claim he killed Lorraine. He fathered her child and she either threatened him with that knowledge or demanded something from him. Either way, he supposedly killed her. If that's true, I want to know who killed him and why."

Devono remained quiet, his eyes scrutinizing Bronson. "The troopers say I killed Mario to avenge Lorraine's death."

"Did you?" Bronson's voice came out rough and dry. He cleared his throat.

"I had the motive, you know that. Whoever killed her, robbed me of half-a-million dollars a year."

Bronson bit his tongue to keep from saying something he'd later regret. He gripped the chair's armrest so tight that his knuckles paled. "Glad to hear you loved my sister so much."

"That I did and still do. But I also loved the money she brought me. Money is always thicker than love."

Bronson forced himself to take a couple of deep breaths before speaking. "Are you admittin' to killing Serafin?"

"I admit to sending someone to beat him to a pulp, but not kill him."

Bronson's shoulder sagged. "So he did kill Lorraine."

"Maybe. Maybe not. I often suspected he had feelings for her. He knew that meant betraying me, knowing that she belonged to me. Being my right-hand man, I assumed he never acted on those feelings. When I found out he fathered her child, I'm afraid I didn't act too rational."

"This person you sent, I'd like to speak to him."

Devono folded his arms and leaned back. "I'm afraid that's impossible. He met with a terrible accident. He won't be able to talk to you or anyone else."

You son of a bitch. Bronson let his eyes drop for just a second before he raised them, glaring into Devono's face. "Serafin killed Lorraine, so you killed Serafin."

"So it seems, except the man I sent to rough up Mario claims when he got to his house, the place was swarming with troopers." Devono stood up, walked around his desk, and perched on it, only a foot away from Bronson. "Why do you need the guns?"

"Someone shot at me yesterday."

"Why?"

"I'm pursuing a totally different angle. Wellington gave Lorraine a paintin' worth a million dollars. It's disappeared. I've been searchin' for it, and I probably stepped on the wrong toes."

Devono whistled. "A million dollars? That's two years payment."

"The paintin' is not yours, and when I find it, it won't be for sale."

"Everything is for sale."

"Not to me."

Devono shrugged and waved his hand dismissively. "Seems like you're onto something, and you're not sharing with the troopers. Mind telling me why?"

"I've been ordered to stop all investigation. Case is closed. Serafin killed Lorraine. I dig further, I go to prison."

"Do you think Mario killed Lorraine?"

"I can't form a conclusion until I have all the evidence in front of me. I'm curious about how the paintin' fits into the picture."

"Funny way of putting it."

Bronson flashed him a fake smile.

"If I get you these guns, you know you will be indebted to me."

"I won't break any laws."

"Except for this minor felony charge." Devono threw his head back and laughed. "It all begins somewhere."

"And it also ends there."

"Troopers are saying I killed Mario. They haven't bothered me for all these years because I never broke the law."

That they know of, and if they do, they turned their backs. Bronson remained perfectly still, wanting to know where this led to.

"That might change now." Devono continued. "I want you to find Mario's killer and you'll have whatever, whomever, at your disposal."

"Including two guns."

"The two pistols I'm thinking about are both nine mm. These foreign weapons are good and reliable. One's the Spanish Model 600. The other is a Russian Makarov. If your partner is a female, I wouldn't let her have the Makarov. The recoil is tight and it requires a strong wrist action to—"

Bronson stared at him.

"Sorry. I forget you know all of this." He straightened up. "One thing I won't forget. From now on, you owe me."

"In that case, throw in the ammo too."

FORTY

BRONSON COULD LIE and tell Mike and Ellen he did the tourist bit, or he could keep his word. He chose two museums to visit, the Carnegie Museum of Art and the Carnegie Museum of Natural History. At the art museum, Bronson didn't learn anything that would help him with the case. The other museum completely captivated his attention. It featured more than four billion years of the Earth's history and Bronson wished he could devote more time to this place. Maybe he'd bring Carol. She'd like that.

As he headed out of the museum, a youthful looking receptionist said, "Thank you for visiting. Come back again."

She looked to be college age, just what Bronson needed. "It's a nice place you have here."

"I'm glad you enjoyed it. We try hard."

"Is your family the museum's curators?"

She opened her eyes wider. "Oh, no, Sir. I'm just an employee."

"Workin' your way through college?"

She nodded.

"Goin' to the University of Pittsburgh?"

"No, I attend Penn Woods College."

"How's its Art Department?"

"Pretty good, from what I've gathered. I'm not an art major."

"I'm lookin' for an art expert."

"Then Penn Woods College is your answer. Our school paper just ran a feature on the Art Department. It hosts several professional art exhibits per year, and there's several art concentrations the student can choose from."

"If I wanted to talk to just one person in the Art Department, someone who really knows the world of art, who would that be?"

"That would be Dr. Rugbie, the newest recruit. The article said the college was very honored that she chose us over the more prestigious institutions of learning."

"Seems you read that article very carefully."

She smiled. "I wrote it. I'm a journalism major."

"Good for you." Bronson saluted her. "You keep writin' those articles."

She nodded, her face beaming with pride.

"How do I get to this college?"

"It's thirty-six miles south of Pittsburgh." She reached under the counter, thumbed through a stack of tourist flyers, found the one she was looking for, and opened it to the map. "Let me show you."

BUILT IN 1893, the forty buildings of Penn Woods College spread over sixty acres of heavily wooded land. The majestic, towering oaks bathed the college with a coat of exquisite beauty and played havoc on visitors trying to locate a building. Even so, due to the receptionist's excellent directions, Bronson easily located the Art Department. Classes were still in session, and that meant that Dr. Rugbie should be somewhere nearby. He'd start by visiting her office.

The directory on the first floor informed Bronson that Dr. Rugbie's office, Room Seven G, was nestled along a row of other art department offices located on the second floor.

Half of the offices had either a strip of light shining under the door or an open door, inviting students in. Music, laughter, and chatter burst out of Room Seven G.

Bronson stood at the door while students hung pictures,

moved furniture, and emptied out boxes. A thin, red-headed, beady-eyed youth disengaged herself from the crowd and approached Bronson. "Something I can do for you?"

"I'm looking for Dr. Rugbie."

"You're lookin' at her."

Really? He would have never pegged her for a professor—a doctor at that. "I'd like to show you some paintings."

"I'm sorry, I don't critique others' work unless they're enrolled in my class." She gave him her back, heading to the center of activity in her office.

"I'm not an artist. These are professional paintings. At least one is a François La Carcé original that has never been publicly displayed." Bronson spoke quickly, hoping to catch her attention.

Rugbie gasped and turned. "How did you get hold of that?"

"It's a long story, but the paintings are in my car which is parked right across from this building. I'd be willin' to pay you for your time." Bronson wondered if she accepted credit cards.

Rugbie looked over her shoulder at her students. "I'll be back in a few minutes." No one seemed to hear her. She followed Bronson to his car. "Tell me about these paintings."

"I've got three with me. There's plenty more. I know next to nothin' about art. Thought maybe you'd be able to tell me if the other ones are as valuable as La Carcé's. I'm also interested in hearing about the forged copies."

Rugbie faltered. "Forged copies?"

"I'll show you."

Bronson opened the trunk and took out the first painting.

"That's a cheap piece of work." Rugbie's face fell. "The kind you buy at a discount store." She looked at the stack of paintings still inside the trunk. She raised the first one and snuck a peek. "So's that one."

"I wanted you to see them the way I found them." Bronson had already removed the back from the first painting. He showed her the first picture hidden under the cheap painting.

Rugbie's eyes slowly widened. She placed her open hand on her chest like the heroine in an old movie. "Is that an original Stuart?"

"You tell me."

She bent down, studying the piece of art. "Looks like it, but I can't be sure. I'd have to analyze it very carefully. How did you get hold of this?"

Bronson flipped the painting to reveal the duplicate under it.

Rugbie looked at Bronson, down at the painting, and back at Bronson. "That's an excellent imitation. Who are you? What do you want?"

Bronson retrieved his badge and flashed it at her. He told her about finding the paintings in an artist's studio and how he had gone there looking for the original La Carcé. As he spoke, he unfastened the paintings, each time revealing a priceless piece of art followed by "extremely good forgeries," as Rugbie put it.

"Tell me what you think is going on," Bronson said.

"The obvious is that this artist duplicates the great pieces. Why? I have no idea. Why don't you ask him?"

Bronson's mind reeled with possibilities. "Say he was going to sell the original underground. He shows it to a prospective buyer who has an art expert with him. The expert verifies its authenticity. At the last moment, he switches the paintings and gives him the forged copy. He's now free to sell the original again. How can he do the switch without arousing the buyer's suspicions?"

"It's not going to be an easy switch. He could carry the original and duplicate in the same portfolio, but different compartments. After the expert verifies its authenticity, he places it back in the portfolio, insisting he must see the money before releasing the painting. He takes the cash, then takes out the forgery, and hands it to the buyer."

Smart, but a risky move, one that would require nerves of steel. Miller would have never been able to pull that off. He had to have an accomplice.

Who?

FORTY-ONE

A COOL BREEZE blew in through the opened car window, chilling Bronson. Students gathered in clumps, their chatter disturbing the serenity of the stately, historical buildings. Lovers strolled by, their bodies close to each other. Somewhere in the background, a dog yelped. Someone nearby grilled hamburgers, filling the air with an aroma that stoked Bronson's hunger. His stomach grumbled.

Long after Rugbie returned to her office, Bronson remained sitting in the driver's seat. Something bothered the heck out of him. A detail. A missed lead. Something.

More students strolled by, some by themselves, others in groups of two, three, or more. Some spoke loudly. Others whispered. Some were silent.

Bronson's thoughts returned to the painting. Focus. Think. Remember.

If he were the buyer and he had an expert verify the work's authenticity, he certainly wouldn't let the painting out of his sight. Rugbie had offered the solution of placing both pieces of art in the same portfolio, but that seemed too risky. How then was the switch being pulled off?

Had to be something simple. Something very obvious. Something…

Hot-digty-dog.

Bronson started the engine, a big smile plastered on his face.

BARBARA CULVERSON WAITED over two hours for the phone to ring. She had watched Bronson and Mike load the paintings they had stolen from Miller's studio. She made the call immediately, only to be put on hold and told to wait. While she waited, her foot tapped to a rhythm only her mind could hear. After waiting for more than a minute, she hung up.

When her phone finally rang, she thought about not answering. Let him sweat. Deep down she knew that wouldn't work. She'd be punishing herself. She was the one who wanted— needed—the order. She picked up the phone. "Yes?"

"It's me."

Like she didn't know that. She chose to remain quiet.

"Look, I'm sorry." Barbara detected no trace of regret in his voice. He continued, "I didn't get back to you right away because I was busy with a client."

Barbara walked over to the window to check on Miller's studio. No activity since Bronson and Hoover left. "You have your job and I have mine."

"And I appreciate you doing your job which is why I suppose you called. What do you have to report?"

"Bronson and Hoover visited Miller's studio, and worse, they carried out what appeared to be three paintings."

She heard the sharp jabs of breath. When he spoke, his voice came out rough and strained. "Which paintings?"

Stupid question. "I'm inside my duplex, watching them through the window. You really expect me to know which paintings they took?"

He remained quiet for a moment. "Doesn't matter. We know very well which ones they are."

"That's the way it seems to me." Barbara picked up a hairbrush and began brushing her long, black hair. One-hundred strokes every day. That's how she kept her hair soft and shiny.

"Bronson somehow figured it out. Damn him. Eliminate him, the sooner the better." Barbara's hand tightened on the receiver. That's the order she'd been waiting for. "Consider it done. Usual price."

"It's the doing that concerns me. I know it's not your style, but you're going to have to make this one look like an accident."

"No problem." She hung up and her hand lingered on the receiver. She would do it her way, and if the trail she left behind led to him, that wasn't her problem.

She'd been ordered to kill and that's all that mattered.

FORTY-TWO

BRONSON HAD ALMOST reached Miller's studio when his cell rang. He didn't recognize the number on the caller I.D. "Hello?"

"Mr. Bronson? Harry Bronson?"

"Yes."

"My name is Maggie."

Maggie? The name clicked. "From Fine Homes Realty Company?"

"Yes."

Bronson felt his breath taken away. He knew what she was going to say, but he wanted that knowledge verified. "Were you able to find out who rented Miller his studio space?"

"Not who, what."

"Meanin'?"

"A corporation owns the duplexes, and not just the ones with the studio, but several others scattered throughout the city."

Not what Bronson had expected to hear. "What's the name of the corporation?"

"Land Development, Inc."

"Who's the head?"

"That's the strange part. Nowhere in the contract could I find a person's name. Even the signature line reads Land Development, Inc."

"How about a contact number?"

"There's none."

"An address?" Bronson's hope faded.

"It's a P. O. Box. Do you want me to give it to you?"

Bronson pulled off to the side of the road. He fumbled in his pocket for his notebook and pen. "I'm ready. Go ahead."

She gave him the information and Bronson wrote it down. "Thanks for getting back to me."

"I'm sorry I wasn't more help."

"You did just fine." He disconnected and tapped the cell on the steering wheel. He really didn't want to bother Mike. On the other hand, he'd want to help.

Mike picked up on the first ring. "Yo, Bronson. What kind of trouble did you get yourself in?"

"No trouble at all. Just needed for you to check on somethin' when you get a chance, and I'm sorry I'm interrupting your date."

"No, you're not. What do you want me to look up?"

"I need to know who owns Land Development, Inc. Their address is a P. O. Box in Delaware, the easiest damn state for a corporation. I want the names of the biggest shareholders, as well as the officers. All I have is the name which I gave you and a P. O. Box number in Delaware."

"Let me get something to write on." A small pause followed. "Okay, go ahead."

Bronson gave him the information.

"And you need this information because why? Oh, wait don't tell me. Let me guess. You're not at the museum."

"This just fell in my lap. I got a call, giving me the information. Carnegie Museum of Natural History is a terrific museum. You should consider bringing Ellen for a tour. You'll both enjoy it."

"Sure, partner, whatever you say. When I get home, I expect full details about the Land Development angle."

"Will do." Bronson pocketed his cell and blended in with the rest of the traffic. Five minutes later, he parked the car in front of Miller's studio. Across the street, Bronson detected the curtains barely moving.

He hurried, jimmied Miller's studio door and quickly entered.

FORTY-THREE

BRONSON SHOWING UP at Miller's studio came as a complete surprise. That had been the last thing Barbara expected Bronson to do. The man was full of surprises.

She liked that. Finally, she had found an opponent worthy of the cat and mouse game they were about to play.

Maybe he had come back to return the paintings he had stolen. This way, no one would be the wiser. If so, he should soon be making trips to the car, carrying the paintings. So far, that hadn't happened. Maybe greed had taken over, and he came back for more. Either way, he had barricaded himself in the studio.

Why? Curiosity poked at her but she knew better than to go sneaking around. Lots of fools had fallen by sticking their noses where they didn't belong. Barbara knew better. She was no fool.

Her mind told her that she should call in this latest development, but the last time she had called the jerk, he had placed his client's need above hers. Screw him. She had her orders.

Kill Bronson.

What an easy target he'd make. Eventually, he would have to head out of the studio and back to his car. At that precise moment, *bang*, one sweet pull of the trigger would end his life.

Barbara studied the display of weapons hanging on the living room wall behind her. For Bronson, she would use only the best. Choosing the correct one meant the difference between stopping power and killing power. If she shot him in the belly with a .25 caliber pistol, his vital organs would look like Swiss cheese after the bullet bounced around consuming its energy. Bronson would most likely die, but that process would take about a week.

A week.

She could drag him to her duplex where she'd lay him in the middle of the floor, chain him, then sit back and watch him agonize and struggle, like an earthworm on a hot sidewalk. She might give him a glass of water once or twice a day just to make sure he hung on longer.

She loved living in this neighborhood where everybody minded their own business. If someone heard a shot, no one would question it. If someone was killed in the middle of the street, the neighbors would turn away. No one knew anything. No one saw anything unless it directly affected him. Bronson's accident wouldn't concern anybody in the neighborhood except her. That meant she could not only just shoot him, but also drag the body inside, for her to enjoy.

A week for her to watch him squirm, sweat, grow weak, and die. The idea caused a tingle of excitement in her body. It began at the nape of her neck and moved down her arms.

A week with Bronson while he died.

She licked her lips.

Barbara grabbed the Beretta .45 and headed for the window. Leaving the curtains drawn, she opened the window and removed the screen. Now she would have a perfect shot.

Soon Bronson would step out of Miller's studio. She was ready. Her anticipation grew.

She had all the advantages.

The perfect shot.

FORTY-FOUR

BRONSON EDGED HIS way toward the front window of the studio. From there, he had a clear view of the duplex across from him.

He watched.

He waited.

Nothing.

More than likely, his overactive imagination blossoming out of guilt made him paranoid. He hated operating outside the law, made him feel like an outcast. It went against all his principles.

He thought of Lorraine.

Don't leave me.

To do her justice, he would turn over the tiniest pebbles if they held the smallest of possibilities that they somehow related to her death. He'd do whatever needed to be done, even if it cost him his integrity.

Don't leave me.

The words echoed in his brain bouncing around with never-ending springs.

Don't leave me.

Maybe this painting angle had little or nothing to do with his sister's murder. Maybe it had everything to do with it. Either way, it was an angle he had to pursue.

He would never get anything accomplished if he spent his time hiding behind the window like a scared rabbit waiting for the mighty hunter to show up. Casting the duplex one last look, he stepped away and focused on the opened briefcase resting between the paintings.

Before touching it, he looked at it from every possible angle. He picked it up and laid it on the floor in the middle of the room, still in its opened state. He walked around it. He bent down and closed it and eyed it some more.

Something clicked.

When he looked at it in its opened position, it seemed only large enough to hold one painting, but when it was closed, it could easily hold two paintings.

Bronson thumped, pushed, pulled, did everything possible to reveal a fake bottom. He couldn't find one. He closed it and stood it upright. He studied the side facing him, then its opposite side. He opened the case. Closed it. Walked around and opened it again. "Well, I'll be," he said aloud even though he knew no one could hear him.

The briefcase opened from each side to reveal only one of the two compartments. The seller would open the briefcase to reveal only one painting. That one, the original one, would be the one the expert would see and authenticate. Then in plain view, the seller would return the painting to the briefcase. He'd collect his money, open the briefcase, take out the painting and place the money in the empty space vacated by the painting.

What the buyer would not see was the seller turning the briefcase one-hundred-eighty degrees so that when he once again opened it, the duplicate showed.

Bronson retrieved his cell, put it on photo mode and snapped pictures of the briefcase both opened and closed. He sent the picture to Mike's, Carol's, and Ellen's cells.

He returned the briefcase to where he found it, felt for the gun hidden in the small of his back, pulled it out, and placed it in his pant pocket where it'd be more accessible. He looked out the window at the duplex facing him. The right hand side curtain billowed in the breeze. Nothing wrong with that. People had the right to open their windows and let the fresh air in.

He watched the place a bit longer. No sign of life. He stepped out, making sure the door remained unlocked.

FORTY-FIVE

BARBARA'S BODY SLIGHTLY stiffened, something it always did prior to killing. She raised the gun and watched.

She aimed.

She waited.

By now Bronson had reached the car.

"Bang," she said and lowered the gun. Had she actually shot him that would have been the end of the game. Way too easy. For Bronson, she had something else in mind.

A little mental torture.

Follow him.

Let him feel her presence.

Let him taste fear.

Then shoot. Bring him home and watch him die.

The game had just begun.

BRONSON SAT IN the car and breathed easier. No action from across the street. He had worried for nothing. He busied himself returning the three paintings. He placed each one on the exact pile he had found it in.

Bronson could taste the sour sting in his mouth. What he had to do next made his stomach grumble with anxiety, but it was the right thing to do. He had no choice.

Forty-five minutes later, he pulled into the troopers' station. He asked to see Cannady.

She frowned when she saw him but invited him to sit. "Thought I got rid of you. What do you want?"

Hello to you, too. "I got some information to share."

Cannady retrieved a notepad and a pen. "Go on."

Bronson explained his theory about fake art being sold underground as original paintings. Cannady listened carefully without interrupting. While Bronson talked, she jotted more notes.

When he finished, he folded his hands on his lap. "Questions?"

She took time to read through her notes. "You said this is happening in Pittsburgh. Why come to me? You know this falls under the Pittsburgh jurisdiction."

"Because this ties to my sister and that makes it your jurisdiction."

Cannady's eyes widened. "How?"

"Wellington gave her an original François La Carcé worth about a million dollars. The paintin' was missin' from her house, so I set out to look for it."

"And?"

"And that's what led me to the discovery."

Cannady tapped the top of the pen against the desk. "How did your sister get involved with these art thieves?"

"Seems my sister, for some reason or the other, wanted or needed money. She thought about selling the paintin' but didn't want to hurt Wellington's feelings, so she came up with this great idea. If Miller made a duplicate for her, she'd hang that one in her house and Wellington wouldn't be the wiser. She'd then be free to sell the original."

"How did she know to go to Miller?"

"I don't know, at least not yet."

"But you do have leads." A statement, not a question.

"Maybe."

"How do we get from your sister wanting to deceive her benefactor to Miller selling the paintings?"

"Miller was a mousey man. He could never pull the deception. Someone else is involved."

"You think your sister was the one who sold the paintings?"

"No, this had been going on way before my sister got involved with Miller. Miller worked for someone else."

Cannady sat up, her features pinched in together. "Miller worked…as in past tense."

"He was murdered."

"I see. Just a minor detail you forgot to mention."

"Actually, I was going to tell you." He handed her Miller's checkbook register. "The Pittsburgh police may be interested in seeing that. It belonged to Miller."

"And how did you come to have that in your possession?"

Bronson's glance slipped away from her, down to the floor, and back up at her.

"Your sister had it." She looked down and wrote something. "So what is it that you're trying to tell me?"

"I'm thinkin' my sister got a whiff of the art theft, so whoever killed Miller also killed my sister."

Cannady bolted out of her seat. "I'm only going to say this once. Mario Serafin killed your sister. It was a lover's quarrel. End of story." Her eyes sparkled with venom. "You have been warned to stay away. If I catch you interfering again, I will drag your sorry ass to jail faster than you can blink. Do I make myself clear?"

The room grew silent. Troopers stopped doing their job and watched with interest as Cannady's voice grew louder. Most moved their hands so that weapons could easily be reached. "I didn't hear an answer."

Bronson stood up. "You made it perfectly clear."

She reached out and shoved him in the chest, pushing him away. "Then get out of here."

Bronson nodded and walked out to the sounds of cheers and clapping for Cannady. He held his head up as he headed for the car. He drove five blocks before he felt safe enough to pull over. He checked the rearview mirror and the side mirrors. No signs of troopers.

When Cannady placed her hands on his chest and pushed him away, she had also done something else. Something, he hoped, no one had noticed.

She had stuffed a piece of paper in his shirt pocket. He pulled it out, opened it, and straightened it out. It read: Tonight 7:00 Jacob's Pizza House Pittsburgh.

FORTY-SIX

Just as Bronson was about to pull out and merge with the traffic, his cell went off. The caller I.D. read Penn Woods College. That had to be Dr. Rugbie. Good thing he thought about giving her his business card before she walked away. He put the cell on speaker mode. "Hello, Dr. Rugbie. What can I do for you?"

"Hello, Bronson. I have some information you'll want to know. It's about the paintings."

"Go on."

"When I saw the paintings—the originals, or at least what I perceive to be the originals— something bothered me, but I didn't want to say anything. I wanted to be sure."

"And what did you want to be sure about?"

"You showed me three paintings."

"I did."

"One was a gift to your sister, an original La Carcé, I believe."

"You are correct."

"The other two have been reported stolen."

Bronson rubbed his forehead. "I suspected as much. Thanks for verifying it and saving me the time."

"You're welcome. I have the names of the museums and names of the owners so you can return the work to the rightful owners."

"I'll take that list. But at least temporarily, the Pittsburgh Police Department will impound the paintings. I'm sure they'll contact the owners and return them their paintings as soon as possible. They won't want to have those any longer than necessary."

"I'm sure the owners will be ecstatic when they get the call."

"Definitely so, and I'll let them know you were the one who pieced it together." Bronson looked at his watch. "I've got some free time right now. I can meet you so I can pick up the list."

"I'm still at the college at my office."

"I can be there around six. Will that be too late?"

"Not at all."

Bronson made a U-turn and headed back. He dialed Carol's number and talked to her all the way to the college.

BARBARA HUMMED AS she prepared dinner for one. Bronson didn't know it, but the game had already begun. She chopped a tomato, savoring the memory of watching Bronson from the parked car's front side window. She set the small pieces of tomato aside and reached for the bag of carrots. She took three out and cut them. She smiled, remembering how Jack, following her instructions, shot at Bronson as he left Miller's house.

Bronson had hunched down, run in a zigzag pattern, and dove into the car that Hoover drove. That showed guts and initiative. She liked that. She took out the chunk of cheese from its bag and grated it.

Bronson shouldn't have expected to be shot at from the side, only from the front. But when the bullet came flying from his left, that didn't cause him to falter. He was running for his life. Not that Jack planned to kill him. He had specifically been told to miss.

It had all been a scare tactic, a test. See how Bronson would react under pressure, a boiling pressure that was just about to heat up.

The lettuce came next. She shredded it and placed it in a salad bowl. She wiped her hands, picked up the phone, and dialed a familiar number by memory.

When Jack answered she said, "I have a job for you and your twin."

"Yeah? What's that?"

"I want you to follow Bronson. Let him know you're there, but don't let him catch you."

"We can do that."

"How long do we follow him?"

"All of tomorrow, maybe the next day, too."

"Mind if I ask what's the purpose of this?"

"Get him agitated, put him on the defensive." The Raven hung up and smiled.

FORTY-SEVEN

FORTUNATELY FOR BRONSON, Jacob's Pizza House was less than a fifteen minute drive from Penn Woods College. He arrived only five minutes late.

The place swarmed with people, old, young, and in-between. They laughed and chattered, but the volume of the noise never reached the roar level. The pictures on the wall depicted the hot actors, actresses, and singers of yesteryear. In the background, the jukebox spit out one Oldie-But-Goodie tune after another.

After checking the place and not finding Cannady, Bronson settled in a booth tucked away toward the back that still had a clear view of the main door. He amused himself by reading the Interesting Facts about the movie stars tucked under the glass that covered the table. Now and then, he'd glance up.

A man threw him mental darts for apparently taking up a booth and not eating. The clock on the wall showed 7:24. Might as well order. He had to eat anyway.

Six minutes later his pizza arrived but still no Cannady. Bronson checked his cell. No messages. He bit into the first slice.

His taste buds screamed in delight. Glad he chose the large even though he knew he couldn't eat it all. He poured himself another cup of coffee. Plenty of sugar. Plenty of milk. Carol would never know.

He finished his first slice, worked on the second. Was it too late to order a side salad? That was healthy. Carol would like that. He was contemplating the idea when a frazzled-looking woman stepped in. Bronson signaled Cannady over.

"I'm sorry I'm so late." She slid in the seat facing him, trying to catch her breath as though she had run from the parking lot inside. She looked around, making sure they were alone.

Bronson indicated the pizza. "I didn't know what kind you like. I ordered pepperoni. I read somewhere it is the most requested ingredient."

"My favorite."

So they had something in common. "Dig in."

She ordered a beer and helped herself to a slice. She gobbled it in four large bites. "Sorry. I haven't eaten all day," she mumbled around a mouthful.

"Have some more. We can always order another."

She grabbed another slice, no hesitation. She wiped her mouth. "Something's going on at headquarters."

"Yeah?"

"We've been ordered to cease all investigation involving your sister's death. As far as the department is concerned, a lover's quarrel ended Lorraine's life."

"But you don't think so."

"Quite the contrary. I'm sure Mario Serafin pulled the trigger."

Bronson set his slice of pizza down. "If he did, then who killed him and why?"

"The who: Devono. They why: revenge. Lorraine was his territory." Her eyes slipped away from Bronson's. "Sorry."

Bronson swallowed hard. He pushed the pizza away. "But now you're wonderin' if maybe Serafin didn't pull the trigger."

"Let's just say that there's something big going on."

"Meanin'?"

"For years now, the law hasn't been able to touch Devono.

Anything came up involving him, it was hands off. An unwritten understanding existed between Devono and the men he controlled. We, as well as the Pittsburgh Police Department, left him alone and he in turn didn't do anything that would call attention to himself. But now we're talking murder and still we're ordered to leave it alone." She paused long enough to bite into her pizza. She took a large swig of her beer. "Serafin wasn't exactly squeaky clean himself. He gets killed, the world's a better place. I could live with that."

"But?"

"But no one should be above the law. Besides, long before you came to me, I followed up on the painting angle. Because I've had to sneak around, I hadn't gotten as far as you. But your story makes sense. Goes along with what I've learned."

"Knowing this, you still feel Serafin is responsible for my sister's death."

"All evidence points to him."

"Includin' the rifle you all found under his bed."

Cannady frowned.

Bronson helped himself to another slice of pizza. "That's mighty stupid, don't you think? Puttin' the murder weapon under the bed. Serafin must have been very stupid."

"He wasn't."

"That's exactly my point."

Cannady leaned forward. "Could be like you suspect. Lorraine got a whiff of the art theft and that is what got her killed. Someone broke into Serafin's house and planted the weapon to frame him."

"That someone is Lorraine's real killer." Bronson stirred his coffee and focused on the half-empty cup. There really wasn't anything to stir, but still he stirred. "Lorraine called me several times, you know. Wanted to tell me somethin'. Wouldn't do it over the phone. She sounded very apprehensive, but I assumed that was because of our estranged relationship. By the time I arrived, it was too late."

Cannady reached for his hand and squeezed it.

Don't leave me.

"We'll get the bastard who did this." She looked into his eyes.

He found kindness there. He nodded.

She removed her hand. "Pursue all leads. I will cover for you as much as I can. Just don't come to the office or expect me to officially support you."

"Do you have a Pittsburgh police contact? Someone who is somewhat of a renegade like you?"

Cannady's eyes widened. "If I'm a renegade, what does that make you?"

A poster of James Dean stared at Bronson from the wall above him. "A rebel without a cause?"

Cannady smiled. "I had a feeling you were going to ask me for a Pittsburgh Police Department contact. Here's his name and cell number. I've already cleared it with him. His name is Joe Randig." She retrieved the paper from her pants pocket and handed it to Bronson. "What I want you to remember is that both Joe and I want to keep our jobs and especially our lives. We won't openly support you or help you. But both of us will do everything possible to help you bring Lorraine justice." She wiped her hands with a napkin. "Basically what I'm saying is that you're on your own. Now go out there and get them. We're rooting for you."

Rooting for me, but I'm on my own. Good thing I bought the gun. Bronson nodded.

FORTY-EIGHT

ALREADY EIGHT THIRTY-SIX and Bronson was barely heading home. The cloak of darkness enveloped the vistas he enjoyed during what had become a daily commute. Now the clusters of trees seemed to be nothing more than dark blurbs. He looked forward to getting to Ellen's and relaxing.

The cell's ring tone told Bronson Carol was calling. "Hi, honey. Everythin' okay?"

"All's well, but I was thinking."

Uh-oh.

"The funeral will be in a couple of days. You're just waiting for me to get there. Right?"

"Yeeeah." Bronson spoke slowly, stretching out the word.

"You haven't told the girls about their aunt. Don't you think they have the right to know?"

Bronson had been dreading this moment. He knew it would have to come, but why now? "Thought maybe I'd tell them in person."

"You don't think they may want to attend the funeral?"

"I don't think either will come. They can't afford it, time wise or financially."

"But at least that's their choice."

As always, Carol was right. "I'll call them."

They talked a few minutes longer before disconnecting.

Bronson called the elder of the two daughters, Little Carol, first. When he heard the phone ring, for the first time in his life, he wished she wouldn't answer.

She did. "Daddy, hi. Good to hear from you. Are you okay? How's Mom? All's well? How's retirement treating you? Hope you're not involved in another case. Are you?"

Bronson smiled. So typical of Carol. Ask a series of questions and don't give time to answer. "Camper broke down. Mom's with the camper, a few hours away from me. I'm in Pittsburgh."

"Pittsburgh? Really, Dad?" Her tone sounded guarded. "Where in Pittsburgh?"

"Actually, a little town close to Pittsburgh."

"Whittle City?"

Had Carol told her? No, she would have mentioned it if she had. "Yes. How would you know that?"

Silence.

"Carol Babel, tell me what you know."

"That's serious business, Daddy, when you call me by my full name."

"Carol Babel."

"Okay, Daddy. Aunt Lorraine called me a few months back. She introduced herself. I wanted to tell you. I really did, but I never found the right time. You never told me about her."

"I didn't even tell your mother."

"Why? What happened between you two? She wouldn't tell me either."

"It's a long story better told in person. Does your sister also know?"

"No, Donna was out of town when Aunt Lorraine started calling. She plans to call her real soon. Maybe this weekend."

Bronson let out a long sigh. "What did you two talk about?"

"She was anxious to know everything about you. I told

her about you retiring and about some of the cases you've gotten involved in after your so-called retirement."

That explained how Lorraine knew so much about him. "You gave her my cell number?"

"Dad, she's your sister."

Dad. A few seconds ago it was *Daddy.* "I need—"

At the same time Bronson started to speak, so did Carol. "We're making—"

Both stopped.

"You go first," Bronson said.

"I was going to say that we're making plans to meet in about a month from now."

The night grew darker, the shadows, deeper. Why did it have to come to this?

Don't leave me.

If he hadn't, would she still be alive now?

"Daddy, you're not mad at me, are you?"

Daddy. She had called him Daddy. His little girl was back. How could he tell her what he had done? "No, of course not, pumpkin." He had no idea why he called her that. She didn't even have red hair. Golden brown highlights added softness to her mostly brown hair. "Is Jim there?"

"Oh, yes. Ever since you talked to him, he's been treating me like a queen. Thank you for saving my marriage."

"Don't give me the credit. He's the one who wanted to change." Bronson cleared his throat. "Could you put him on speaker phone? I have something to tell you both."

"Oh my God. Is Mom okay?"

"Yes, honey. She's perfectly fine. Now go get Jim."

Bronson heard her set the phone down. A few seconds later Carol came back on. "We're both here."

"Hello, Bronson. What's this about?" Always the man of few words. Get down to business immediately. That was Jim.

"Daddy, you're scaring me."

"I'm sorry, sweetheart." Bronson hesitated and wished with all his might, he didn't have to do this. "I'm here in Whittle because Lorraine died."

Carol gasped. "Oh my God. What happened?" Her voice broke.

"She was murdered. She died in my arms." Tears welled in his eyes, and Bronson hated this weakness.

"Are…you okay, Daddy?"

Bronson swept away the tears with jerky, clumsy movements as if his hand had a mind of its own. "As well as expected. And you?"

Jim answered. "Carol was very excited about her new aunt. They would talk on the phone for hours. Carol couldn't wait to meet her, and now… Mind if we call you back? I need to comfort Carol."

"Sure. Do me a favor?"

"Name it."

"Hold her for me."

"I plan to."

Bronson punched the end button. He started to call Donna but found he had neither the strength nor energy to face her now. He'd call her tomorrow.

FORTY-NINE

THE TREES AND buildings muted colors created by the street lights swirled around Bronson. Every inch of him felt wretched. He stomped on the accelerator, and the car shot ahead. He dared the police, or the state troopers, or the county Mounties to catch him.

By some miracle, Bronson reached Ellen's house ticket free. He sat in the car rubbing his forehead and forcing his body to relax. He looked at his image in the side view mirror. His eyes were droopy and his complexion pale. Did he really feel as tired as he looked? He sat up straighter and practiced smiling. He looked fine.

Mike must have heard him drive up as he opened the front door even before Bronson reached the porch. "You look like hell."

"Shiiiit."

"Museums are that taxing?"

Bronson flashed him a fake smile, swept past him, and flopped down on the couch. He unlaced his boots and kicked them off.

"You're a true Texan," Ellen said.

"Meanin'?"

"You always wear boots."

"These are special boots."

"How's that?"

"When I was still active, I bought a pair of boots that had a pocket on the inside of the right boot. It held a knife, the type that with a flip of a switch, opens. I got the laced up version of the boots because I get a tight fit, but at the same time, I have enough space for the knife. Ever since I purchased that first pair, all of my boots have had that pocket."

"Where's the knife now?"

"In the camper, along with my gun." He sighed and looked away.

Ellen sat beside him and Mike across from them. "Tell us why you're so sad." Ellen squeezed Bronson's shoulder. "Is it Lorraine?"

"That and the fact that I've just finished talkin' to Little Carol. I told her about Lorraine."

"She took it hard, I gather." Mike sat straighter, leaning toward Bronson.

Bronson massaged his eyebrows. "Harder than I expected. She and Lorraine had apparently struck up a relationship."

"So that's how the kids at the school she worked at knew about you," Mike said.

Bronson nodded. "Lorraine and Little Carol planned to meet in a month."

"How about Donna?" Ellen asked. "Did you talk to her too?"

Bronson shook his head. "I couldn't. Not after talkin' to Little Carol. I'll call Donna tomorrow."

"She knew Lorraine too?" Ellen asked.

"Not according to Little Carol."

Mike kicked off his shoes. "Okay, partner. I'm in for the long haul. Tell me about your day, and you can leave off the museum part."

Ellen stood up. "If you boys are going to talk shop, I'm going to head to bed and curl up with a good book. If either of you need anything, help yourselves."

Mike stood up and kissed her goodnight. "I'll be in shortly."

"I bet." She looked at Bronson and winked.

Bronson waved goodnight and threw her a kiss.

Mike waited until Ellen had left before he sat back down. "I'm listening."

Bronson began by telling Mike about his visit to Devono's. He included every detail he could remember, with one exception. He failed to mention getting hold of some guns.

Bronson then told him about meeting with Dr. Rugbie and about his theory regarding forging expensive art pieces and selling them as originals. To support his hypothesis, Bronson told him about finding the two-sided portfolio.

Mike got his cell out and showed it to Bronson. "I got the pictures you sent. Couldn't figure out what they meant."

"Now you do."

"Now I do." He pocketed his cell. "Anything else?"

Bronson told him about Cannady. First her harsh treatment when he went to return Miller's checkbook register, then her explanation and offer at dinner time.

"Amazing. You did all that, and you still had time to visit two museums."

"I told you I would."

"You are a man of your word."

"One of my many wonderful characteristics."

"Including modesty."

"That, above all." Bronson stretched out. Mike had a way of making him feel at ease. "Your turn. Tell me about your day. Skip the gooey details."

Mike smiled. "There were plenty of those."

"I said skip them."

"Can't give you the full picture unless I mention them." Mike looked down the hallway, toward Ellen's bedroom. "I think we have a chance. A real chance." His eyes sparkled.

"If I wasn't so tired, I'd get up and give you a hug."

Mike waved his hands in front of him. "Don't get gooey on me."

"Wouldn't think of it."

"I do have other news."

"Yeah? What's that?"

"Shortly after you called and told me about that P. O. Box, I told Ellen. She immediately called in a favor. We got the Special Eight O'clock Tour of County Records, and we got an answer for you."

Bronson's eyebrows shot up. "Really? You did that for me on your special date night?"

"All I did was drive. Ellen's the one who insisted on calling in the favor."

"Must have been one heck of a huge favor that person owed Ellen."

"Ellen says they're even now."

"I could kiss you both."

"You're getting gooey again."

"It's my nature."

Mike cast him a weird look. "Since when?"

"Quit stallin'. Who owns that P.O. Box address?"

"Give it one wild guess."

Bronson audibly exhaled. "Our attorney friend, Sam Glass."

"None other," Mike reassured him.

FIFTY

THE LEGAL SECRETARY pressed the intercom button. "Mr. Glass, a Mr. Bronson and a Mr. Hoover are here to see you."

Glass smiled. Life had reached the age of perfection. "Tell them I have a phone conference, but will see them immediately after. It shouldn't be more than half-an-hour or so."

The lawyer heard his secretary talking to them. A few seconds later, she spoke to him. "They'll wait."

Glass released the intercom button and leaned back on his leather chair, a tight grin spreading across his lips. He reached for his private line and punched number one. He heard the phone ring three times before The Raven picked up.

"Yes, Sam?"

"We're in luck. I thought maybe you were wondering how to locate Bronson. He and Hoover just walked into my office."

Two for the price of one. "It'll cost you extra."

"It's worth it. One accident, two lives lost. That's not a bad deal."

A silence followed.

"You're not planning on doing anything foolish, are you?" Glass knew The Raven was as dangerous as she was beautiful. He bit his lip.

"I'll send the twins over to get Bronson's car ready."

Glass relaxed. A hole in the brake line. Not a bad idea. The Raven would come through. He looked out the window toward the parking lot. "I see only three parked cars. My secretary's, mine, and a silver Chevy Cruze. That's got to be theirs."

She knew the car. She had followed it often enough. "Keep them in your office long enough for the twins to do their job."

"How long is that going to take?"

"They're less than half-an-hour away from you. Add a few minutes to do their thing and get away."

"I'll keep Bronson and Hoover busy."

"Just to be sure, I'll call you to let you know when it's okay for them to leave. I'll call your private line and let the phone ring twice. That'll be the signal."

"Get to it, then." Glass disconnected and worked on a deposition he had to prepare. Twenty-five minutes later, Glass told his secretary to let the two men in. Soon as the door opened, Glass bolted to his feet and greeted them. "Mr. Hoover, so nice to see you again." He offered him his hand.

Mike accepted it. "This is my partner, Harry Bronson."

"Mr. Bronson." Glass pointed to the two leather-covered chairs facing his desk. He walked around and sat down. "Bronson." He tapped his lip with his index finger. "I've heard that name before." He snapped his fingers and his eyes widened. "You're…you're…"

"Lorraine's brother."

"Yes, I'm very sorry about your sister's death. I really didn't know her, but Mr. Wellington is one of my best clients and a close friend."

"I'm sorry, too," Bronson said.

"What can I do for you gentlemen?"

"We'd like to know about your relationship with Larry Miller."

Glass' eyebrows furrowed. "The artist?"

Both Bronson and Mike remained quiet.

"He's a great artist."

"So you are familiar with his work?" Bronson took out his spiral notebook and jotted something down.

Glass nodded.

"Anything you can tell us about his paintings?" Mike asked.

"No, I'm sorry. I never dealt with him or his work."

Bronson stared directly into his eyes. "I followed him to your office just recently."

Glass didn't blink. "I remember the day he came. Was it yesterday? The day before? Doesn't matter. It was recently." Glass shifted in his chair, made himself more comfortable. He knew the importance of body language. Let them think he had nothing to hide. "Mind if I ask why you were following him?"

"I'm tracing a paintin' he did. Mind if I ask why he came to visit you?"

"I own a number of duplexes not very far from here. Mr. Miller is one of my tenants. A real estate company handles all of the maintenance and upkeep work. They also handle the rental fee. Other than being the owner, I have nothing to do with my properties." He paused and placed his intertwined fingers on his chest. "Miller came because he couldn't make this month's rental payment. He wanted a two weeks' extension. Said he's going to come into a lot of money, and he'd pay me with interest. Naturally, I agreed."

"Did he tell you where he was getting the money?"

Glass' private line rang. He looked at the caller I.D. It read Raven. After the second ring, it stopped.

"Aren't you going to get that?" Bronson asked.

"It's my wife. I'll call her when we're finished. You were saying?"

"I asked if you knew where Miller planned to get a large amount of money."

"Didn't say and I didn't ask. Sorry."

Bronson stood up. "In that case, we won't take any more of your time. Thanks for seeing us. I'm sure you have a lot of work to do."

Glass swept his arm over his desk pointing to all the papers scattered in various piles. "That's an understatement." He stood up. "Thank you for coming."

"One more thing." Bronson stepped around the chair. "You'll have to collect your rent from Miller's estate."

Glass frowned. "Meaning?"

"Miller was murdered."

A little grunt escaped from Glass as though he had suddenly lost all his wind. "I'm…I'm sorry to hear that. He seemed like such a nice man. Was it robbery?"

"It's an ongoing investigation. You understand why we're not at liberty to discuss the details."

Glass slowly nodded.

Bronson and Mike walked out, closing the door behind them.

Glass walked over to the window and watched them get in the car and drive off. A sharkish grin spread across his lips.

FIFTY-ONE

"WHERE TO?" MIKE pulled out of the parking lot.

Bronson thumbed through his pocket-size spiral notebook. He stopped several times to reread the notes he'd scribbled. "The state troopers have been ordered to drop the case. Mario Serafin killed my sister and that's that. He lived outside the law so no one's interested in solvin' his murder. Who has that kind of power to enforce a ruling like that?"

"The better question would be: who has that kind of money?"

"Devono, but I rule him out."

Mike's eyes squinted and his eyebrows furrowed. "Why?"

"Because someone with power ordered the troopers as well as the Pittsburgh police to stay away from Devono, and that happened a long time before this began."

"That was then. This is now."

"Okay. Call it a gut feelin'." When Bronson was still active with the Dallas Police Department, he relied heavily on his gut feelings.

Mike came to respect them and not question them. "Fine by me. We can rule Devono out. Who's left? And before you answer that, tell me first where we're going."

"Let's head back to Ellen's."

Mike made a U-turn. "Back to the original question. Who else beside Devono has that kind of money and power?"

"There's Wellington."

"Maybe at one time, but now, he's an old man on his deathbed. Isn't that what you told me?"

Bronson nodded. "He's not a good candidate. He loved Lorraine too much. Besides, he's got all the money in the world. Why would he deal with stolen art pieces?"

"Could be out of boredom. You know, the man who has everything." Mike glanced at the rearview mirror.

"Nah." Bronson shook his head. "Doesn't sound like him. He's been too busy keepin' up with the steel industry. But his daughter—now there's a candidate. She's desperate to get her hands on that La Carcé paintin'. She can't sell the forgeries without havin' the original."

Mike slowed down and glanced at the side mirror. "She would have the power and the money to buy the troopers and the Pittsburgh Police higher-ups."

"I'll go talk to her next."

"*I*? What happened to *we*?" Mike sped up and divided his attention between the road ahead of him and the rearview mirror.

"There's someone else I'd like for you to investigate. This someone also possibly has the clout and the money." Bronson lowered the visor and adjusted the mirror so he could see the road behind him.

"And who is that?" Mike executed an unexpected right turn.

"Glass." Bronson's gaze didn't leave the mirror.

"Our lawyer friend." Mike took a left. "I tend to agree with you. He puts on a good show, but I think he knows a lot more about those art pieces than he admits. I wouldn't be surprised if he's orchestrating the whole thing."

"That's why I want you to check him out. See if there's a way to link him to the art thefts." Bronson tightened his seat belt. "I see the Camry."

"Same green Toyota Camry LE that was parked across the street from Miller's house."

"Yep."

"I'm going to lose him."

"Go for it."

Mike sped up and made a quick left, then two rights. A left. Another left. A right. He drove down the same street for three blocks. "I don't see him."

Bronson used both the side mirror and the vanity mirror to watch the street behind them. It looked clear. He swiveled and looked out the back window. "We lost him."

"Why is he following? Who is he?"

"Excellent questions. Somehow we've got to find the answers including what's his motive? He's followed me—us—often enough to get a clear shot, but he's never taken it. In my book that makes him more dangerous than the guy who aims and shoots."

"I hear you, buddy." Mike worked his way back to the main road. He constantly glanced at the mirrors but he saw no trace of the green Camry.

Bronson kept an eye on the road behind them. "If either Amanda or Glass is the ring leader, I don't think either of them would get their hands dirty. Someone else pulled the trigger."

"And it wasn't Serafin." Mike checked the mirrors but saw no trace of the Camry.

"That someone else stuck the rifle under Serafin's bed and killed my sister."

"You're thinking the guy in the Camry is the shooter."

"Shiiit."

Mike glanced at his mirror. "We've got company."

FIFTY-TWO

LIEUTENANT JOE RANDIG doodled while the chief-of-police talked. Somehow this helped him concentrate. At first the other officers thought Randig was being rude, but soon learned this was his way of focusing.

Unlike other times, Pittsburgh's crime rate had dropped and the streets, for once, were relatively quiet. Their biggest case centered on the murder of a local artist. Surely a tragedy but since he had criminal connections, this low priority case didn't ruffle anyone's feathers. Still, the chief-of-police said they would devote time to solving it, as time permitted.

Someone's mobile rang, causing the chief to frown. During these short daily meetings, he demanded everyone's full attention.

Randig felt the blood rush to his face. He always remembered to turn the damn thing off even though no one hardly ever called. Today, he forgot and here it was, embarrassing the hell out of him. He looked at the caller I.D. and recognized the number as the one Cannady gave him that belonged to Bronson. Great way to make his acquaintance.

Randy stood up. "I'm sorry, sir, this won't happen again." He walked out, the cell insistently beeping out a tune. Out in the hallway, Randig pushed the send button. "Bronson?"

"Yes, that's me. I'm being—"

"This isn't a good time. Mind if I call you back later and get things sorted out?"

"Sure."

Randig disconnected, put the cell on vibrate, and returned to the meeting.

"WE'RE ON OUR OWN." Bronson looked out the side view mirror. The green Camry remained several car lengths behind. Too far to identify the driver but close enough to let Bronson and Mike know he drove alone.

"Got any brilliant ideas?" Mike kept the speedometer at a steady thirty. "I'm not about to lead him to Ellen's."

"Don't blame you."

"So what do we do?"

"Divide and conquer."

"Meaning?"

"Pull into a crowded parking lot. Get out. Call Ellen. She'll come pick you up. Leave her at a mall or somewhere. Call me and together, we'll corral the animal."

"In the meantime, what are you going to do?"

"Drive around, look for the perfect place for this to go down. I'll also make sure I don't lose him."

Mike ran his opened hand over his cheek. "How wise is that? You don't even have a gun to protect you."

Bronson kept his eyes glued to the mirror, watching the Camry.

"Damn it, Bronson. What have you done?"

"That parking lot coming up to our right looks pretty crowded. It should be safe enough."

"I see it." Mike slowed down so he could maneuver the turn. He let the engine idle as he pulled in and parked directly in front of a large clothing store. "Stay safe, my friend."

Bronson scooted over to the driver's seat. "I plan to."

The Camry stayed at the opposite end of the parking

lot, still visible. The driver made no attempt to get out or otherwise move.

"I'll wait for your call," Bronson said.

Mike dodged into the store and disappeared behind the closed doors.

Bronson switched the gear from park to drive. He drove out of the parking lot and maintained the speed the other drivers used.

The Camry followed behind.

FIFTY-THREE

JACK WOULDN'T PUT it past Bronson.

He and his twin had been asleep when the Raven called. Soon as the Raven told him she wanted a listening device put inside Bronson's car, Jack sprang out of bed and immediately drove to the lawyer's. No time for breakfast, not even a bagel and a soft drink.

Now, as though deliberate, Bronson led him down three blocks of restaurants, one after the other. *Tonight! Succulent Prime Rib* one sign read. Like throwing gas on a flame, the smell of cooking steaks traveled like waves and ignited Jack's hunger pangs.

A bit further down, the aroma of hamburgers grilling over an open fire almost forced Jack to stop. The bakery down the road released the scent of freshly baked bread.

Jack slowed down. On his own, he had decided that besides bugging the inside of Bronson's car, he could also place a tracking device. This way, he could pick him up anywhere, anytime. That meant he could answer the lure of the bakery. Grab some freshly made bread or one of those tantalizing, still steaming, sweet rolls. Top it off with a soft drink. Jump back in the car. Pick up Bronson's trail. Continue to follow him. That would work.

Except that Bronson had told Hoover he'd make sure he wouldn't lose him. Bronson planned to ride around until Hoover arrived. Then they would trap him.

Not quite the way Bronson had phrased it. They would *corral the animal.* That's what Bronson had actually said.

Corral the animal.

Yeah, like that was going to happen.

Corral the animal. As if he were an animal. Bronson would get his due. The Raven had heard every word Bronson and Hoover said while both were still in the car. Jack had called the Raven and put her on speaker phone.

It hadn't been his idea to put a bug in the car. The Raven had come up with that. Not only was she drop-dead gorgeous, she was brilliant. And dangerous, but that was part of what attracted him. That danger drove Jack. He'd do anything for her, including risk his own life. Not that he would have to worry about that.

The Raven would never hurt him.

THE RAVEN FOUND herself living two distinct lives. As Barbara, she was the normal person who existed in an average, boring world. She was beautiful and constantly attracted attention, but that concluded the extent of her excitement. Whenever she worked, the Raven took over. Like now.

She and John, the younger of the twins, sat in her car at the mall's parking lot, the same one where Bronson had dropped Hoover off.

Through Jack's cell, she heard a mobile ring.

"Here we go," Jack said, listening to the goings on inside Bronson's car. "That's Bronson's cell."

The Raven looked around the parking lot, hoping to spot Hoover. "I can hear it ring."

"Yo, buddy," Bronson said. "Where are you?"

A pause followed while Mike spoke.

"The mall where I dropped you off, right?"

Another pause.

The Raven saw a man help an attractive woman get out of a car. The Raven recognized him: Hoover. The woman with him had to be Ellen. The man and woman headed toward the mall. The Raven indicated for John to get out and follow them.

The Raven's concentration broke when Bronson spoke again.

Bronson said, "Yes, I did. Not far from here is a row of restaurants. Behind them is a narrow alley. I'll pull into the alley. The Camry will follow. You come in behind the Camry. I stop. He can't back up because you'll be blocking the animal. We rush him, one from each side."

The Raven stuck her thumb up in the air. Brilliant plan. So simple in its efficiency.

Bronson would be a worthy opponent. She was definitely going to enjoy this.

She rushed inside the mall to join John. Ellen would be right in front of him.

FIFTY-FOUR

BRONSON EYED THE rearview mirror. The Camry hung three car lengths behind. While waiting for Mike to call him, he did everything possible to kill time without arousing the driver's suspicions.

He filled up the gas tank even though the gas gauge read three-quarters full. He used the drive-through window and chose one with a long line. He ordered coffee and put the bill on Wellington's credit card. He figured a credit card would take longer than cash. He pulled off to the side while he fixed his coffee and checked the mirror for the Camry. He drove through a residential area and slowed down several times, pretending to look for a particular address.

About the most useful thing he did other than getting his coffee was to stop at a variety store and purchase a knife with a five inch serrated blade. He put it in his pocket and made a mental note to transfer it to his boot. When he stepped out of the store, he saw the Camry parked four spaces behind his car.

Soon as he was inside the car, he took the knife out of his pocket and put it in his boot. Just as he started the engine, his mobile went off. Mike. Finally, they'd be able to trap their prey. "Yo, buddy, where are you?"

"I just left Ellen at the mall. She loves to shop, so she's happy. Told her I'd pick her up later, and we'll go eat. I didn't tell her what we're doing, but I'm sure she knows something's up. I'm back to Ellen's car and I'm getting in. Tell me where to go, and be nice about it."

"It would never cross my mind not to tell you exactly where you should go."

Bronson and Mike agreed to meet on the corner of Hercules and Diana Dr. From there, Bronson would lead them to the alley behind the row of restaurants. Mike would follow the Camry. "Give me about fifteen minutes to get there."

"I'll be there in fifteen minutes too. We'll call each other as we get close." Bronson turned to head toward the intersection. His cell beeped once. Someone had just texted him. He pulled over, giving the rearview mirror a glance. The Camry had also pulled over.

Bronson retrieved his message. No words, a picture instead. Ellen, obviously enjoying herself at the mall. Bronson looked at the picture carefully. He sat up straighter. He recognized the blond man beside her. He'd been the one who had followed him to Lorraine's house and later showed up in front of Miller's house.

Assuming the picture had just been taken, that meant that the blond-headed man was with Ellen right now. Bronson had assumed that the blond man was driving the Camry, following him. He looked through the rearview mirror. The Camry had disappeared.

Couldn't worry about that now. He had to call Ellen and Mike. He reached for his cell when it began to ring. The digital display read Unavailable. It had to be the blond. How had he gotten hold of his cell number? Bronson punched the send button. "Yes?"

"I suppose by now you've figured out we have Ellen."

A woman's voice. Who the hell was that? The black haired beauty who hung around with the blond? Bronson's full attention focused on her voice. Could he detect a trace of accent? He paid close attention to the background noises. Someone nearby honked and a rush of wind swirled. Whoever this woman was, she was outdoors, possibly in a car. Bronson looked at the cars around him. No one seemed to be paying attention. "Who is this?"

"No reason not to tell you. I'm known as the Raven."

Bronson held his breath. She had given him her name, even if it was a nickname. Knowing your adversary's name always put the victim at an advantage. She would know that. Yet she had told him. Why? "Okay, Raven, tell me what you want." His smooth, calm voice betrayed no sign of fear or apprehension.

"My friend is with Ellen right now."

"That would be the blond."

"Yes."

"What's his name?"

"You're asking too many questions. Ask only what's important."

"What do you want?"

"You."

Bronson shook himself. "Apparently you have me, or at least you have my attention."

"Then listen carefully. You do as I say and nothing will happen to Ellen. In fact, she doesn't even know she's in danger. Only thing that has happened to her is that my friend, who's an excellent pick-pocket, lifted her cell. Contacting her will be a waste of time but by all means feel free to try. Then there's Hoover. I know you're to meet him on the corner of Hercules and Diana."

How in the world did she know that? Bronson ran his hand under the car seat, then under the driver's unit. He located the bug. "Seems like you have me at a disadvantage."

"Indeed I do because I have someone else waiting at that corner. He will shoot Hoover if I tell him to."

"You said you wanted me. You've got me. What must I do so that you leave Hoover and Ellen alone?"

"Simply step out of the car. Walk half-a-block north and you will see the green Camry. I know you know which car I'm talking about. I'll be waiting for you."

"What guarantee do I have that you won't harm Hoover or Ellen?"

"You don't know me yet, but you will. You will find that I'm a woman of my word. Now start walking, and Bronson, we know you got a gun. It would be very wise of you to leave it on the passenger floor. We'll walk by your car. Make sure it's there. Leave the passenger door unlocked."

Bronson felt like a bird whose feathers had been plucked. What else did she know?

"One more thing," the Raven said.

"Yes."

"You've got exactly seven minutes to reach my car. That gives you plenty of time to get rid of the gun and do whatever else you need to do. If I even think I see the police, I'll give the order to kill Hoover and Ellen."

The Raven disconnected. Bronson looked at his watch. He had seven minutes to come up with some kind of a plan.

FIFTY-FIVE

Soon as Bronson headed away from the car and reached the intersection, Jack crept out from the shadows and approached Bronson's car. He slipped on a pair of gloves and opened the front door.

He smiled. The Raven had said that Bronson would do as told. He'd leave the gun on the floor and there it was, just as the Raven had predicted. She was always right and so beautiful.

So, so beautiful.

He picked up the pistol, one of those foreign jobs. The Raven would love that. She'd add it to her collection of trophies. The guns decorating her living room walls had come from the men and women she'd killed, and each had carried a gun. Some had been hoods, others, hunters. She'd even killed people who carried concealed weapons.

But never a policeman. Bronson would be the first, and Jack could see the Raven's anticipation pouring out of her like sap dripping out of a tree. That thought thrilled Jack.

He couldn't wait to hand her the pistol. He pocketed it, and then speed dialed the Raven. When she answered, he said, "I got the gun. He's ahead of me. He should be there shortly. I'm coming up behind him."

"You better move it. I may need help with Bronson, but afterwards, I want you to leave. Bronson is all mine." She watched the sidewalk through the side mirror. Seconds later, she spotted Bronson. "I see him." The Raven stepped out and leaned against the car. She held her cell in her hand.

WHILE STILL IN the rental and after getting his instructions from the Raven, Bronson put himself on speed mode. First, he called Ellen, knowing it would go to voice mail, hoping it didn't. Bronson left a generic message. "Hope you're well and having fun." Bronson disconnected and called Mike.

As he waited for the connection, he took the Makarov and emptied it, putting the rounds in his pocket.

"You sure got there fast," Mike said. "I'm—"

"Turn back. The blond-headed man who's been following us is with Ellen."

"What—"

"The Raven promised me neither you nor Ellen would be harmed as long as I go with her. I'm on my way to meet her now."

"The Raven? Who…what… Talk to me. What's going on?"

Bronson opened the glove compartment, tore a page from his spiral pocket notebook, wrote down *Blond twins?* and stuffed the paper in the glove compartment. "The Raven knew about the Makarov. She made me leave it behind. Call Devono and tell him I'm sorry, I won't be returnin' his pistol. I'm headin' for the Camry now. I'm leaving our car parked on Vulcan Avenue. Also, there's no use callin' Ellen. Our blond guy lifted her cell. Be happy with Ellen."

Bronson disconnected and rummaged through the glove compartment. He found Ellen's fingernail file, but nothing else that might be useful. He put the file in his pocket. His cell played the tune he had assigned to Mike. He let it go to voicemail.

He scooted down and reached under the driver's seat, his fingers searching for the Astra. Chances were the Raven would frisk him, and he'd lose this gun too, but at least carrying made him feel better, somewhat safer. He tucked the pistol between the small of his back and his jeans. He patted his boot to reassure himself that the knife was still there.

Bronson reached for the door handle and took his time getting out of the car. He put on his sunglasses and glanced around, looking for anything out of place. A man, half-hidden by a store's columns, could be the blond. Bronson headed in a northerly direction for approximately ten feet. He took off his sunglasses and used the mirror side to look behind him.

A man walked toward Bronson's car, probably to retrieve the weapon. Bronson slowed his pace, put his sunglasses back on, took out the cell, and dialed Joe Randig's number.

The voice message informed him that Detective Randig was currently unavailable, but feel free to leave a detailed message and a phone number. "This is Bronson. I'm being kidnapped by a woman, code name the Raven. She works with at least one blond-headed man, possibly two. My partner's name is Mike Hoover. He knows about the blond and about the car." Bronson gave the detective Mike's cell number. "I see a woman standing by the Camry where we're supposed to meet. She's got black hair down to her waist. Around five-seven, knock-out looks, late twenties or early thirties, about one hundred and twenty pounds. I'm almost there so I need to disconnect. I'll keep the cell on as long as I have service. You can track me through the phone." He disconnected and put the mobile in his pants pocket.

He walked at a steady pace the rest of the block. He stopped when he reached the Camry. The woman stepped in front of him.

"I assume you're the Raven."

Her eyes scrutinized him, from top to bottom. "Take your sunglasses off. I like to see a man's eyes when I speak to him."

Using slow, deliberate movements, Bronson removed his glasses, folded them, and placed them in his shirt pocket.

She raised her hand, revealing the cell. "I report in every fifteen to thirty minutes. I do that, all's well. If I fail to call, my friends have instructions to kill Ellen and Hoover."

"Understood."

"Good. In that case, you'll behave and won't give me any problems."

"I'll be on my best behavior."

The Raven looked at Bronson's shoes. "Are those boots?"

"They are. I'm from Texas."

"Soon as you get in the car, take them off, and I don't care where you're from."

"Yes, Ma'am."

"Get on the backseat, facing down, hands behind your back."

Bronson took a step toward the Camry.

"I'm not a fool, Bronson. Everyone will be looking for you in this car. We're ditching it." She indicated the four-door, silver Ford truck parked in front of the Camry. "That's our new ride."

Shiiit.

FIFTY-SIX

TEN MINUTES.

Mike had been searching the mall for ten frickin minutes and so far, no trace of Ellen. With each passing second, his heartbeat accelerated. Bronson had been assured Ellen wouldn't be hurt, but could he be sure?

He tried her mobile three times, only to have the answering machine direct him to voice mail. Bronson had told him it would, but still, he had to try.

Logically, it would be nearly impossible to find anyone in the mall. The three-story, one block long mall offered dozens of stores Ellen could get lost in.

Mike headed toward the security booth. "I'd like to talk to the head of security."

The youth inside the booth couldn't possibly be more than twenty years old, if that. "He's not here." He popped his gum.

"Then page him."

"Uh." He looked around as though searching for someone to tell him what to do.

Mike pounded the counter with his opened hand. "Now."

The youth jumped and let out a little grunt. "Sure. Sure."

While waiting for the head security man to show, Mike focused on the security screens that highlighted various parts of the mall. The image blinked every thirty seconds, exposing a different part of the mall. Mike hoped to spot Ellen in one of those.

"May I help you, sir?"

Mike pivoted to face a gray haired man. "You're head of security?"

He nodded.

"My name is Mike Hoover." He retrieved his badge and showed it to him. "I'm a detective for the Dallas Police Department."

"You're a little out of your jurisdiction."

"I am, but I'm working with the Pittsburgh Police to solve a crime mutual to both of our cities." Not quite true, but Mike didn't mind stretching the truth in this case. "We believe that one of your shoppers may be in danger. We received a lead that the killer is also here in the mall."

The security guard's eyes widened and his bushy eyebrows bobbed several times.

Better calm him before he panicked, if he hadn't already. "He's not stupid enough to draw attention to himself, but we do need the woman paged."

The guard's jaw moved up and down as though he were a cow chewing. "Her name?"

"Ellen Biebesheimer." For once, Mike was glad she had reverted to her maiden name after their divorce.

The head of security led Mike back to the main control room located near the other mall's offices, behind the storefronts. He handed Mike the microphone. "You page her." He flipped the switch and nodded, indicating he was live.

"Attention, shoppers." He paused long enough to allow shoppers to listen. "Will Ellen Biebesheimer please report to the security booth on the second floor? Repeating: Ellen Biebesheimer, report to the security booth on the second floor." Mike handed the head of security the microphone and hoped Ellen had heard him.

His insides grumbled with apprehension. "Thank you." He dashed out, heading for the booth.

Ellen, be there. Please, be there.

The head of security followed him out, keeping pace with him. "This…this killer…"

"Is only interested in Ellen. He won't do anything foolish." Or at least Mike hoped not. They took the escalator heading back to the booth. They reached the top.

Mike maneuvered his way around the unconcerned shoppers, the guard close to him. One more turn and Mike would be able to see the booth.

Be there.

Somewhere from behind him, he heard his name. "Mike."

He turned and saw Ellen rushing toward him. Mike let out the air he'd been holding. He breathed through his mouth, forcing his nerves to calm.

"What's wrong?" Ellen looked behind Mike, to his left, to his right. "Is Bronson okay?"

"I…don't know. I'm not sure." He wrapped his arm around her and led her toward the exit. "I'll explain everything. Let's get you home."

Behind them, the head of security stared at them, then at the people around them.

FIFTY-SEVEN

BRONSON DID AS TOLD.

He removed his boots and placed them on the floor in a way that the boot pocket remained hidden. He lay down in the truck's backseat, his hands behind his back. The Raven climbed into the driver's side and the blond who had been stalking Bronson hopped up into the front passenger seat. Both closed the truck doors. She turned to face Bronson, pulled the gun, and pointed it at him. "You try anything cute, and you're dead. And so are your friends."

"Best behavior, remember?" Bronson's mind popped with possibilities, but as soon as each came, he discarded each idea. He wouldn't take a chance on the Raven and her soldiers hurting Mike and Ellen.

The blond leaned over and handcuffed his hands. He grabbed the cloth bag from the passenger seat and attempted to put in on Bronson's head.

He thrust his head back. "Tell your goon he doesn't have to do that. The way he handcuffed me, I won't be going anywhere."

"And the bag on your head won't allow you to see where we're going. Now shut up." Using her free hand, she showed him the cell. "Do you really want for me to miss making that call?"

Bronson closed his eyes and allowed her to put the bag over his head.

After making sure the bag was loose enough to allow him to breath, but tight enough so it wouldn't come off,

Bronson felt the blond grab his ankles and place leg irons on them.

The front passenger door opened. "I'm out of here. Enjoy your time with Bronson."

"Oh, I plan to."

Something about her tone sent a chill running down Bronson's spine.

The front passenger door closed and the Raven said, "We're ready to rock 'n roll."

Maybe she was, but Bronson sure wasn't. The truck hadn't even moved and already Bronson felt as comfortable as a man lying on a bed of ants. He hoped the ride was smooth and short.

It wasn't. The first part of the trip began with a few stops here and there. Bronson attributed those stops to stop signs and traffic lights. To make the time pass and to forget about how uncomfortable he felt, he counted the number of stops the truck made even though he figured that would be of little help since he had no idea which direction they headed.

Approximately ten minutes later, the Raven made no more stops. Apparently, they had entered the freeway, as she drove at a steady rate. Bronson strained to listen. He heard tire noises as they sped up, a horn honking, the squeaking of brakes, and someone's loud radio.

Bronson heard her talking, more than likely, on the cell. He tilted his head, hoping for better reception, wishing he could get the damn bag off his head.

"I got Bronson in the truck," she said. "Everything is going according to plan. Keep an eye on Hoover and his main squeeze. If they become a threat, kill them. I'll check in after I make that last turn."

Bronson hoped that wouldn't be too long. His muscles screamed for relief.

ELLEN SAT QUIETLY listening to Mike's explanation of the day's events. Several times she closed her eyes as though attempting to keep tears from gushing out.

Mike stroked her upper arm. "Are you okay?"

Ellen sat without moving, staring at the scenery through tears that blurred everything. Mike drove like a maniac in his hurry to get her home. She sighed.

"Hon?" His voice rang with concern.

"I'm the last person you need to worry about. Bronson needs you. Go to him." She flashed him a weak smile.

"You're sure?"

"Of course I'm sure. This is Bronson we're talking about."

"I love you." Mike turned into her driveway and let the engine idle.

"Don't bother getting out." Ellen opened the car door but then stopped and turned to Mike. "Do what you need to do, just please come back safely to me and bring Bronson back." Ellen leaned over and kissed Mike. "Go, now."

FIFTY-EIGHT

Tires squealed when the Raven made a sharp left turn. From there, the smooth ride disappeared. Gravel crunched under the tires, leading Bronson to believe they had turned onto a dirt road.

As promised, the Raven made the call after she had straightened the truck. Once again, Bronson strained to listen but at best, he could only catch a phrase or word. The bouncing truck made it hard for Bronson to focus.

"...just made my turn...off range...depends. If he's... three days at the most...kill...Ellen, then Hoover...calling again."

Agonizing silence filled the air. An occasional groan escaped out of Bronson each time the truck bounced over a rougher section of the road. The Astra jabbed his back each time the tires found a pothole.

After what seemed to be several hours but in reality was only a bit over an hour, the truck came to a stop. So did Bronson's heart. He heard the Raven open the front truck door then slam it shut. He waited a second.

Two seconds.

Three.

His heart beat wildly and he started breathing through his mouth.

Four.

Five.

The front passenger door opened.

Bronson lay still, listening.

The Raven unfastened the leg irons. Bronson stretched his legs.

"I'm going to take the bag off your head. Then we'll head to the cabin. Before I do, need I remind you that I'm supposed to make a call to my friend?"

"I remember." Bronson's lips felt dry, and he wet them. He waited for her to remove the bag. He thought he heard her walk away. He waited some more. Nothing.

He yanked his hands, hoping to release the cuffs. Nothing happened, but he had known that all along. He wished he could remove the bag from his head. But even if he could, he wouldn't tempt fate.

She had to make that call.

The fact that she had plenty of opportunities to kill him, but hadn't done so, bothered him. That meant she was keeping him alive for some purpose, a complicated ritual they both needed to follow. She had killed before, and she would do it again.

KNOWING BRONSON, MIKE expected his ex-partner would leave a trail of hints for him to follow. Mike had picked up on the one about leaving the car parked on Vulcan Avenue. He'd begin there. Someone must have seen something, heard something, or knew something.

Cannady had followed up on the Camry. She knew who owned the car. He would call her. As he reached for his cell, it rang. He didn't recognize the number. "Hello?"

"Is this Mike Hoover?"

"Who is this?"

"Detective Joe Randig from the Pittsburgh Police Department. Bronson called and left me a message. He said he's been kidnapped? He gave me your contact information. What can you tell me?"

"Some woman known as the Raven told Bronson she had

two shooters. One aimed at me, the other one at my ex-wife. To prove it, the Raven sent a picture of my ex to Bronson. Next to her was the blond headed man we've been following. To keep us safe, Bronson willingly left with the Raven."

"Is your ex-wife okay?"

"God, I hope so." He massaged his forehead. "I drove her home."

"I'll send a patrol unit to make sure she's all right. What's the address?"

"I appreciate that." Mike gave him the address. "There's something else that needs to be done."

"What's that?"

"Bronson's cell is equipped with a GPS. Do you have his cell number?"

"My caller I.D. does. Besides, Cannady gave it to me. I'll get someone to start tracking him. Can you hang on?"

"Sure." Mike waited a few seconds then heard Joe pick up the phone.

"Where are you?" Joe asked.

"Bronson and I were setting a trap for a Camry that had been following us. We were going to meet at the corner of Hercules and Diana. Before we could do that, Bronson got the picture text. He said he was leaving the rental parked somewhere on Vulcan Avenue and would head toward the Camry where the Raven told him to meet her."

Joe remained quiet for a few seconds. "Looked it up. Vulcan is a very long street. Any chance of you narrowing it down a bit more? Do you have a name of a cross street?"

"Bronson said he was about a ten minute drive from the corner of Diana and Hercules. That gives us a narrower range to focus on."

"I'm on my way," Joe said. "In the meantime, fill me in and focus on all the details."

FIFTY-NINE

FRESH AIR NEVER felt so good. Bronson swallowed large gulps of it.

"Really, Bronson, was it that bad?" The Raven still held the canvas bag she had just removed from his head. "You're to put your boots back on and head toward the house." She raised her hand, revealing a Glock. She pointed it at Bronson's head. "Just a friendly reminder. I'm supposed to report within the next five minutes. If I don't, the twins know what to do, and you definitely don't want that kind of death for Hoover and Ellen. Besides, if I get even the smallest of a whiff that you're considering doing anything stupid, I'll shoot. I won't hesitate."

Bronson believed her.

The Raven locked her eyes on him and stepped away, a safe distance from his reach.

Bronson wiggled his way to a sitting position and assessed his situation. He could feel the Astra rubbing against the small of his back. Why hadn't she frisked him?

He put his boots on but without the use of his hands, he couldn't lace them. As he slid his foot in, he felt for the hidden compartment. The Raven hadn't found the knife. He scooted out of the truck, making sure he kept his balance.

The single room cabin nestled into a shadowy stretch of the woods. Creature sounds surrounded Bronson, but somehow they seemed more guttural. Unreal. Menacing. The vast woodlands seemed to swallow him whole.

"Get moving." The Raven jerked the gun, letting Bronson know he better do as he was told.

Bronson headed toward the cabin. As he neared the door, he noticed a baseball bat and ball resting against the wall close to the entryway. The bat might be a possible weapon, if he could convince the Raven to uncuff him. Not that he thought she would.

He stepped in, his gaze searching, his mind memorizing every detail. Off to his right a single bed and a dresser represented an entire bedroom. Nothing there. An opened doorway revealed a compact bathroom. A dining table, large enough to accommodate four comfortably, sat directly in front of him. Behind that— A flashing pain exploded in his head. Bronson attempted to focus, but everything around him whirled at great speed. He felt his knees buckle and saw the floor rushing up at his face. He collapsed like a rag doll.

His world turned gray, then solid black.

MIKE AND JOE located not only Bronson's Cruze, but the Camry as well. Joe radioed dispatch to get the cars towed to headquarters and processed for fingerprints and other evidence.

Wearing the latex gloves Joe had provided, Mike felt under the Cruze's seats for anything Bronson might have left behind. He found the bug. He tried to remember if they had said anything important. He couldn't think of anything, but at that point, all that they discussed was important.

He opened the glove compartment, found the note, and read it.

Twins. It made sense. One to be with Ellen, the other, to follow them.

Joe's cell went off and Mike looked up. He saw Joe talk

briefly on the phone and disconnect. From the look on his face, Mike knew the call had brought bad news.

Joe headed toward Mike. "We can't pick up Bronson's signal. He must have turned his phone off."

"Bronson wouldn't do that. He knows better. He must be in a dead zone. Anyway we can locate those?"

"Oh sure. In our tiny city of Pittsburgh, there are only a million dead zones. Add another million if you include drivable distances outside the city limits. How would you suggest we tackle this task?" Joe flashed him a wide-eyed look.

Mike semi-smiled. Tacky, but cute. "We'll have better luck canvassing the neighborhood. Someone had to have seen something or heard something." Mike indicated the buildings to his right. "I'll start with these."

"Good idea." Joe nodded. "I'll do those on the left, but first, I'm calling Cannady. She might be able to shed some light onto this."

Mike handed Joe Bronson's note. Joe read it. "So we're dealing with twins. That may work to our benefit. Twins often attract attention. Let's hope someone saw the twins."

SIXTY

BRONSON OPENED HIS eyes and wished he hadn't. The pounding inside his head crashed like waves against a sea wall. His hands, now free from the cuffs, fumbled toward his head. Maybe if he helped support it, the dizziness would evaporate.

The Raven stood, looking down at Bronson. "You're finally awake. I was getting worried. Thought maybe that the baseball bat did real damage."

So that's what happened. He tried to sit up, but the spinning sensation forced him to stay on the floor.

"I have extra strength aspirin. Here's the pills. The bottle is unopened so you won't think I'm trying to poison you." She set a glass of water and the bottle of aspirins on the floor next to Bronson. She stepped away.

Bronson looked at them. He could see two, three glasses and bottles. He closed his eyes and tightened them, hoping to clear his vision. The pain volleyed in his head. He had to get his faculties back. He reached for the aspirins. His fingers felt like lead pegs. He gave up trying to open it.

The Raven smiled and removed the protective wrap, unscrewed the lid, and took two pills out. "You're going to spoil my plan if you don't clear your head. I need you wide awake and alert." She handed him the aspirins and the water.

Some of the water dribbled out on his chin and onto his shirt as Bronson gagged and swallowed the pills. He too wanted to be wide awake and alert. His life depended on it. A silver bolt of pain attacked his head, forcing Bronson to throw his head back and grind his teeth.

Still, the pain persisted. He gave in to it. He closed his eyes.

"YEAH, I SAW someone suspicious," the comic book store owner said. "This blond headed dude right out there." He pointed to the outside of the store. "Used the store's columns as though he were hiding. Creeped me out. I was about to call the pigs—oops, excuse me—the police, when the dude in that Chevy—" He indicated the Cruze Bronson had rented. "—steps out. He heads that way." He tilted his head to his right, showing Mike the direction Bronson had headed. "Soon as the guy walks away from the car, the blond dude is all over it. Seems he picked up something from the car. Not sure what. He makes a call then heads the same direction as that dude." He shrugged. "I lost interest. Besides, a customer came in. Bought two hundred dollars worth of comic books. That made me real happy."

"If you saw the blond man again, would you be able to recognize him?"

"Yeah, sure. He was creeping me out. I remember him."

"I'll have Detective Randig come talk to you. He might want you to go to headquarters and do a sketch or maybe even go through some pictures for possible identification."

"Really, man?" He combed his thinning hair with his fingers. "I got a store to run, you know."

"We appreciate your co-operation."

"Don't mind co-operating as long as it doesn't mess up my business, you know?"

Mike nodded and walked out. He looked for Joe and found him talking to a man across the street. While he waited for him to finish, he'd call Devono.

SIXTY-ONE

THROUGH PAIN-BLURRED EYES, Bronson could make out a shape of someone fluttering back and forth through the tiny kitchen area like a bird trapped indoors, her movements deliberate and precise. Who was she? He closed his eyes, remembering.

The Raven had whacked him on the head. He had passed out twice, if he recalled correctly. He snapped his eyes open as the memories rushed in.

"It's supper time." The Raven approached, but stood several feet away from him. "You wasted most of the day sleeping."

Bronson still lay on the floor where he had fallen. He moaned as he sat up. His head still bounced with pain, but at least now if he didn't move too fast, he could function. "You got any more aspirin?"

"Sure do." She headed back toward the sink, filled a glass with water, and grabbed the bottle of aspirin.

Bronson looked at his feet. While he'd been out, the Raven had removed his boots and placed the leg irons back on. A heavy chain no more than eight inches long connected the two. It would be difficult to walk. Worse, another thick chain connected the leg irons to a ring bolt on the wall. He could only go maybe fifteen or twenty feet.

The Raven set down the water and aspirins on the floor within his reach.

Bronson grasped the opportunity to look past the aspirin bottle and toward his boots. She had obviously jerked them off his feet and discarded them. If luck was his companion, the knife would still be there. He had no way of knowing. He opened the aspirin bottle and swallowed two pills.

"I saw you admiring your new ankle bracelets. I'm sure they're not very comfortable, but they're ideal for me. You won't be going anywhere in a hurry."

"Not that I planned to."

"Are you saying you want to be the perfect guest?"

"Of course."

"The ideal guest would never bring an Astra to the dinner table. So I took the liberty of relieving you of your gun. You are a naughty boy."

"Can't blame a person for tryin'."

The Raven smiled. "You're going to be a formidable opponent. I'm looking forward to our game."

"And what game is that?"

"I made us supper. Can you stand? I'll explain the game as we eat."

Getting up posed no problem, other than his head still feeling like a lead ball. Walking, on the other hand, proved to be a major dilemma. The heavy chain clanked with each step he took. He was as quiet as a two-year-old turned loose in a room filled with drums.

It took him twenty baby steps—he counted them—to reach the table. Under normal circumstances, he would have made it in five. He sat down and stared at his plate. The chicken was appetizing, but he never really cared for them. He ate them only because Carol insisted.

Carol.

He felt a hallow space in his chest.

The Raven opened the oven and took out some freshly made dinner rolls. She placed them on the table. "If you want yours buttered, let me know, and I'll do it for you. I don't quite trust you with knives."

Bronson thought of his boots. There had to be some kind of irony there. "Plain is fine. Less fattenin'. You get to live longer."

"Only if you survive." The Raven opened the refrigerator. "I have lemonade, tea, or Coke. Which would you prefer?"

What? No coffee? What kind of a last supper was this? "What kind of tea?"

"Peach."

"I'll take that."

She poured them each a glass and set Bronson's in front of him. She sat down at the opposite end of the table. "Ground rules of our game."

Bronson nodded. Ate some chicken. Delicious.

"Tomorrow morning, I open the door, and you walk out."

Bronson tore his dinner roll in half and took a bite. Nothing like fresh-baked bread. "And the catch is?"

"An hour later, I walk out. I'll have my guns and my tracking gear. When I find you, I will shoot you in the gut. That won't kill you, but if you're real lucky, a black bear or a pack of wild dogs will finish you off. I will sit with you until close to nightfall. This way, I can watch you squirm with pain. Right before leaving you for the night, I'll set up a video camera so I can continue to watch you. I'd stay, except that I don't want to spook the bears or wolves away. Oh, and one more thing, before we part for the night, I will shoot you two more times. Once in each knee. At the very most, you might be able to drag yourself, but I doubt it. None of the others before you have been able to. But then again, you are a worthy opponent—something none of them were." She took a large piece of chicken and ripped it with her teeth. She wet her lips and outlined them with the tip of her index finger. She smiled at him in a way that under normal circumstances would have made a man salivate.

Bronson continued to eat as though unaffected by her revelations. "What if I manage to drag myself?"

"That means you'll be a few feet away from where I left you. You won't be able to get away. That's for sure. I'll be back in the morning. I'll bring my bat with me and use you as a ball. I am very handy with it, don't you think?"

Bronson's head still pounded with explosive bolts of pain. "Adequate, I'd say."

She threw her head back and laughed. "You have no idea how much I'm looking forward to tomorrow."

"I have a question, if I may."

The Raven set down her fork. "Ask away."

"You're callin' your friends on a regular basis, and that's keepin' Mike and Ellen safe."

"You are correct."

"Tomorrow, when you release me, what happens when the hunter becomes the hunted and you can no longer call?"

The Raven resumed eating, a tiny smile plastered on her face. "Prior to my leaving the cabin to resume my role as the hunter, I will call them for the last time. At that point, they'll release Mike and Ellen." The Raven served herself more vegetables. "I noticed you're not eating your vegetables."

"Don't like them. You say this is my last supper. I want to carry good memories of it."

"That's the right attitude. For the record, this is your last supper. No one has ever survived. No one ever will. I'm that good. You're a dead man." She raised her tea glass as if toasting. "Here's to your very slow, painful death."

"If you don't mind, I won't be toasting to that." Bronson ate his chicken and wished for a cup of coffee.

SIXTY-TWO

"You said you used to be Bronson's partner before he retired," Devono said.

"I did." Mike stood on the sidewalk in front of the comic book store, wondering who else might have seen something.

"Good for you, but why call me? I have nothing to do with Bronson."

Devono's voice came through so loud that Mike had to pull the cell away from his ear. "I was there that night you invited him to your office at the restaurant."

"I don't deny knowing him. We had a nice long conversation that night. But that's the end of our relationship."

Mike stood behind the same column the blond man had used to hide behind. He had spied on Bronson, and now Mike turned the tables to watch the police work on Bronson's rental. In order to do so, he had to step away from the column, an inch or two. Enough to be seen. Bronson had to have seen him. "Mr. Devono, I'm calling you not as a policeman but as Bronson's friend. I'm worried about him."

"He's a big boy. He can—"

"He's been kidnapped." Silence met Mike. He wondered if Devono had hung up. He looked at his cell. The connection was still active. "Bronson left a couple of hints. One involved you."

"Explain."

"He told me to tell you that his kidnapper had forced him to leave the gun behind, and he was sorry but he wouldn't be able to return it to you."

"Why would he say that?"

"My question precisely." Mike watched the police haul Bronson's rental away. "I'm not looking to get you into trouble or anything like that. I'm doing this on my own, and all I want is information that may be able to save Bronson's life."

A small pause followed. Then, "Did he say gun?"

"He did."

"I lent him two."

Oh, Bronson. What were you thinking? That meant he was possibly armed, but any person in her right mind would frisk him. He'd lose the gun in a matter of seconds. Bronson would have known that. There had to be another reason Bronson wanted him to talk to Devono. *Think.* "Could you possibly know the kidnappers?"

"Mr. Hoover, if you're insinuating that I had anything to do with the kidnapping, think again." Devono's harsh tone came through loud and clear.

"No, that's not what I meant at all. I'm simply suggesting you might know of the kidnappers. Here's what I know. There are three of them. A set of twins, blond, males, in their late twenties, early thirties. Their ring leader is a woman whose code name is the Raven."

"The...Raven?"

"Yes."

"I'm afraid I can't help you much. I've heard of the Raven, but I don't have any connections with her. I know she's pure evil and sadistic. And yes, she works on-and-off with the twins. She does them both, sometimes separately, sometimes simultaneously. They're fiercely loyal to her. That makes them very dangerous."

"Do you have any idea where I can find them?"

"Unfortunately, no. But I do have extensive files. Let me check my folders and see what I can find."

Mike knew no such folders existed. What Devono meant

was that he would get his men digging up the information. Bronson must have somehow known that. "I appreciate your help."

"Don't thank me. I haven't given you anything, and I can't guarantee that I will."

"I understand."

"Is this the number where I can reach you, the one you're calling from?"

"Yes."

"I'll get back to you. I have a vested interest in Bronson. I don't want anything to happen to him. Knowing the little that I know of the Raven, if I were you, I'd find him now. You may already be too late."

SIXTY-THREE

"THE BULLET IN your gut will explode inside you, burning you from the inside out." The Raven droned on in great detail about how horrible Bronson's death would be.

He still sat at the table eating, his appetite lessening with each bite. He had long ago tuned her out, choosing to hear only a word here, a phrase there.

"Your agony…beg for mercy…want to die…pain…horrible, agonizing pain…" She used each carefully selected word to eat away at Bronson's will, just like she had probably done with the others. Raw nerves had driven them crazy. By the time she freed them, insanity dictated their actions. They had been easy prey.

She expected Bronson to be no different, but he would have a surprise for her. *Ignore her. Focus on something else.* Bronson thought of Carol. Little Carol. Donna. The grandkids. Lorraine's beguiling smile the last time he saw her.

Don't leave me.

Tears pearled in Bronson's eyes, and he blinked them away as quickly as possible.

The Raven leaned back in her seat. The smile she wore spoke of triumph. She wiped her mouth, and set the napkin down. "I got a new drug. I forget what it's called, but it's very effective, and it cost me a bundle."

Bronson decided to listen. His gaze met hers.

"I chose you to be my first experiment."

Lucky him.

She picked up the knife she had used to carve the chicken. She stroked the blade like a lover seducing her mate. "You see, I've never cut anyone, but always wondered what it would feel like." She ran her tongue around her lips.

Sadistic bitch. Bronson swallowed hard, causing his Adam's apple to bob. He made sure she saw that. He raised his head just a bit and repeated the action.

"Uuuhh." She sang the letters. Seductively. She bit her lip.

Bronson looked away. He should have been an actor.

"Even after I've shot you and you're writhing with pain, you wouldn't be able to lie still while I carve you out. No one would." She leaned forward, elbows on the table, an intent look in her eyes. "So I'll shoot you with my dart gun. In seconds, the poison will work through your system. You won't be able to move, but you will feel everything." She wrinkled her nose. "Every...thing."

Bronson considered taking her down. The chains around his ankles limited his moves. But if he could get her to come close to him, he could overpower her.

Surely by now Mike had gotten control of the situation. Both he and Ellen were safe and would be safe even if the Raven didn't make that call. Should Bronson chance it? "You're a beautiful woman, and every inch of you is seductive."

Her eyebrows shot up her forehead. "You are a live one. I'll give you a treat. Each time I cut you tomorrow, I'll remove one article of clothing. I'll do that until I'm naked." She stretched out the word *naked.* "Then I'll straddle you."

Bronson pushed his plate away. "Do that now." He forced his voice to come out low, throaty.

She stood up. Walked to the corner of the table and stopped. "And miss the chase tomorrow?"

"Now, and then. Twice the fun."

She took two steps forward. Stopped. "I have a call to make."

"Make it now." *Please make it now.* "Make it later. It's your call."

Two more steps forward.

Bronson eyed her from top to bottom. He stared extra long at her breasts.

She took one more step forward. "Your ring finger shows you're married."

"Out of sight. Out of mind."

She smiled and took one more step forward. She had reached the halfway point. "Oh, you're naughty." She shook her finger at him as though scolding him. "Naughty, naughty, naughty."

"Very."

She took another step. Paused. Then another step. She stopped. She smiled. "More power to you, Bronson. I knew from the beginning you'd make a perfect opponent, and you just proved me right. You almost had me going. Almost, but not quite." She flipped him a finger and returned to the head of the table.

Shiiit.

SIXTY-FOUR

JOE'S HAND LINGERED on the phone, his fingers drumming the receiver. He had just finished talking to Cannady. He frowned. He picked up the phone once again and punched in the appropriate numbers. "Mike Hoover?" he asked once he had made the connection. "Detective Joe Randig here. I just got off the phone with Cannady."

"What did she have to say?" Mike hoped she had co-operated.

"Unfortunately, nothing we can use. A Frederick Parsons rented the Camry. The computer showed no criminal record for him, but strangely enough, Frederick Parsons had cancer and died at age thirty-two."

Damn. "A case of stolen identity." And a dead end.

"I'm afraid so. Then, to top it all off, those sons of bitches must have worn gloves every time they used the car. We lifted not even one useful print."

Dead ends. Why did it always have to be a dead end? "If we can find the twins, we can find the Raven."

"My thoughts, too," Joe said. "Based on what we know, we place the twins to be somewhere in their mid-twenties to mid-thirties. We've got our computer experts to gener-ate a list of twins in the area. First, we're checking crimi-nal records, then birth records in the area."

"That must be one heck of a list."

"We're doing everything possible to narrow it down. We've keyed in males only. Blond, both still living in the area, but as you say, the list is astronomical. We're hoping we find something that will help us." Joe paused. "We're not giving up. We're on top of this. We've put the word out on the street. Anyone knows about the twins or the Raven, they'll get in touch with us."

"Is there something I can do?"

"Yeah, I could use help with those lists."

"You're at the station?"

"Sure am."

"Give me about forty-five minutes to get there."

"I'll be here," Joe said.

Mike hung up and looked out the window. He didn't see any unaccounted for cars or suspicious persons lurking around. Still, he didn't want to leave Ellen alone.

She wrapped her arms around his waist and leaned her head on his back. "I'm a big girl. I can take care of myself. You need to be out there, looking for Bronson. He's counting on you. You're the only hope he has."

He turned around and held her. "You're forgetting Detective Joe Randig. He's doing everything he can. I'm impressed with him." He kissed the top of her head.

"Then go help him."

"You can come. You know your way around the police station. Maybe later on we can grab something to eat."

"Or maybe you can go by yourself." She broke the embrace and walked out of it. "I've been at the station hundreds of times. Why would I want to go there on my days off?" She pushed him away. "Now go."

BRONSON LAY ON the make-shift bed pretending to sleep, wishing he could remove those ankle bracelets. Due to them, he hadn't been able to move, and his body felt stiff. He hadn't slept much. He took advantage of the situation and forced his mind to spit out one scenario after another.

Problem with each one centered on his lack of wood

survival skills but somehow, today, he would have to accomplish what others before him failed to do.

Think.

Think, think.

"Quit faking." The Raven stood at the foot of the bed. "It's time to begin our game." She reached for Bronson's ankle bracelets.

SIXTY-FIVE

MIKE BLINKED SEVERAL TIMES, pushing the sleep away from his eyes. He sipped his coffee while waiting for the light to turn green. He had stayed at the police station until past midnight, first calling sets of twins, and then when it got too late, checking the list. To those he managed to get hold of, he had told them about a "priceless piece of artwork" he owned, and that he wanted their advice. Out of the nearly one hundred calls he made, only eight seemed promising.

The light was about to change when he noticed a blue sedan speed in order to beat the light. The signal turned when the sedan was halfway through the intersection. Drivers like that were menaces. If Mike had the time, he would follow and pursue. Instead, he accelerated and blended with the rest of the traffic, eager to reach the police station and continue making the calls.

Out of yesterday's eight calls that warranted a follow-up, Joe eliminated five after he paid them a visit. That left three possibilities. For two of those two sets, neither twin was home. One set remained a loose wire that had led to a bogus address.

Today Mike and Joe would follow up on all three leads, focusing their main energy on the missing link. But first, Mike would spend some more time on the phone talking to more twins, adding to the list of possibilities.

In the meantime, Joe would attend his mandatory daily meeting. Soon as that was over, they planned to trace the twins with the missing address.

In an attempt to drive sleep's embrace away, Mike rolled down the car window. Mother Nature seemed to be promising to release a storm, and he inhaled the scent of the impending rain. He always enjoyed a nice, steady rain, but not if it meant slowing him down in his search for Bronson.

A bolt of lightning sizzled in the sky just as he turned into the police parking lot. His mobile went off at the same time. At first, Mike failed to answer the call, thinking it somehow related to the soon-to-be-here rain.

He shook his head as he grabbed the cell, upset at himself for reaching such an illogical conclusion. That meant he felt more tired than he was willing to admit. The caller I.D. read Unknown, but Mike recognized the number as belonging to Devono. His heartbeat accelerated as he answered the call.

"I may have something for you." Devono's tone revealed his pride in his sense of accomplishment.

"I'm listening."

"As I told you, I asked my, uh, steady customers at the restaurant to dig up anything they could find on the Raven and the twins."

Mike locked the car and headed toward the police building. At that moment, the heavily laden clouds released their burden. The steady downpour drenched Mike as he ran inside the police headquarters. Once indoors, he wiped the water away and felt guilty when he saw the mess. Mike no longer felt guilty. "What did your contacts tell you?"

"Don't know the exact location, but the Raven got herself a small cabin in the woods. Word is that she takes her guests there to play a cat-and-mouse type of game. Her guests are never seen after that. The cabin, built about ten years ago, is somewhere off Highway 422, close to Lake Arthur. The woman you know as the Raven is really Barbara Culverson."

Mike's eyes widened as he pumped the air with his arm. Yes! "Now that we have her name, finding her cabin will pose no problem. Thank you for the information."

"No thanks are required. I have a vested interest in Bronson. I don't want anything to happen to him until I can collect."

You bastard. Mike shrugged. At least he came through. "Either way, thanks anyway."

"Bring him safe to me."

Yeah, like he was really going to hand Bronson to him. "I'll find him." Mike hung up.

His walk had a bounce as he approached Joe's desk. Joe set down his pen and looked up at Mike. "Something's got you going." Joe stood up to greet him. "What's up?"

Mike told him about the cabin.

"And your source?"

"Someone in the streets."

"Reliable?"

Mike nodded. "I believe so."

"In that case, let's download the county map, get the address, and head that way."

"I was hoping you'd say that." *Bronson, we're on our way to you. Just hang on, buddy.*

Just hang on.

SIXTY-SIX

"I TALKED TO my friends." The Raven stood at the foot of Bronson's bed, the key to unlock his chains in her hand. "The twins told Hoover and his lady they would be released today just as soon as you're set free. Hoover didn't believe them. She did, but it doesn't matter what they think. They will be released, provided I make that final call."

Bronson's eyebrows wrinkled. "Why wouldn't you make the call?"

"Maybe you're planning to do something stupid."

Bronson tilted his head and blinked several times. "I wouldn't think of it."

"That's the opposite of what I'm thinking. The little I know of you tells me you've considered jumping me several times and will do so as soon as your hand and leg restrictions come off."

She was right, but Bronson would never admit it, not as long as she dangled the phone call above him like a piece of meat being offered to a starving dog. "I want you to make that call. I won't try anything."

"After you have walked out the door and before I go hunting for you, I'll make the call. From there on, it'll only be you and me." She picked up the Astra, and pointed it at Bronson. "I was thinking what a hoot it'd be to shoot you with your own pistol, but first I'll have to find you." She walked toward Bronson and tossed him the key to the leg irons.

Bronson grabbed it in mid-air.

"You know what to do." The Raven stood as far away as possible from Bronson's reach.

Bronson sat up in the bed without moving, wondering if this was some type of a trap.

"My, my. I see you don't trust me." The Raven smiled and stepped further back.

"Unfasten the ankle bracelets and stand up."

He did as told.

"Good, now take off your shirt."

Bronson hesitated.

"Do it."

He removed his shirt.

"Now drop the pants."

Bronson glared at her, unfastened his pants and stepped out of them.

"I like what I see. Now get rid of the shorts."

Bronson glued his eyes on her as he removed them.

"You hang well."

Bronson kept his arms by his side, making no effort to hide himself. He'd be damned if he let her intimidate him.

"Just for your information, all the others kept their clothes on. You're special."

Lucky him. "You're thinking you're not going to win this game, and you're right."

The Raven's eyes narrowed, sending invisible darts at Bronson. "What does that mean?"

"You said I'm the only one you've sent out naked. That means you don't trust yourself to win under normal circumstances. So you strip me down."

The Raven kicked a chair, sending it flying toward the dining table. The dishes rattled but didn't fall. "I don't need any advantages." Her deep voice came out dry and strained. "I'll prove you wrong. I'm a hell of a lot better than you.

Get dressed and get out of here. Your time starts now." She turned over the egg timer, and the sand began to trickle out.

JOE AND MIKE studied the rural map spread before them. They had found four cabins in the area, all owned by women, but none by Barbara Culverson. Best they could hope for was that Barbara Culverson bought it under an assumed name.

Joe focused on the map and circled an area with a red pen he had picked up from his desk. "Best I can figure, all four cabins are located in this general area."

Mike pointed to the area Joe had circled. "These are the dirt roads that will lead us to the cabins. They should be easy to find."

"Don't fool yourself. Looks like a snap on the map. Once we're there, from what I remember, there'll be so many twists and turns, we won't know which road leads to the correct path. We'll have to do a trial and error thing."

Mike tapped the map with his index finger. "That'll take up precious time we don't have. Do you have any suggestions?"

"Yes, I do. We'll have to get the troopers involved. Each can cover different areas. Pittsburgh is considered a Class One city and that gives us statewide authority, but as a matter of courtesy, I'd like to notify them."

Mike knew that had to be done, but he didn't want to waste the time required to jump through the proper hoops. "That'll take too long."

"Not if we call Cannady. She can drive out to and rescue Bronson while we're still at headquarters making our request."

"Let's go for it."

SIXTY-SEVEN

BRONSON, FULLY DRESSED, opened the cabin's front door and stepped out. The cool, morning air hit him with full force but also invigorated him. For the moment, freedom enveloped him but the threat of death hovered above him like a suffocating cloud.

He had only an hour to execute the plan he had devised last night. Yet, he stood as still as a tree spreading its roots.

An hour.

That meant the road to safety lay further down the hill, more than an hour's distance. The four door silver Ford truck parked in front of the cabin lured him. He could hot wire it and drive out, but the Raven would have thought of that. She had probably disabled it, and if he spent time trying to connect the wires, he would have lost precious minutes.

His attention shifted from the vehicle to the gigantic pines, white fir, and quaking aspen that whispered in the wind and cast deep shadows as though protecting the evil vines that promised to strangle him. That way, toward the cluster of trees, laid the best chance of survival.

He could head toward the brush or follow the road that surely led to the main highway. He could see the rough shape of the trail that had brought them to the cabin. Rocks protruded from the ground and enough vegetation had been smothered to qualify this as a dirt road, a crude one at best, but still a road.

He followed it down the hill, pausing only long enough

to cast one last look back at the cabin. He pushed on, faster and harder. When the cabin vanished from view, he stopped and made a sharp right, heading away from the road, deep into the forest's concealing shadows.

His movements identified him as a city dweller not familiar with the dangers the shadows hid. He stumbled. He picked himself up, pushed forward, trying to put as much distance as possible between him and the Raven. He moved like a blind man on the run, not sure of his destination.

He traveled this way for five minutes. He timed it. He stopped. Ten feet ahead of him a branch had recently fallen. Its leaves screamed for water and the green chlorophyll that had kept them alive and green, but now the leaves had started their slow starvation. Perfect. Exactly what Bronson sought.

He picked it up and walked backwards, retracing his footsteps as much as possible. As he headed away from the road, he had memorized each rock and each root that broke the surface.

He had mentally marked the places he had stumbled.

Almost five minutes later, to the dot, he once again reached the road. Once satisfied these ruts were the same ones that led back to the cabin, he retraced his steps again heading toward the thickets of chokeberry and clusters of trees that made up the forest.

He knew for sure he followed the same path he had previously taken. Behind him, he dragged the branch obliterating as many of his footsteps as possible.

A stitch at his side reminded him that the Bronson of yesteryear had aged. He breathed through his mouth. He'd be damned if he allowed the years to slow him down. He paused only long enough to study the trees that surrounded him.

The one a little to his left fit the bill. Its lowest branches hung low enough for him to climb and its foliage thick enough to conceal him. He used long steps to reach the foot of the tree.

Still clinging to the branch, he walked away from the tree, brushing the path behind him, making sure the leaves obliterated his trail. This time he paid attention to details so that even the smallest of hints disappeared.

Bronson sat on the ground and removed his right boot. He took out the knife—thank God the Raven never found it. He practiced opening it four, five times. Feeling confident he had the required skill to snap it open at an instant's command, he set the knife down. He hoped he didn't need to use the knife this way, but he better be prepared.

He took off his sock and something stabbed his thigh. He looked at the ground. No sharp rocks or twigs that would hurt him. He reached in his pants pocket and felt the fingernail file Mike had given him to put in the glove compartment. He probably wouldn't use the file, but he'd keep it anyway.

He filled his sock with rocks ranging from pebbles to small fist size. He snuck a peek at his watch. Time had lapsed and his hour had almost run out.

He better hurry. His thoughts turned to the tree that would conceal him.

SIXTY-EIGHT

A THIN LITTLE giggle escaped out of the Raven's mouth. Only a minute or two at the most, and the sand would release its last grain. Death had already begun its waltz with Bronson.

Hurry, sand.

Hurry.

Unburden your load.

The last trickled out and a mad rising laugh filled the tiny cabin echoing off the walls, announcing the Raven's impending victory.

Already dressed in hiking shoes, brown Khakis, and an earth-colored shirt, the Raven walked out the door. She carried a small backpack which held the extra gun and the camera which would record yet another victory.

She had also prepared a special sandwich, had even added two slices of cheese, something she never did. But this called for a special celebration. Killing Bronson would add an extra mark on her Wall of Success, but this carving would be deeper and bigger. Maybe even the same size as good ol' Dad's. Or maybe not. Bronson called for a larger carving. It was, after all, a bigger victory.

The Raven could almost taste the sandwich now. Her mouth salivated. As with the others, she'd eat her sandwich and drink her water after she had shot her victim. While Bronson squirmed and yelled in agony, she would be eating and recording each scream to savor later, over a steak.

But none of this would happen if she didn't focus. She pushed all thoughts aside and studied the ground.

Bronson had also stood here in this same spot evaluating his circumstances. She liked that. All the others had dashed out of the cabin running like scared rabbits. Not Bronson.

Others had headed for the truck, trying to find a way to start its engine. None succeeded. How could they? The distributor cap lay carefully hidden inside the cabin.

Filled with frustration, her previous captors ran down the road, hoping it would lead them to other cabins or the main road. Fools. They should have known they couldn't cover the distance in an hour's time. Yet, they followed the road.

So did Bronson.

That bothered the hell out of her. She had thought him smarter. Maybe she had expected too much out of him. She hoped he wouldn't let her down.

The Raven moved down the road with the confidence of a lioness following the scent of prey. She stopped and smiled. Bronson had left the road here. She looked behind her. She could no longer see the cabin.

Bronson had followed the road only long enough to make her think he'd continue down this path, just in case she was watching from the window. Not that she'd ever do that. She wouldn't cheat.

But that dubious Bronson wouldn't know that. He had to assume she had. So now that the cabin lay concealed behind the dense forest, Bronson deviated from the path and headed north.

She could see his trail. A broken twig here, a partial footprint there. He ran like a madman, not giving much thought to anything but escape. But at least he had been smart enough to use something to erase his footsteps, probably a branch to sweep the ground, thinking that would obliterate his prints.

The fool. He had erased most, but not all. An expert like her could read the deception with the ease of a parent playing hide-and-seek with a one-year-old.

I'm coming to get you, Bronson.

She turned and followed his trail deep into the woods.

SIXTY-NINE

A FAT SOCK bulging with rocks and tied with a knot at the top rested beside Bronson. He sat on the ground and removed the shoelace from his boot. He held the shoelace, one end in each hand, and pulled. Good, it didn't tear. If luck held, it would serve its purpose.

He set the piece down and picked up the branch he had carefully chosen because of its width, length, and shape. He used the knife to remove any side branches so that when he finished, the wood resembled a semi-smooth, straight limb. He catapulted the discarded pieces of branches as far away as he could, all in different directions. Anyone crossing the forest would think the branch had fallen off one of the neighboring trees.

Several large droplets of sweat trickled across his forehead. With the back of his hand, he wiped away the sweat only because he didn't want it running into his eyes. Using the shoelace as a rope, he secured the opened knife to the limb. He stood up and threw the spear he had just designed, aiming for a tree. The blade held and embedded itself into the tree trunk.

Success. Sweet success. He thought of the fingernail file he could use as a backup just in case. Maybe he should make it into a mini spear too, but time was tight, best be spent doing other things. He retrieved his spear and froze.

Goose bumps formed on the back of his neck and traveled down his spine. Something had changed. He cocked his head, listening...listening to a deathly silence. The forest had grown eerily quiet. The goose bumps spread down his arms. The silence of the forest yelled at him, warning him a predator approached—the worst kind of predator, human.

He had run out of time. Bronson bit his lip.

Two things still needed to be done, both equally as important if he were to survive. He looked at his chosen tree, the one that would be easy to climb. The one whose full foliage could easily conceal a full grown man. He wished he had the time to study the surrounding trees, maybe choose a better one. But time had become his enemy. He had to go with this one. He had to trust his original instinct. This tree would serve his purpose. God, it had to.

As quickly as possible, he picked up some dirt and rubbed his hands. He then grabbed his homemade spear and the sock filled with rocks, and headed toward the tree. His muscles tensed, demanding rest, but Bronson knew that luxury would not be his.

He wished he could bolt, but the circumstances dictated he pay special attention to small details. He took three steps and paused only long enough to wipe his footprints away. If only he had the time to double check his work. After all, his life depended on his ability to erase all the evidence. He cast one quick look. Satisfied, he moved on to the next three steps and repeated the process. He did this until he reached the base of the tree.

Already he could hear the approaching footsteps, each whispering its urgency. Each narrowing the distance between the two of them.

Bronson climbed the tree.

SEVENTY

CONFIDENT IN HER knowledge of the forest and in her ability to read the trail Bronson left behind, the Raven advanced at a steady rate. Now and then, she would lose sight of the trail, just like she had at this moment.

She stood still, her gaze zooming in on the ground. She analyzed it, inch by inch. She took a step forward and then did it all over again. She saluted herself when she once again picked up his trail. Bronson probably thought she had let him keep his boots on to give him a bit of a chance. What a fool. Boot prints were always easier to track than bare feet.

Lately, that hadn't happened as often as it did at the beginning. The deeper Bronson penetrated the woods, the more reckless he got. In his desperation to flee, he hadn't been erasing his footsteps as carefully as he should have.

Too bad for him. So good for her.

Halfway up the hill, she once again paused. She hadn't lost sight of Bronson's footprints. That wasn't the problem.

Seconds ago, the air vibrated with birds' songs. The wind blew and the leaves whispered as they captured the breeze. A rabbit dashed from one place to the other. A squirrel chirped as it glided through the trees.

All that came to an abrupt stop as though Nature had waved her magic wand and silenced the forest. The Raven smiled and breathed hard through her mouth. She knew the significance of the strangling silence.

Bronson was near. Perhaps just right up the hill. She

had finally caught up with him. Time had come to unburden herself of the extra gear. Normally, she didn't take this precaution, but she would for Bronson.

The Raven allowed her backpack to slide down her arms. She set it down on the middle of the trail where she could easily find it. She unzipped it, reached for her gun and stuck it in the large right hand side pocket of her Khakis. She left the pocket open, assuring her easy access.

She climbed the rest of the hill and right before reaching the crest, she paused for the last time. She listened as alert as a bird ready to take flight.

Only silence greeted her.

Every inch of her body warned her Bronson waited for her at the top. What kind of trap had he devised? Anticipation caused her to lick her lips.

She squatted and waited. Nothing.

She dropped to the ground and slithered the rest of the way up the hill.

She reached the top, her sight darting from place to place. Searching, searching. Always searching.

She couldn't see Bronson. Had she been wrong? No, impossible.

He was here, somewhere, hiding like a coward.

She would lure him out.

The Raven looked down at Bronson's trail now almost too easy to read. She took out the Astra, held it at the ready. Up ahead, Bronson had made a sharp turn, hoping to confuse her, no doubt. But his footprints didn't lie. The cluster of trees to her right concealed him.

She stood up and quickly began to follow the trail that led her to a large tree whose full foliage added a touch of beauty to the forest. Its grandeur awed the Raven, but better yet, Bronson's footprints dead ended at the foot of the tree. She looked around, double-checking to make sure Bronson hadn't tricked her.

He hadn't.

He had climbed the tree.

Her sight rested at the foot of the tree. Slowly her gaze traveled up, inch by inch, absorbing each detail, captivated by the moment.

She looked up and saw the bottom of Bronson's boot halfway sticking out of the foliage.

Her lips slowly formed into the shape of a smile.

She raised the Astra and fired into the tree.

SEVENTY-ONE

CANNADY'S BRONCO FOUND another deep rut in the road, causing her to almost hit her head against the roof of the car. This road had deteriorated tremendously since the last time she'd driven it, which was a heck of a long time ago. She knew she should slow down.

Should, but wouldn't. Bronson needed her and if she could save him, that would be reward enough. She liked Bronson and hated the brass who ordered her to stay away from him and anything relating to his sister's death.

Someone with a lot of clout had orchestrated this, and she aimed to find and expose that person, but first she'd focus on Bronson. Detective Joe Randig had told her only four cabins had been built eight to twelve years ago. A lot more cabins had gone up around the lake and in other developed areas close to Lake Arthur, but only four in the rural areas. "Let's focus on those first," Joe had suggested.

She agreed. The little Cannady knew about the Raven told her that Barbara Culverson, alias the Raven, would have chosen to build in an isolated area. Two of the four cabins utilized the same road even though more than a couple of miles separated the two. The third and fourth cabins lay at the end of completely different roads. Trooper Hunsicker headed toward the third cabin while Trooper Swanson covered the fourth.

Cannady wished Hunsicker and Swanson were with her while other troopers searched for the other two cabins. But the three of them were doing this on their own without the brass' approval. In fact, in spite of direct orders to leave things alone.

No matter. At least they were able to cover the areas and hopefully reach Bronson before it was too late.

Cannady's hopes soared. Through the trees she could see the first cabin. She parked, pulled the .40 caliber semi-automatic Glock out and held it at the ready. Weaving between the trees, she advanced toward the cabin even though it seemed deserted. She plastered her back against the wall and stuck her head out only far enough to see through the window.

In its prime, the place must have adequately served its owners. It offered all the necessary creature comforts one would need. But now the upholstery of the sofa had faded, and it looked dirty and worn out. A layer of dust impregnated the room. It had been a heck of a long time since this cabin was used.

Scolding herself for wasting valuable minutes, she put the gun away and bolted toward the car. She started the engine and sped out.

She wondered if Hunsicker or Swanson had met with luck. For Bronson's sake, she hoped so. She stomped on the accelerator, pushing the Bronco almost to its endurance point. She had to close the distance between her and the other cabin.

If that's where Bronson was being held captive, she needed to reach the place now. Every second that ticked away brought Bronson closer to death.

Forty-three minutes later, Cannady heard the crack of a pistol being fired.

SEVENTY-TWO

JUST AS THE Raven sent the bullet speeding through the tree, Bronson stepped out from behind the cluster of trees located several yards away.

The Raven gasped and cocked her head, hearing the crunching of leaves, the sound of approaching footsteps. With the speed of a jaguar, she did a one hundred and eighty degree turn. When her gaze landed on Bronson, her eyes popped open as huge as saucers. Her lower lip dropped. She shook herself and looked down at her hand that held the gun. Like a robot, she raised it.

But by then, Bronson had twirled the heavy sock filled with rocks, and with all his might aimed it at the Raven's chest.

A *hmmph* escaped her mouth as she tumbled down, the gun landing a foot away from her. She squirmed to reach it, her arm stretched out toward it.

Bronson pushed forward, not an easy task, wearing a boot on his right foot and only a sock on his left foot. Every cell in his body focused on reaching the gun before she did. His mind screamed for him to hasten. His logic told him he'd never make it. She was a foot away. He, ten feet.

The Raven's lips formed a thin line of success. She wrapped her hand around the Astra's handle. She gasped in pain but managed to raise the gun an inch.

Two inches.

Bronson raised his spear above him, aiming for the Raven. He released it into the air and continued to advance.

The spear found its home in the Raven's chest. She screamed as she pulled out the bloodied knife. The wail pierced the woods, sending a flock of birds into a frightened flight.

She inched toward the gun, her hand wide open, closing the distance between her and the pistol.

Bronson, three feet away from her, launched himself forward, landing on top of the Raven's legs. He retrieved the fingernail file from his pants pocket and stabbed her leg.

The Raven screamed and slowed down only enough to give Bronson the advantage.

His arm stretched out, grasping for the weapon.

She squirmed, reaching for the gun.

They both grabbed it at the same time, both pulling it toward themselves.

A shot rang out.

THE LAST THING Joe Randig wanted to do was create animosity between himself, as a representative of the Pittsburgh Police Department, and the State Troopers. They often had to work together and each department always fully co-operated with one another.

That's why he couldn't understand the reason why the troopers were so obviously stalling. Again, Joe explained the urgency of the situation.

Mike Hoover stood beside him. His hands at his sides formed fists that trembled. He opened his hands, only to close them into fists once again. He leaned toward Joe's ear. "This is a total waste of time. I've got to go help Bronson."

Joe nodded and handed him the keys to his car. "Go with God and take caution. I'll be in the lead trooper's car. It shouldn't be much longer."

Mike nodded and made a mad dash toward the door.

SEVENTY-THREE

THE SHOT IN the woods that Cannady heard could have come from any direction. She had an idea that its origination point lay somewhere in front of her. If so, she would continue on a northerly direction. With luck, she might notice something that would lead her to Bronson. She hoped she wasn't too late.

Unlike before, she drove slower, her gaze scanning the area. Five minutes later, she stopped. She saw something unusual halfway up the hill. A boulder? Couldn't be. This was black with a red band across its width.

She slowed down to a crawl, focusing on the item. A backpack. What the heck was a backpack doing there? She parked and as fast as she could, ran up the hill.

Halfway up, she heard another shot. This one a bit to her right but somewhere in the general vicinity.

"CONGRATULATIONS, YOU...WON." The bullet had pierced the Raven's chest and blood oozed out.

Bronson sat up and attempted to apply pressure to the wound. His efforts made no difference.

"Your reward...for winning. Listen...carefully. Sam Glass...you know him?"

Bronson nodded. "The lawyer?"

The Raven closed her eyes and nodded once. "He ordered...your death."

"Why?"

"Was afraid...you'd find out...about the paintings."

Bronson's eyes narrowed and his eyebrows furrowed. His sister had died because of a stupid painting. "Glass ordered Miller to paint the forgeries, and then Glass sells them. He tricks the buyer into thinking they're buying the original."

Slowly, the Raven nodded. Her breath came in shallow puffs. She breathed through her mouth. "Makes…millions. Glass knew…Miller was weak. If…he talked…to you… he'd tell you…everything. Glass had…me kill…Miller."

"Lorraine, my sister, had a La Carcé original. Miller was in the process of painting the forgeries so they could be sold. Lorraine must have found out about it. Is that why Glass had her killed?"

"She threatened…to go to the police." The Raven gasped and her eyes widened. "Glass arranges…the sales, but… reports to…" Once again she gasped. She gave Bronson a weak smile. "You won." Her lips formed the words as she closed her eyes.

Shiiit! "Don't you dare die. We're not through. Finish your damn story first." He pounded her chest.

The Raven didn't respond.

He pounded again and again. He continued to pound until his energy gave out.

With a loud *thud*, he sat back, his legs folded in front of him. He wrapped his arms around them, and rested his head on his knees, his thoughts drifting from one subject to the other.

He raised his head and listened to the sound of approaching footsteps.

SEVENTY-FOUR

SAM GLASS SLAMMED the phone receiver down into its cradle. This marked the fourth time he had called the Raven, and she didn't have the courtesy to return his calls. He grew more and more agitated as the minutes ticked away.

He drummed his fingers on the phone. The twins could reach her. They always did. Glass flipped the pages of his rolodex to the letter *J*. John, Jack—that's them. One and the same. If you dealt with one, you dealt with the other. Even the Raven enjoyed them both and sometimes at the same time.

Jack answered on the third ring. "Mr. Glass, good to hear from you. I hope you have an assignment for us. We're kinda low on cash."

"Sorry about that, but all I need right now is some information. I've been calling the Raven, and she hasn't answered my calls."

"She's at the cabin. No cell connection up there."

"The cabin?" Glass sat up straighter. "What about Bronson?"

"She took him with her. She's enjoying him, if you know what I mean."

That fool. He had specifically told her to make Bronson's death look like an accident. And what of Hoover? Wasn't she supposed to take care of him too? He should have hired the twins to do the killing, not the Raven. That pervert. She had probably messed everything up.

Glass' gaze slid to the locked file cabinet. Maybe he

should consider getting rid of the evidence. Maybe he should leave the city.

Maybe.

BRONSON DROPPED TO the ground and rolled toward the pistol. His fingers grabbed the handle, and he rolled again so that now he lay on his stomach, the gun pointing toward the approaching footsteps.

He waited for someone to crest the hill. Two seconds went by. Three. Nothing.

Four.

Bronson could see a shape emerging. He readjusted his grip on the pistol. He waited.

"Don't shoot!" Cannady lowered her gun. "It's me, Cannady."

Bronson put the gun down, stood up, and then pocketed the Astra.

"You got a permit for that?" Cannady indicated his pocket.

"Sure do. When I retired, I registered."

Cannady smiled and winked, letting Bronson know she was kidding. "You okay?"

"A bruise here. A bruise there. Not much else. How did you know to come here?"

"Joe Randig called." Cannady approached the Raven's body, bent down, and checked for a pulse. "What happened to her?"

"She got herself killed. We were wrestling for the gun. It went off. The bullet chose the victim, a matter of luck it got her instead of me."

"That gun in your pocket. Is that the weapon used?"

Bronson nodded.

"I'll bag it."

Bronson reached for his pocket.

"Not now. Bags are in the car. Let's walk down the hill so I can call this in. While we wait, you can fill me in on the details."

Bronson threw a rock at his boot still stuck in the tree. It took him three tries before he knocked it down. He dusted the boot off and put it on. It felt good walking with shoes. "On the way to the cabin would you mind if I call Mike, my ex-partner?"

"I know who he is—and where he is."

"Oh?"

"He's with Joe."

Bronson nodded. "Mike won't admit it, but I'm sure he's concerned about me."

"He is."

Bronson smiled. "Can I borrow your cell?"

"You could but it won't do you any good."

"Why not?"

"This is a dead zone."

"For all providers?"

"That's what I hear."

Shiiit. He could have overpowered the Raven at the cabin. All those calls she supposedly made had all been fake. Double shiiit.

Cannady and Bronson reached the area where the Raven had discarded the backpack. Cannady grabbed it and continued walking down the hill. "Once we reach my car, I'll send word to Hoover. Soon as he arrives, he can take you to the emergency room."

"Thanks, but I'm fine."

"That lump the size of an egg on your head concerns me. Besides, you're going to have an adrenaline crash. Later, you can give us a statement and fill in all the gaps."

"I'm fine, really. If you don't mind, I'd like to hang

around and answer any questions you and your team will have. After that, I'll have Mike take me to see a doctor."

"Suit yourself." They reached her car and, as promised, she relayed a message to Hoover. She set the mike down and looked at Bronson. "What can you tell me about what happened?"

Bronson took a deep breath, trying to drive away the sudden fatigue that enveloped him. He rubbed the bridge of his nose. "You know about the paintings and the forgeries."

She nodded.

"One of the top culprits is a lawyer named Sam Glass. He may have been the one who ordered my sister's death. I'd like to get my hands on him."

Cannady cleared her throat.

"But since I'm a good, law-abiding citizen, I'll let the troopers handle it."

"Yeah, I bet." Cannady opened the glove compartment and retrieved some plastic bags. She opened the bag and Bronson placed the Astra inside. "Before we get to Glass, tell me what happened here."

Bronson groaned. He'd rather put the incident behind him but knew he had no choice. "The Raven has an egg-timer back at the cabin. When the sand runs out after it's turned over, she said she'd come hunting for me. That gave me an hour to set up the trap I devised the night before."

Cannady took out a notebook and recorded the information.

Bronson led her twenty-feet from where they stood. He pointed to the ground. "I followed the road until this point. From here, I ran and stumbled up the hill, all the time searching for an ideal tree. When I found it, I back-tracked to the beginning, carefully wiping away every footprint. Following that path as much as possible, I erased some footprints and other give-aways, but left enough for the

Raven to follow. She suspected, I imagine and hoped, that I ran like a frightened man with no destination in mind."

"And all the time you had a goal."

Bronson nodded.

"Oooh, you're a devious man."

"I've been called worse."

"I imagine."

Bronson nodded and continued the narrative. Ten minutes later, they heard the crunching of tires and saw a trail of growing dust as vehicles approached.

The cavalry had arrived.

SEVENTY-FIVE

"BUDDY, YOU DO this to me again…" Mike and Bronson stood staring at each other for the first time since the kidnapping ordeal began. Mike ran his fingers through his hair. "I swear every gray hair I have is because of you."

Bronson cocked his head and flashed him a wide-eyed look. "Does this mean I won't get a hug?"

"Wouldn't think of it."

They looked at each other, smiled, and hugged.

Several yards in front of them, Cannady and Joe talked as officers and EMT's swarmed around the forest or flocked near the Raven's body.

Joe looked back at Bronson and Mike but continued his conversation with Cannady. Joe nodded and they both headed toward Bronson and Mike. "I thought you were going to get checked out," Joe said.

"I am, but I wanted to be here to answer all of the questions you have."

Joe puckered and nodded. "You've cleared up most of our questions. But there is something we'd like you to do, if you're willing." He pointed to Cannady and himself. "But first please go get yourself checked out."

"What do you have planned?"

"Cannady tells me you would really like to reel Glass in."

"Yeah." Bronson's curiosity peaked.

"What about if we wire you and you confront the lawyer? I think you'll get him to talk a lot easier than we could."

"I'm all for that."

AFTER BEING RELEASED from Pittsburgh's St. Joseph Medical Center's emergency room, Bronson and Mike sat in Joe Randig's office. Mike watched as Joe and Cannady wired Bronson and told him how they and Mike would be parked across the street from Glass' office. They would be listening to every word being said.

Bronson nodded, walked out, and drove himself to the lawyer's office. He kept a close eye on the police van following him. Half-an-hour later, Bronson had reached his destination. He watched as Joe parked the van and waited a few minutes for them to set up.

The Sam Glass, Attorney at Law office occupied the entire first floor of a four-story office building. Not only was the place huge, but an interior designer must have earned a hefty sum to create the eye-pleasing effect the reception room had. Leather-bound sofas invited potential clients to relax while waiting to see Glass. Abstract art paintings consisting of various colors and shapes adorned the walls. Generally, Bronson preferred realistic art to abstract art, but these paintings complimented each other and added a touch of elegance. The receptionist desk could easily accommodate two secretaries at the same time.

Bronson approached the receptionist, an attractive heavy-set woman in her mid-thirties. "Cindy." He read her name plate. "I'm Harry Bronson. You tell Sam Glass I'm here to see him."

The receptionist thumbed through the calendar. "Do you have an appointment?"

Bronson took a step forward. "I don't need an appointment. I assure you, Glass will want to talk to me."

The receptionist fluttered her eyelids. "Oh."

Bronson leaned forward, placed both hands on her desk, and smiled. "That means you're supposed to take me to him."

Cindy bolted to her feet. "Oh, sure. Sure." She pressed the intercom button. "A Harry Bronson is here to see you. He assured me you'd want to talk to him."

"He's right. Send him in."

Cindy opened the door almost directly behind her and indicated for Bronson to go in.

By the time he entered, Glass had walked around his desk, greeting him with an open hand and a warm smile. "Mr. Bronson, it's good to see you again." He pointed to the leather cushioned chairs facing his oversized desk. "Please, sit." He walked around and sat in his overstuffed chair. "What can I do for you this time?"

Bronson sat bolt upright, his features firm. "I'm here to discuss the Raven." Bronson studied the lawyer. Except for a tiny twitch in Glass' forehead, the lawyer remained passive.

He squinted as though attempting to search the files in his memory bank. "The Raven? As in the bird? Is that a musical group?"

Bronson leaned back and smiled, a man in complete control of the situation. "Cut the crap. I know you're familiar with the Raven."

Glass raised his hands as if surrendering. "Believe me, I have no idea what you're talking about. Would you care to fill me in?"

"Does the name Barbara Culverson mean anything to you?"

Glass' Adam apple bobbed once, a movement that didn't escape Bronson's attention.

The lawyer's eyes darted from side to side, as if he continued to search through his mental files. "I can't seem to recall anyone by that name. Should it be familiar to me? I meet hundreds of people each month. It's hard to keep track of all the names." His wide-eyed innocent look gave credence to his words.

He's good, Bronson thought. He's not going to be easy to break. "Let's talk about the paintings."

"The paintings? The ones in the outer office?"

Two could play the game. Bronson's eyes locked on the lawyer. "What are the twins' names?"

"Ah, Jack and Jill?" Glass shrugged. "What twins? Please, back up and explain what you're talking about."

"I'll be glad to do that. I'll begin by telling you that the Raven is dead."

Before he could stop himself, Glass' eyes widened and he took small, sharp breaths. He shook himself and looked away. "And what does that have to do with me?"

"It has everything to do with you. Before she died—I killed her—she told me how you hired her to kill me. She told me about the paintings and the forgeries. She also told me about the twins."

Glass crossed his arms and looked down as though studying the carpet for a secret answer. "I've never heard of the Raven, and I never hired anyone to kill you or anybody else."

Bronson leaned forward on his seat. "You're a lawyer. You know that a dying declaration will hold up in court. If I were you, I'd come clean, or you'll end up taking the rap for everything."

Glass let the air out through his mouth, giving him the appearance of a deflated balloon.

Bronson scooted over so he'd be even closer to the lawyer. "The cops are on their way. Thought I'd give you the heads up and give you a chance to save yourself."

"Why would you do that?"

"Because I'm sure you answer to someone. I want to know who that is."

Glass bit his lip.

"Fine. Have it your way." Bronson stood up.

"Wait," Glass said.

Bronson sat back down.

Once sitting tall and proud, Glass now hunched over, holding his head in his hands. "I'm not taking the rap for this. I want it known I'm willing to co-operate. I want your word you will talk to the police who in turn will talk to the judge about my willingness to fully co-operate."

"That, I can do."

Glass hesitated and bit his lips. "As far as the scheme of things go, I'm the one at the bottom of the totem pole." Silence filled the room. Glass ran his finger inside his shirt collar. "Wellington." He whispered the name.

Bronson frowned. "The old steel magnate? With all the money he has, why would he want to get involved with this?"

"Mr. Wellington has been critically ill for a long time. He's always thought his daughter Amanda to be worthless. When he passes on, she will only inherit one hundred thousand dollars, and she'll be allowed to keep her personal possessions. The rest of the billions will be donated to charity. Amanda was livid. She wants to prove to her father she has—how should I say this?—nerves of steel. The master mind isn't Mr. Wellington, but his daughter, Amanda."

SEVENTY-SIX

SHORTLY AFTER BRONSON walked out of Glass' office, Joe and Cannady stepped in. Bronson smiled at the irony. The lawyer would soon need a lawyer.

"Ready to head home?" Mike opened his hand and wiggled his fingers.

Bronson nodded and handed him the car keys. Minutes later, they headed down the freeway toward Ellen's house.

Bronson drew a deep breath, filling his lungs to maximum capacity, and slowly exhaled. He rolled down the car window and focused on the variety of trees, black cherries growing among red and white oaks next to a cluster of hard and soft maples. Amazing how the same type of trees that now enveloped him with peace had several hours ago, filled his world with terror.

As usual, Mike drove and Bronson sat in the passenger seat. "You doing okay now?" Mike sped up so he could keep up with the traffic in the freeway.

Bronson nodded. "Sure, even though I would really like to know who ordered Lorraine's death."

"You figure it's got to be either Wellington or Glass?" Mike cast a glance at the car's digital clock. He pressed the gas pedal a bit harder. The speedometer needle climbed.

"If that's the case, then the Raven or one of the twins pulled the trigger. I can't imagine either Glass or Wellington getting their hands dirty."

Mike changed lanes. The next exit was his. "Between the Raven and the twins, who do you think was the assassin?"

"More than likely, one of the twins. If the Raven had done it, she would have told me. She made no mention whatsoever of Lorraine's death."

"That leaves the twins."

"Yeah, maybe."

Mike snuck a glance at Bronson. "Maybe? Tell me you're not thinking of pursuing this any further."

"I'm not thinking of pursuing this any further."

"Now say it like you mean it."

"I'm not thinking of pursuing this any further."

"That sounded the same."

Bronson shrugged.

"You need to let Joe Randig and Cannady unravel the last threads in this case all by themselves."

"Fine with me. I told you I don't plan to interfere."

"You don't?" A trace of doubt crept into his voice.

"Nope."

"Uh, oh. What gives?"

Bronson shifted positions. "Nothin'. Even though I've just met Detective Randig, I feel he's very competent. So is Cannady. We've led them to this art theft ring, so we've done our share. It's up to them to wrap up the loose ends."

Mike frowned. "Tell me what you're not telling me."

"Nothin' to tell." Bronson turned away from Mike.

"I hope so, because I have a surprise for you."

"Oh?"

"Carol's here."

Bronson's eyes lit up, then immediately dimmed. "Does she know about what happened out there in the forest?"

"No, she doesn't. I figure if you wanted to tell her, that would be up to you."

"How did you explain my absence?"

"Told her you were having trouble with the cell and had gone to get it fixed."

"Thanks, buddy."

"You're welcome, especially since you know I hate to lie, even little white lies bother me."

"I know." Bronson caught the name of the next exit. He tried to orient himself, figuring out how far they were from Ellen's house. "When did Carol arrive?"

"She hasn't yet. She's due in half-an-hour. That's why I've been speeding, trying to get you home in time."

"Once again, I'm indebted to you."

"And I will collect."

"I'm sure." Mike executed a right and turned into Ellen's street. "I know you called Little Carol and told her about Lorraine, but did you ever call Donna?"

Shiiit. He'd forgotten about his youngest daughter. He pulled out his cell.

SEVENTY-SEVEN

A SOLITARY FIGURE sat at the far side of the bar, nursing his beer, rubbing his chin. Above him, a neon sign advertising Coors flashed with bright red and white letters and served as the bar's main source of light. The wall to his right bore the names of the troopers who had been killed in the line of duty. Several framed pictures, mostly of cops in uniform and most with their families, adorned the bar's walls.

He was neither a policeman nor was he in any way associated with the police force, but he liked this bar and the regulars accepted him even though none spoke to him. That's the way he liked it. Often, his business brought him to My Kind of Place Bar, and he felt confident in the knowledge that he'd be able to conduct his business without any nosey troopers interfering with him. Today would be no exception.

Two plain clothed policemen, whom he knew were detectives, entered the bar and stood by the door. Both squinted, allowing their eyes to adjust to the darkness.

The man, waiting for them, picked up his beer and chose an empty table close to the bar. He sat down. The detectives approached and waved a hello as they pulled out the chairs and sat beside him. The man nodded a hello.

They sat in silence while waiting for the bartender. Seconds later, he stood by their table, took their orders and left.

The man took a swig of the beer he had been nursing. "What's the word?"

The younger of the two detectives, who looked more

like a teenager than an adult, spoke first. "Word has it that Bronson killed the Raven. He knows about the art theft ring and was informed his sister found out about it before she was killed. Had she lived, she would have come to us with that information."

The man leaned back on his chair, smiled, and drank his beer. He set the mug down and rubbed his chin. "That's wonderful news."

"We thought you'd like that."

The college age bartender placed two more beer mugs on the table and a plate filled with pretzels. Once he was out of hearing range, the man reached for a pretzel and ate it. "What else do you have?"

"Randig is working the case." This time the other detective answered. "He's traced the thefts to a lawyer by the name of Sam Glass."

"I know him." He continued to rub his chin. "He's quite an influential man."

"Not anymore." The detective laughed and raised his beer mug.

The other detective did the same and both clinked glasses. "One less thug loose in the streets."

You should talk. He kept the comment to himself. He was about to rub his chin but stopped himself. Somehow, he'd have to break that habit. "Anything else?"

"Yeah, seems this whole deal wasn't orchestrated by the lawyer. He's simply the man in the middle. He arranges the meetings between buyer and seller. That makes him a pawn in the theft world. The real ring leader is Amanda Wellington."

"The heir to the Wellington steel wealth?"

"None other."

The man emptied his beer mug and stuffed more pretzels in his mouth. "This is perfect. Absolutely perfect."

"That's what we say."

"Thank you for the information. As always, I would like to compensate you for your time and efforts." He reached into his pocket, retrieved two envelopes, and handed each policeman one. He rubbed his chin and stood up. "I'll report your findings to my boss. I know this news will be welcomed." He ate one more pretzel and walked out.

SEVENTY-EIGHT

HALF-AN-HOUR after Bronson and Mike pulled into Ellen's driveway, Carol arrived. By then Bronson had showered, shaved, and changed. He felt human again. Mike and Ellen opted to watch T.V. while Bronson sat on Ellen's porch, rocking the time away, waiting for Carol to arrive. Soon as he saw the camper, he stood and sprinted toward the sidewalk, a big smile plastered on his face.

Carol parked the van and got out. Her eyes danced with anticipation as she ran into his opened arms.

She felt warm and comfortable. It felt so good and natural to hold her. He kissed her lips. "I missed you." He gently stroked her hair.

"Me, too, and frankly, I was scared."

Bronson stepped back to see into her eyes. "Scared? Why scared?"

"I thought…I don't know what I thought."

She knew. Dang it, somehow she knew. "Let's go inside and greet Mike and Ellen. Afterwards, we'll go into the bedroom, and I'll tell you the whole story." He wrapped his arm around her and led her inside.

THE SIGN BLINKED each word separately. My…Kind…of… Place…Bar. Then all together the phrase flashed several times. Then back to each individual word. The man stood under the sign, contemplating what he should do. The more he thought, the harder he rubbed his chin.

He knew his boss was at this very moment surrounded

by a fast growing group of friends. If his boss were to accomplish all his goals, then tonight's events must be the focus of attention.

On the other hand, his boss had given him specific instructions. If he were to learn the smallest of details, he was to immediately report his findings.

What the man had learned tonight was huge. His boss would want to know immediately. That knowledge would even make the evening more enjoyable. Yet something told him to wait, verify the information.

He went against his gut feeling and made the call. The cell rang three times before the boss picked up. "I'll call you back." Didn't even wait for a response, simply hung up.

The man waited twelve minutes before his boss returned the call. He wanted to let the jerk know that his time was also valuable, but he bit his tongue and accepted it as part of the job.

At least his boss was apologetic. "I hated to keep you waiting, but you know how it goes. Those were the longest twelve minutes of my life, not knowing what you had to say. I hope you have good news for me. Again, I apologize for the delay, but I'm here now. I'm all ears."

"I have better news than you could possibly imagine." He explained about the art theft ring and how Lorraine threatened to expose them.

"That's fantastic news." The boss remained silent for a moment. "You've worked for me through thick and thin all of these years. I'm gearing up for the big event—it's going to happen, no doubt about it."

"Let me be the first to congratulate you."

"Let my so-called better half be the first. You can be second."

Both laughed.

The boss continued, "I'm giving you full freedom. Do

as you see best. You don't have to check in with me any longer. I trust you will make the right decision and know that whatever you choose, I will support you."

"Even if it means killing Bronson?"

"That may be the best route to go."

ELLEN ROLLED OVER in bed and kissed Mike goodnight on the cheek.

A goodnight kiss on the cheek.

That's how it had started the last time, right before she told him she wanted a divorce. He rolled over, his back to Ellen. Outside, the shadows cast by the full moon and prodded along by the gentle breeze, danced across the window.

Maybe it wasn't meant for them to be together. Ellen would always hate and fear his job. He would always love and sacrifice all for his career.

Maybe the forbidden nature of their relationship lured him. Even as a kid, his desire for what he wasn't supposed to do or have fueled him. He imagined that had been the reason he became a law officer—always dipping into the darker side, the forbidden side.

He knew Bronson's ordeal would chip away into Ellen's fortitude, but he had hoped it wouldn't happen this fast. His gaze strayed to a photo Ellen kept on top of the nightstand. It had been taken when both were young, when innocence still filled their lives. At that time, dreams and ambitions dictated their actions and filled their thoughts and souls.

Mike closed his eyes, wishing the picture would fade away. He still loved Ellen, even more now than then. But he also loved his job.

His damn job.

Tonight, sleep would pass him by, and he'd be doomed to spend the night analyzing his life and the decisions he'd made from the perspective of distance. From that angle, he saw his world as an empty shell.

In the next room, Carol probably lay in Bronson's arms and for that instant, Mike hated Bronson.

SEVENTY-NINE

BRONSON, CAROL, MIKE, and Ellen sat around the breakfast table in Ellen's dining room. Mike wiped his hands and pushed the empty plate away. "Oh yeah, I remember everybody in the force thinking Bronson was the man. Nothing would faze him. He was unbeatable. Then it came time for Carol to deliver. The man fell apart."

Bronson sipped his coffee. "Oh come on, now. I wasn't that bad."

Ellen let out a hearty laugh. "You weren't that bad? I had to drive Carol to the hospital because you drove yourself and forgot to take Carol with you."

The ringing of the doorbell prevented Bronson from defending himself.

"Who could that be?" Ellen stood up and glanced at her watch. "It's only eight-thirty." She left and returned a few minutes later. "It's for you, Bronson. A man wants to talk to you."

"Did he say what he wanted? Who he was?"

Ellen shook her head. "I got the impression he would only talk to you."

Bronson stood and Mike followed him.

Ellen had left the front door open and Bronson could see the man through the screen door. Even though he was in his late thirties or early forties, he had taken good care of himself. His firm stomach and bulging biceps revealed he spent time in the gym. He stood firm and tall, a man accustomed to getting what he wanted. "Mr. Bronson?"

Bronson nodded.

"My name is Willis Durango."

With the man's light brown hair and cool, ice-blue eyes, Bronson would have never pegged him for a Hispanic. "What can I do for you, Mr. Durango?"

"I'm here to talk about Lorraine. She and I worked together."

Bronson took a step back, opened the screen door, and pointed to the couch.

Durango not only sat on the couch, but leaned back on it, a man at ease with the world.

Bronson waited until everyone sat down. "You said you and Lorraine worked together?"

"At the school." Durango brought his hand toward his face and scratched his chin.

Mike cleared his throat. "I talked to Claudine, the school's secretary."

"I know who she is." Durango studied Mike and puffed himself like a proud peacock. "What I don't know is who you are."

"Sorry," Bronson said. "This is my good friend, Mike Hoover."

"Your former partner." A statement, not a question.

Still, Bronson nodded. "Seems you have me at a disadvantage. You know a bit about me."

"Lorraine and I kept no secrets from each other."

Mike leaned forward. "If you and Lorraine were as close as you claim, then why didn't Claudine mention your name when I asked her to give me the names of those Lorraine was closest to?"

"I'm sure Claudine doesn't even know about me." Durango continued to rub his chin. "I'm not a full time faculty, only a substitute teacher. I don't ever deal with Claudine."

"Now that we settled that, what can we do for you?" Bronson asked.

"It's the other way around. I know tomorrow's the funeral, and I know you and Lorraine were not on the best of terms. I know she called you, repeatedly, and you ignored her. By the time you decided to pay attention, it was too late. She died in your arms, I understand."

Bronson swallowed the large lump in his throat. Mike clutched the arm rest so tightly that his knuckles turned white. Bronson narrowed his eyes, telling Mike to let it go. Mike focused his attention on his shoes as though that was the most interesting part of the living room.

Durango continued, "When the past haunts you, you're consumed with guilt and remorse, and at the same time, you must be riddled with unanswered questions. Ask me anything."

"Why was my sister afraid?"

"Mr. Wellington, Lorraine's benefactor, worshipped Lorraine, but I'm sure you know that. Mr. Wellington gave Lorraine an original La Carcé painting. Amanda, Wellington's daughter, was furious. She felt it belonged to her. Lorraine was going to give it to her, just to keep peace in the family. That's the kind of woman Lorraine was."

Mike's glance traveled from his shoes to Durango's cool blue eyes. "Why did she decide to keep it?"

"She found out Amanda passed the originals to a lawyer named Sam Glass. He hired a local artist to duplicate them. Glass then sold the duplicates as originals. Lorraine was going to go to the police, but she was petrified what Glass and Amanda would do to her."

"Who ordered her death?"

"I'm sure Amanda told Glass to do whatever was necessary. We see how Glass took care of it."

"Who pulled the trigger?"

"A hired assassin, I'm sure. Unless Glass opens up, we'll probably never know. I personally suspect one of the twins."

"How do you know about the twins?"

"Lorraine told me. I guess she did her homework so that when she went to the police, she'd have a full picture."

Bronson and Mike exchanged looks. Bronson said, "All the evidence at the scene pointed back to a pimp known as Matthew Devono and his right-hand man, Mario Serafin."

"Mario was a set up. Glass figured Mario takes the blame, the heat is off them. The police never find out about the paintings. Amanda and Glass are free to continue with their little scheme." Durango leaned back as though pleased with himself. He no longer rubbed his chin. His hands lay still by his side.

"With all that you know, why didn't you go to the troopers with all the information?"

Durango covered his eyes and rubbed them. "I'm... ashamed of myself. I too feared Amanda and Glass, especially after what happened to Lorraine. I didn't want to end up like her." His chin quivered as though he were ready to cry. "These last few days, I've hated myself. I've been a coward, but this morning I decided to do what's right. So here I am."

Bronson remained quiet, absorbing what Durango had said. Nothing Bronson hadn't heard before, but this guy sure knew a lot. Who was he and how did he know so much? "Lorraine had a baby. What can you tell me about that?"

Durango's eyes widened. "A baby? When? Maybe she didn't tell me everything after all."

Bronson nodded. "She never mentioned the baby to you?"

"If she had one, that must have been way before I met

her, while she was still a teenager. She must have given the baby up for adoption and forgot all about him."

"How long have you known Lorraine?"

"Long enough to know she was a highly paid escort. Then she decided to turn her life around. She applied for a job as a nanny for an up-and-coming lawyer, now a congressman, by the name of Daniel Jenkins. You might know him."

Bronson nodded. "I know of him. Who doesn't? Think he'll be our next President?"

"I think so." Durango began to rub his chin again. "Any other questions?"

"Just one. Why would a preeminent lawyer hire an ex-hooker to be his son's nanny? Surely, for a job like that, he would have investigated her thoroughly."

"Wellington is a very powerful man and his influence runs deep, especially when he's your main campaign contributor."

EIGHTY

"Everything all right?"

Bronson turned away from the opened front door to face Carol. He wrapped his arm around her and drew her toward him.

Mike looked away.

Bronson kissed the top of Carol's head. "He was a friend of Lorraine's. Confirmed what we already knew but mentioned a couple of things I'd like to verify."

Mike reached for the doorknob and closed the door. "Do you think he knew about the baby?"

Bronson nodded. "His reaction seemed a bit staged."

"My thoughts, too."

By now Ellen had cleared the breakfast dishes and put everything away.

"Got more coffee?" Bronson asked.

Ellen indicated the kitchen. Carol eyed him.

"What? It's only my second cup."

"And it's not even nine." Carol tapped her watch.

"It's still only my second cup."

Carol threw her arms up, and Bronson headed for the kitchen to refill his cup.

Mike followed him. "Do you think Durango might be the baby's father?"

"That's a hard one." Bronson offered Mike some coffee. Mike shook his head. Bronson quickly scanned the area. Carol was nowhere in sight. He poured three teaspoons of sugar. "Why would he deny his son?" For good luck, he added one more teaspoonful.

"Son?" Mike raised one eyebrow.

"Durango always referred to the baby as *he*, but then again, it could have been he wasn't being politically correct."

"Maybe so, but Durango did make a couple of statements I'd like to verify."

"Like what?" Bronson poured enough cream to turn his coffee the color of sand.

"Durango mentioned he was a substitute teacher. Then he suggested Wellington pressured Jenkins into hiring Lorraine."

Bronson set his cup of coffee down. "I was thinkin' of payin' Wellington a visit. I need to update him. Want to come?"

"Yeah, it'll give the girls a chance to talk. I think Ellen needs that." Mike grabbed the car keys lying on the kitchen counter.

"And I'll call Wellington to let him know we're on the way." Bronson gulped down his coffee, being a firm believer that no coffee should ever go to waste. He rinsed the cup, set it in the sink, and made his call.

THE AIR FELT damp and oppressively hot even though the car's digital clock told Bronson it was only 7:28. The day promised to be a scorcher, unless it rained. The bright blue sky smiled down at Bronson. Not a cloud in the sky.

Mike, normally chatty, sat silently behind the steering wheel, maneuvering the car around Pittsburgh's early morning heavy traffic.

Bronson leaned his head on the headrest. "You and Ellen doing okay?"

Mike shook his head. "I thought this time maybe we had

a chance, and then the Raven went and messed everything up. Ellen quickly remembered why she hates my job. Drove a wedge between us."

"Thanks for blamin' the Raven and not me."

"You didn't ask to be kidnapped."

"And you and Ellen didn't ask to be put in danger, yet it happened."

"And that's what freaked her out. She hasn't mentioned a single word, but since it happened, things haven't been the same between us."

"Sorry, buddy."

"Yeah, me too. But life goes on." Mike rolled up the windows and turned on the air conditioner. "Since we're being personal, are you still on a guilt trip about your sister?"

Don't leave me. Bronson shook the chill away. "Yeah. Always will be."

"You've got to let it go. It's not healthy. You solved her murder, not much more you can do."

"Did I solve it? Who pulled the trigger?"

Mike shrugged. "One of the twins, we suppose."

"And is the right twin in prison servin' a life sentence?"

"No, not yet, but he will soon be arrested."

"And tried for art theft, not Lorraine's murder." Bronson recognized the bitterness in his tone.

"Chances are one thing will lead to the other. Give it time."

"Not sure I can."

EIGHTY-ONE

WELLINGTON ROAMED AT death's door. His pale yellow complexion and his sunken cheeks made him look like a wilted flower. One gentle breeze and he'd crumble to the ground. Yet, still he sat in his wheelchair, Lorraine's blanket covering him from the waist down. He hunched over a bit but still managed to hold his head high.

The three of them, Bronson, Mike, and Wellington sat in the mansion's palatial living room with a ceiling to floor glass pane that offered spectacular views of the multi-colored flower gardens complete with a creek running through them. The gleaming hardwood floor in the living room complemented the room's high ceilings. Both Bronson and Mike sat on separate striped silk Queen Anne chairs. A massive mahogany coffee table separated them from Wellington. Bronson inwardly cringed. What purpose did the coffee table serve if not to serve coffee? So where was it?

"Mr. Bronson, Mr. Hoover, I want you to tell me everything in detail, and Mr. Bronson, you haven't been making any charges to the credit card I sent you. You're going to force me to pay you."

"You may not want to after we report our findings."

Wellington's eyes widened and a coughing spell that lasted well into the minute mark ensued. He coughed into his hand, his frail chest collapsing and expanding with each effort. When he finished, Wellington took several deep breaths. "Sorry about that. Expect that to happen on a regular basis. Please begin and don't leave anything out, even if you think it'll hurt me."

Bronson and Mike took turns with the narration. When Bronson got to the part about Amanda's involvement, he hesitated, swallowed a breath through his mouth and plunged on. He figured it'd be better for Wellington to hear it from him rather than Detective Randig or Trooper Cannady.

As Bronson spoke, Wellington's eyes watered. "I won't be around to help her. Maybe that's the problem. I always bailed her out. Not this time. I knew she was insanely jealous of Lorraine. I can't believe her jealousy drove her that far."

"Maybe it wasn't all jealousy," Mike said.

"Meaning?" Wellington coughed.

Mike waited until he finished. "Maybe it was greed and anger."

"Is that a reference to me disinheriting her?"

Both Bronson and Mike nodded.

Wellington continued, "I thought I'd be teaching Amanda a lesson. She's getting a hundred thousand dollars and she'll be allowed to keep all of her personal possessions. She could make something good out of that. Instead, she chose this." A tear ran down his cheek. "Do you think my daughter really ordered Lorraine's death?"

Bronson shook his head. "Like I said, that's what the police suspect, but at this point, they don't know for sure."

Wellington nodded and coughed. He took out a handkerchief and wiped his mouth. "I'm going to Lorraine's funeral tomorrow."

Bronson gave him the thumbs up signal. "You're welcome to sit with us. Lorraine would have wanted you to sit up front next to me." Bronson closed his eyes for a second.

Lorraine's funeral. Lorraine's death. The pain that grabbed him caused him to gasp.

Wellington studied Bronson, but said nothing about his pain. "I appreciate the offer, but I will gladly give up my seat to that nice Jenkins boy. Do you know him?"

Bronson remembered his meeting with Daniel Jenkins Jr. He recalled how the youth had impressed him. "I do know him."

"Then you know that Lorraine practically raised him. They had a very strong bond, those two."

"I gathered as much." Bronson waited for Wellington to finish coughing. "Does the Jenkins boy know about her past?"

"Not to my knowledge, but then Lorraine didn't tell me everything."

"I'm glad Lorraine grew up to earn an honest living. Thank you for doing that for my sister."

"Why would you thank me?"

"Aren't you a major contributor to the Daniel Jenkins Campaign for President?"

"I am."

"And were you one of his contributors when he first got involved in politics?"

"I was his only contributor."

"At that time, as a special favor to you, did you make a call to Jenkins or in any other way suggest he hire Lorraine as his son's nanny?"

"No, I didn't. I could have easily, but Lorraine never asked me to. All I know is that one day she came in, grinning from ear to ear and told me she had applied for the nanny's position and had been hired."

Bronson and Mike exchanged looks. He knew Mike was thinking the same thing he was. *Why would Jenkins hire an escort to be his son's nanny?*

EIGHTY-TWO

As BRONSON AND Mike walked down Wellington's driveway, Detective Joe Randig and Trooper Cannady met them as they headed toward the mansion. When their paths crossed, each nodded a hello and kept on going.

When Bronson reached the car, he watched as the butler opened the door and allowed Randig and Cannady to go in. "I feel sorry for Wellington," Bronson snapped his seat belt on.

"Because he's dying?"

"No, because he has a daughter like Amanda. Being a father, every instinct in me orders me to protect Little Carol and Donna."

"Which, by his own admission, is what Wellington has done his entire life. I'm with him, it's time to let go."

"It's called tough love which reminds me, I need to call Daniel Jr." Bronson reached for his cell.

Mike placed his hand over Bronson's phone, preventing him from using it. "Are we heading back to Ellen's?"

Bronson nodded.

Mike removed his hand from the mobile. "Okay, I'll drive and you call Daniel Jr."

Bronson flipped the cell open and punched in the numbers.

Daniel answered on the second ring. "Mr. Bronson, I'm glad you called."

"Drop the mister. My friends call me Bronson."

"Thank you, Mr.—uh, thank you, Bronson. Did anybody ever tell you you're very much like Nanny?"

"Nanny?"

"That's what I called her. Lorraine didn't sound right, and I certainly couldn't call her mom. As it is, my real mother resented her all of the time. That would be like adding gasoline to the fire."

Bronson noticed that Mike put his Bluetooth on, took out his cell, and made a call. "Why did your mom resent my sister?"

"I don't know. My dad denies she does, and Mother and I—well, we've never been close. I know it sounds like sibling rivalry, but Mother always preferred my brother and sister over me. I would like to think Mother resented Nanny because we were close and Mother and I have never been."

"I'm sorry you feel that way. Would you like for me to talk to your mother on your behalf?"

"No, that would only create more problems. Dad aspires to be President and as such, we must be the perfect family. What I told you is in strict confidence."

"I will honor that and keep my mouth shut, but know that if you ever need a friend or a word of advice, I'm here for you."

"I know you are. Thanks, that's comforting to know."

Bronson scratched the bridge of his nose. Every time he thought of the funeral, he began to shiver. "Tomorrow is Lorraine's funeral."

"I…know."

All of a sudden, Daniel sounded like a little kid. Bronson mentally whipped himself for not making the effort to visit him and talk to him in person instead of over the phone. "You mentioned before that you'll go to the funeral with your family. Has anything changed? I'm still willing to pick you up early tomorrow morning so you can ride in the limousine with us."

"I'd like that, but like I suspected, my parents are coming to the funeral to show the world how they support me. My dad would be furious if I didn't arrive at the funeral with them."

Bronson's eyes widened. Daniel Jenkins Sr. would be attending his sister's funeral. Who would have thought that a future President would be one of the mourners. *Ah, Lorraine, you did good.* "I understand your dilemma. By all means, be with your parents."

"I'd rather not. Would you mind saving me a seat next to you at the funeral service? I'd like to be considered part of the Bronson family."

Bronson's Adam's apple bobbed. "You are part of the family." He sat back in the passenger's seat. A fleeting thought bombarded his mind but before he could capture it, it vanished.

EIGHTY-THREE

Soon as Bronson hung up, Mike said, "Bet you didn't even notice that I made a call while you were talking to Daniel Jr."

"I did. I noticed. You shouldn't drive and talk on the cell, you know."

"So arrest me."

"I can't. I'm retired."

"So you say."

"Who did you call?"

"The school. Checked to see when the last time Durango substituted. I pretended to be a loan officer and was checking up on his employment status."

"Very smart. Proud of you. When was the last time he subbed?"

"That would be never." Mike cast Bronson a sideways glance. "Wonder what else he lied about."

"And why he lied."

Bronson's phone chirped. He recognized the number that flashed on the screen— Devono's private line. Bronson showed it to Mike. He arched his eyebrows, and Bronson got the feeling he was saying, I told you so.

"Bronson here."

"I understand congratulations are in order."

"And why would that be?"

"Don't be so modest. You exposed an art theft ring and in the process you found the reason Lorraine was murdered."

That wasn't common knowledge. The news hadn't yet been released. "And how did you know that?"

"I've got my contacts. They also tell me that *Mother Nature's Anger* is worth over a million dollars, and that painting belonged to Lorraine. I want you to get me that La Carcé painting, the original and all the copies."

Shiiit! "I'm not sure I can do that."

"Of course you can. You owe me, and this is one of the ways you're paying me back. So yes, you can and will do it."

Shiiit.

DURANGO SLAMMED DOWN the phone. All the administrative personnel at the Daniel Jenkins School for Boys were informed that if anyone called about him, they were to hail him as the greatest substitute teacher. But apparently someone wasn't told, or that someone refused to follow orders. Either way, Durango would make sure she would get her ass in trouble, then fired.

Not that this would help him any. The damage had already been done. Somehow he'd have to rectify the situation.

Bronson should take the full blame for this mess. He couldn't leave it alone, could he? He had to talk to the Jenkins kid, not that Daniel Jr. knew anything, but Bronson could find a hidden cabin by just looking at a twig.

Durango rubbed his chin as he recalled what his boss had told him. "You make the decision, and I'll support you." Fine. He'd been itching to get Bronson, now he had the excuse. But he would check with his boss, make sure the orders remained the same.

Durango took out his cell, punched in the familiar numbers, and heard the phone ring. After exchanging pleasantries, Durango said, "Bronson is creating waves."

"You're taking care of it, right?"

"Tomorrow's the funeral, a very stressful time for Bronson. After the funeral, there'll be a gathering—especially since the future President of the United States will be there. Bronson is a coffee drinker. I'll drug his drink, take him with me, and that's the last time anyone will hear from that meddling son-of-a-bitch. At first when people notice he's gone, they'll think he wants time to himself. By the time they realize he's gone for good, he'll be dead. Then, Hoover, if need be, will meet with an unfortunate accident."

"You know your business, so I won't question you other than to ask, how you plan to dispose of the body?"

"Remember I told you I'm getting a new swimming pool?"

"You mentioned it, yes."

"They're coming to lay the cement day after tomorrow. Bronson will be rotting at the bottom of my pool while I enjoy doing my laps."

EIGHTY-FOUR

LAUGHTER DANCED THROUGH the playground, filling the air with its soft melody. "You can't catch me," six-year-old Lorraine teased Bronson, then pranced away.

Bronson could catch her all right, but he pretended not to. Let her live in her child world. He was, after all, two years older and much more mature.

Her laughter filled the air and warmed Bronson's heart.

BRONSON, DRENCHED IN perspiration, sat bolt upright, Lorraine's laughter still echoing in his mind.

Carol sat up and wrapped her arms around him. "Is there anything I can do?"

Bronson turned and kissed her lips. "It was just a dream. Go back to sleep. The funeral is in the morning."

The funeral is in the morning.

"Sorry I woke you up." Bronson planted both feet on the floor and stood up.

The funeral is in the morning and he was to blame. If only he'd come when Lorraine first called.

He parted the bedroom drapes just enough for him to glance out. The leaves of the black cherry tree in Ellen's front yard barely swayed as though listening to the same laughing melody embedded in his memory. He closed the drapes, stepped away, and headed for the bed.

Carol had gone back to sleep. Bronson watched her chest slowly rise and lower with each breath she took.

Bronson tried not to move so he wouldn't disturb her.

He wished he too could fall asleep, but for the rest of the night, sleep evaded him.

AT EXACTLY NINE O'CLOCK, the limousine arrived. Mike, Ellen, Carol, and Bronson, all silent, one by one, got in. Bronson found refuge in the scenery as the driver maneuvered the limo in and out of the shadows of the buildings, homes, trees, and shrubs. The green grass in people's yards still dazzled from the early morning dew. The sun's rays ignited the trees causing them to shimmer with a brilliant light, Lorraine's light.

She would never again enjoy any of these sights.

Fate had robbed him of his sister and erased the time they could have spent together. All memories he had of her were those when she was a little kid.

Bronson closed his eyes.

Don't leave me.

THEY WERE THE first to arrive. Bronson heard Carol gasp when she saw the various sizes of the numerous flower arrangements. Bronson, Carol, Mike and Ellen stood by the entrance. Bronson finally stepped forward, leading Carol toward Lorraine. He saw the body, but didn't recognize it. In his mind, Lorraine would always be that little girl he adored.

Bronson felt Mike come up and stand behind him. He placed a supporting hand on Bronson's shoulder. "They say killers like to attend their victim's funerals." Bronson spoke only loud enough for his friend to hear.

"Don't worry, buddy. I've got your back."

Bronson nodded once and reached for Carol's hand, pulling her toward him. "Sis, this is Carol. You would have loved her."

Carol placed her hand on Lorraine's shoulder. "Hi, Lorraine. I know I would have loved you too."

Bronson and Carol stepped aside and busied themselves reading the cards attached to the flower arrangements. Some names Bronson recognized, others, he didn't. Daniel Jenkins and family had sent the largest display, naturally.

By now people had formed a line to pay their respects. Some introduced themselves and briefly talked to Bronson.

"It's hard, saying goodbye to someone you cared for."

Bronson turned to face Devono. "Thank you for caring for my sister."

Devono acknowledged Bronson's statement with a single nod of his head. "Have you done anything about getting me those paintings?"

Bronson's eyes narrowed and his lips formed a thin line. "It's only been a day. Today, I'm burying my sister."

"Precisely why I'm not putting the pressure on you. I'm giving you a couple of days. Then I expect delivery." He walked away.

Bronson's gaze followed him. Devono sat on the third row next to a strikingly beautiful twenty-odd-year-old. She raised her head and Devono kissed her lips. She then laid her head on his shoulder, and Devono wrapped his arm around her.

That S.O.B.

While Devono made himself comfortable, Detective Randig approached. "Didn't know you knew Devono."

"Yeah, I know that scum."

"Considering all the ways to describe him, *scum* is possibly the nicest compliment he's received."

Bronson half-smiled.

"I've been after that scumbag for years," Randig said. "But he's always one step ahead of me. Wish I knew who his sources were. I'd like to nail them and Devono. Seems to me the only way I'll accomplish that is to get him for a small charge—even an unpaid parking ticket. That would lead to more serious charges. But as long as he remains Mr. Squeaky Clean, he's beyond my reach."

"Like Al Capone?"

Randig tilted his head.

"He was caught for income tax invasion."

"I've already checked. Devono pays his taxes on time and the full amount."

"Maybe he's heard of Al Capone too."

The hushed tones that filled the room silenced. Heads swiveled toward the back of the room. Daniel Jenkins, his wife, and their son entered the room. Except to occasionally stop to shake hands or pose for a picture, they worked their way toward Bronson.

"Dad, Mother, this is Harry Bronson."

Jenkins' strong and firm hand shake revealed the strength behind the man. "A pleasure, Mr. Bronson and our condolences."

Mrs. Jenkins, who stood a bit behind her husband, stared at the ground. Her tight lips lightly trembled and her eyebrows furrowed. Either Lorraine's death affected her tremendously or something or someone had angered her. Bronson suspected the latter.

Jenkins said, "We're so sorry for your loss. Lorraine was so special to us. She'll surely be missed."

The pastor approached the podium and people headed for their seats. Bronson placed his hand on Daniel Jr.'s shoulder. "I saved a seat for you on the first row. I know Lorraine would have wanted that." Bronson looked at the congressman. "You don't mind, do you? You can sit behind us, in the second row."

Mrs. Jenkins' lips formed a small smile.

The congressman shook himself in an attempt to cover

his surprise. "Ah, no, of course not." He looked at his son. "You go on up there."

Once his parents were out of hearing range, Daniel leaned toward Bronson. "Thanks."

Bronson put his arm around him and squeezed him. "My pleasure." As they turned to sit, Bronson caught sight of Durango. Lorraine's best friend. A substitute teacher. A liar.

He was one person he wanted to talk to.

The service began and only one chair remained vacant: Wellington's.

EIGHTY-FIVE

During the service, Bronson couldn't help but observe Daniel Jr. The way he raised his head, defiant, but at the same time a whisper of doubt intruded. Looking at him reminded Bronson of Lorraine. He could see her in his actions, his mannerisms.

Of course, he could. From what Bronson gathered, Lorraine raised him, not his real mother. Bronson cast his glance toward her. He caught her staring at him.

After the cemetery service, more people gathered around Jenkins Sr. than Bronson, and that was fine with Bronson. He had wanted Lorraine's funeral to be intimate, only family and close friends. Apparently, Lorraine had a lot of close friends who had a lot of other close friends. At a snail's pace, people headed for their cars. Bronson wondered how many of them would head to Ellen's.

Bronson waited until the last person walked away from the casket before he approached it. He placed his hand on the coffin. "Sis, you asked me not to leave you and I won't. Wherever I go, I'll carry you in my heart. Even though we've been apart for all of these years, I never stopped lovin' you. It was stupid, bitter anger that kept me away. Now I wish that just one more time we could play tag, or see which one of us could leave the best note at the Glacier Valley State Part Covered Bridge. Hell, I wish we could've just talked, gotten to know each other all over again. Sis, I'm so sorry I wasn't there for you. I love you. I already miss you." He lowered his head and his tears rolled down onto the coffin.

He didn't know how long he stayed like that. He only wished...

Someone placed a hand on his shoulder. Bronson straightened up, expecting to see Carol or Mike, maybe even Ellen. Instead, he looked into Daniel Jr.'s tear-filled eyes.

"I c-can't let...her go." Daniel sobbed. "Teach me...to let go. I don't know h-how." A big sob shook his young body.

Bronson wrapped him in his arms and held him. If anyone really loved Lorraine, this kid did. "I want us to sit down together and you fill me in on all that I missed with my sister."

Daniel broke the embrace and took a step back. "And you tell me what she was like as a kid."

Bronson nodded. "Together we'll form a complete picture."

Daniel wiped his tears away. "That sounds really great. I'm looking forward to that day." He turned and his eyes widened.

His mother headed toward him.

He took a small step forward, paused, and then headed her way. When they met, she increased her pace as she walked toward Bronson. She didn't bother to cast a glance at her son. Daniel looked down and continued toward the limousine that had brought him to the funeral. He looked for his father, but as always, a group of people had gathered around him.

Bronson watched the transaction, and then focused his attention on Mrs. Jenkins.

"Ma'am."

"I've been analyzing you. You seem like a good man."

"Thank you, Ma'am."

"Unlike your sister."

Bronson's jaw dropped, and then stiffened. "If you're—"

She waved him off. "I'm not going to sugar coat anything, but I have the answers you're looking for."

"Go on."

"Not here. When we get to Ellen's house. My husband will be too busy campaigning, and Daniel will be busy with his friends." She turned and walked away.

EIGHTY-SIX

BRONSON HAD NEVER seen so much food. Pasta plates, chicken, shrimp, sandwiches, tacos, enchiladas, sweet and sour pork and beef—they were labeled—along with several other types of Oriental food overflowed from the table. The china buffet held a variety of desserts, salads, and breads.

Bronson stood in front of all the food, an empty plate in his hands. All of this for Lorraine, and she couldn't enjoy a bite.

Detective Randig grabbed a plate and stood next to Bronson.

Bronson pointed to the food. "Help yourself."

"I will, later. But first, I have some news."

"Go on."

"We arrested Amanda. She confessed to the art theft and forgery scheme. She implicated the lawyer, Sam Glass. She's willing to do anything to get a deal."

Bronson liked it when the criminals did that. Didn't happen often enough. "That's good. Glad that's over."

"Not quite over. Amanda gave us a list of paintings. Matching the paintings to the buyers greatly reduced the numbers that are unaccounted for. In fact, only eight are still missing and that includes Lorraine's La Carcé piece. I believe that stolen painting is the one that started your investigation."

Bronson played with the rim of his paper plate. Interesting news. Randig hadn't yet discovered Miller's studio. *Mother Nature's Anger* and probably the other seven masterpieces laid scattered among the lesser ones. "Yep, that's the painting that started it all. So it's still missin'?"

"Stolen is the word you're looking for." Randig shifted positions and stared deep into Bronson's eyes. "Is there something you're not telling me?"

Bronson put on his poker face. "No, nothin' at all." At least not yet.

Randig puckered his lips and slowly nodded. "There's more."

Bronson braced himself. He knew he wouldn't like what he was about to hear. "What else?"

"Amanda denies having anything to do with Lorraine's death, either directly or indirectly."

"Do you believe her?"

"If she admits to theft, she's facing prison time. If she admits to murder, she's facing life without parole. She's a smart woman. I'm sure she realizes this. She could be lying."

"Between you and me, what does your gut instinct tell you?"

"She's innocent, but before you say anything, Sam Glass did a lot of things without asking permission. He only let her think she was running the show."

A woman and her teenage son approached them but stopped at a respectable distance. Bronson recognized the boy as being one of Daniel's friends. Bronson nodded a hello. Detective Randig excused himself and began filling his plate. The woman introduced herself and they talked for a few minutes before she and her son wandered off.

Bronson spotted Durango and grabbed the opportunity to talk to him.

Durango sat on the couch, his plate filled with food. When he saw Bronson, he set his plate on the end table, stood up, and waved. "I owe you an apology."

Bronson saw Mike heading toward him. He waited until Mike joined them. "Why do you owe us an apology?"

"I told you both that I met Lorraine at the school and that I sub there. That's a lie."

"Why would you lie?" Bronson asked.

"Because of my real job."

"Which is?"

"I work for Congressman Daniel Jenkins. I handle his career. When I tell people that, they always want something: an introduction, a picture, or an autograph for their great aunt who just worships him. They want me to relay a message to him about one of their causes—something, they always want something, anything. I didn't want to put up with all the B.S. that comes with the job."

Bronson scratched his chin just like he'd seen Durango do. "Mike, you have any causes you want the congressman to support?"

"Can't say I do."

"You want an introduction?"

"Too late. I already met him."

"Yeah, me too. Maybe you want an autograph or a picture?"

"Can't say I do. What about you?"

"Nah, not me."

Durango frowned. "Okay, so I misjudged you both. I already apologized."

"You haven't told us how you actually met my sister."

"As you might suspect, it was my idea that Daniel donate a lot of money to help the struggling school for boys. Daniel always follows my advice, so he poured money into the sinking school. The personnel were so thankful, they changed the name of the school to carry his name. The school became an instant success, and Daniel continues to draw great publicity from that."

"I like stories with happy endings." Bronson glared at Durango. "But that doesn't tell me how you met Lorraine."

"She volunteered her time at the school. She taught music. I made it a point to meet all faculty and staff members, make sure they'd vote for Daniel."

"How well did you know my sister?"

"Very well." Durango stressed the word *very*.

Mike took a small step forward. "Enough to be her lover and be the father of her child?"

Durango rubbed his chin, then noticed Bronson was staring at him. He dropped his hand.

"Mr. Bronson, why don't you and I finish this conversation later on tonight? We can talk after most of the people have left. You never know who's eavesdropping." Durango picked up his plate, sat back down, and continued to eat.

Mike and Bronson walked away. Mike waited until Durango was out of hearing range. "What do you think?"

"I wouldn't want to have him as my brother-in-law."

EIGHTY-SEVEN

BRONSON RETURNED TO the dining table, picked up another plate—he couldn't remember what he did with the one he had before—and stared at the food. It all looked and smelled delicious, but truth be told, he didn't feel hungry. He put the plate back on the stack.

"Since you're not eating, what if we talk?" Mrs. Jenkins bit her lip and quickly glanced around the room. "My husband is very busy. He won't notice that I'm gone."

Jenkins stood among a group of men. He laughed with them and occasionally patted their backs.

"Daniel and his girlfriend have disappeared," Mrs. Jenkins continued.

Bronson's eyebrows arched. Daniel Jr. had a girlfriend? He made a mental note to ask him about her.

"And Willis is busy networking."

Bronson s searched his mind's file where he kept people's names. Nothing clicked. "Willis?"

"Willis Durango, Daniel's campaign manager." So he hadn't lied this time.

"If we don't talk now, I'm afraid I'll lose my nerve. I've got to get this off my chest, and you need to know what I have to say."

"Ellen is lettin' Carol and me use the spare bedroom. We can talk there." He turned and Mrs. Jenkins followed him.

He opened the door and closed it behind her. "Sorry. We don't have any chairs here, but you can sit on the bed."

"Thanks, I'd rather stand." Mrs. Jenkins twisted the

strands of her long blond hair around her index finger. "I'm not sure where to begin."

Bronson also chose to remain standing. From where he stood, he could see the bathroom door closed almost all the way. Bronson always liked to have it open, but Carol always shut it. "Best place is always at the beginning."

"That would be before Daniel and I got married."

"Then begin there."

"Daniel has always been a lady's man." She removed some imagined lint from her sleeves. "I was sure once we married, things would change, but they didn't. They never do. He continued to have a string of affairs—one nighters, you could say. So when your sister came along, I thought it'd be the same."

Bronson froze as his mind spun one question after the other. His sister and Jenkins. Not Durango, but Jenkins. "How long did this affair last?"

"It never ended. She loved him until the day she died."

"And your husband?"

"He loved her too." Mrs. Jenkins' lips quivered and she looked away. "Don't get me wrong. He loves me too, but never the way he loved Lorraine."

"If you don't mind me asking, why didn't you divorce him?"

"A month after we got married, my father got very sick. He had some financial difficulties, and he let all of his insurance lapse. Daniel picked up the bills and provided him with the best care. And he never let me forget."

"He'd pay all the bills as long as you two stayed married."

She nodded.

"Why was it so important that you stay married?"

"Even back then, he had aspirations to be President. He craved a perfect image." She paused and walked toward the window and looked out. Without turning around, she continued. "I too had my foolish pride. I dreamed of being the First Lady, and I knew I would be one day. All I had to do was let her be the mistress. I convinced myself that was all right. She was the mistress, but I was the one who had him."

Bronson sat hard on the bed. He felt a cold wash break out of his face and the vein in his forehead pulsate.

Mrs. Jenkins pivoted to face him. "Once he started the affair with Lorraine, he never again strayed. That, more than anything, really hurt me. He could be faithful to her, but not to me. Our sex life became almost nonexistent, and I hated your sister for that."

Bronson massaged his forehead. "I'm sorry. I don't know what to say."

"You haven't heard the worst."

Bronson looked up at her.

"She got pregnant."

Bronson forced himself to breath in and out through his mouth. He formed a fist and it shook. "What became of the baby?"

"He grew up to be a strong, young man. His name is Daniel Jenkins Jr."

Bronson's eyebrows furrowed. "But he told me he has pictures of you when you were pregnant with him."

"What he has are pictures of me wearing a pillow." She covered her eyes and for a minute Bronson thought she was going to cry. "I know I have taken my anger and resentment out against Daniel, and he's really the only one who's innocent. I owe him the truth." She gnawed her lips. "What I'm about to tell you is going to end my husband's and my dreams of living in the White House, but truthfully, neither of us deserves the honor."

Bronson waited for Mrs. Jenkins to compose herself. He

was afraid to move or ask anything. Even now she seemed reluctant to continue, afraid she had already said too much.

Mrs. Jenkins smiled, actually smiled. "Did you know Daniel will turn eighteen in three days?"

Bronson made another mental note. "No, I didn't."

"Originally, my husband and Lorraine agreed to tell him the truth when he reached legal age. But at this point, we're so close to the White House, Daniel can taste it. He was sure he could convince Lorraine to wait until their son's twenty-first birthday, but when he mentioned it, she refused. He promised her all sorts of things, including divorcing me and marrying her after he became President."

"Would he have done that?"

"Of course not. She was a hooker. The First Lady certainly can't be a former hooker." Her frown twisted into an ugly grimace. "Did you know that's how they met? When he was still just a lawyer, she was his Lady of the Night." Mrs. Jenkins spat out the words as though they left a bad taste in her mouth. "For some reason, though, he fell hard for her. He did everything she wanted and thought she would return the favor by not revealing Daniel's secret until he turned twenty-one. She would have nothing to do with keeping silent, even though she knew it would ruin my husband. He pleaded and pleaded with Lorraine, but she wouldn't change her mind. Then he made a terrible mistake. He told Willis—that's Durango."

Bronson nodded but otherwise sat as stiff as a statue. "And?"

"And I heard them talking. They didn't know I heard. Then Willis…" She wiped the tears away. "He suggested they get rid of Lorraine. Daniel went berserk, no way would he allow anyone to harm his precious Lorraine. But still she wouldn't give in even though she knew it was going to ruin him. Why couldn't Lorraine let him have that? Eventually, my husband…he…he told Willis…to go ahead." She covered her mouth, stifling a large sob.

The door to the bathroom opened and Daniel Jr. stepped out. His wide, tear-filled eyes searched the face of the woman he once had called Mother.

EIGHTY-EIGHT

ALTHOUGH MIKE STOOD three inches shorter than Bronson, he was still big enough to cover most of the door frame leading into the dining room. He quickly scanned the area. Not finding what he was looking for, he moved on into the kitchen, opened the back door, and stepped out. He looked around. He returned inside, walked through the kitchen and dining room and into the living room.

He saw Durango pouring himself a cup of coffee, moving slightly so that Mike could no longer see him pour the cream and the sugar. Mike shifted his eyes away from him. He caught Ellen staring at him, a question mark stamped on her face.

Mike mouthed the word *Bronson*.

Ellen scanned the room and shrugged.

Mike turned and headed down the hallway. He saw the door to Bronson's bedroom slowly open. Bronson stepped out and closed the door behind him.

Mike let out the air he'd been holding but immediately held his breath when he saw Bronson's features. His stiff jaw and firm eyes told Mike something was wrong.

Terribly wrong. He approached Bronson.

"Where's Durango?" Bronson spoke through clenched teeth.

"I saw him a few minutes ago out in the living room."

Bronson nodded and brushed past Mike.

"Whoa." Mike grabbed Bronson's shoulder. "What's going on?"

"That son of a bitch killed my sister. He's the one who pulled the trigger."

Mike thought that nothing in this business would ever surprise him. Yet, he still felt the air sucked out of him. He gasped. "How do you know that?"

Bronson indicated the bedroom. "Mrs. Jenkins confessed. She's there with Daniel Jr."

"Detective Randig and Trooper Cannady are here. I'll go get them."

It was Bronson's turn to hold Mike back. "Not yet."

"Why not?" Mike's eyes narrowed. "What are you planning to do?"

"I only need three minutes at the most alone with Durango. I want to hear what he has to say. Then I want to beat the shit out of him."

"That's not a good idea."

"Then get Randig and Cannady there, but not before I get the chance to throw at least one good punch."

"Bronson, don't."

But Bronson ignored Mike. He turned and headed for the living room. Soon as he entered, he spotted Durango, sitting on the couch. Bronson caught his eye and signaled for him to join him outside. Durango's twisted grin didn't get past Bronson.

Durango picked up the cup of coffee he had prepared and headed outside. "I was just going to get you." He led Bronson down the driveway and to his car, a black Mercedes. He opened the car door for Bronson. "I know you like coffee and you probably have been too stressed to fix yourself a cup. So I took the liberty of pouring you a cup." He handed the still steaming cup to Bronson. "Hope you like it."

Bronson stared at the cup. Durango was right about that. He hadn't drunk his coffee, and it did smell good. He reached for the cup.

EIGHTY-NINE

WELLINGTON HALF-SMILED at the chambermaid. "How long have you worked for me?"

"Twenty-four years, sir."

Twenty-four years, and he couldn't remember her name. He was sure that at one time he had known it. "You'll find that my will takes very good care of you, and the butler, and the cook, and the chauffeur, and the downstairs maid."

"Thank you, sir, but we aren't expecting anything."

"You should be. You and the rest of the staff have always been kind to me, even more so than my own daughter."

"I'm sorry about Ms. Amanda, sir."

"It's my fault. Lorraine used to tell me that I spoiled her too much. As always, Lorraine was right." A tear pearled in his eye. "Today is her funeral."

"I'm sorry your health prevented you from going."

"Don't feel sorry for me. Lorraine is here with me. She's ready to take me home."

The chamber maid gasped. "Oh, sir, don't say that." She placed her opened hands on her chest like the heroine of a silent movie.

"Before I go, I need for you to promise me you'll give Bronson the letter."

"Of course, sir." She patted her pant pocket. "I have it right here, and I will personally give it to him."

"Thank you." Wellington smiled and focused his gaze at the far end of the wall in his bedroom. "I'm ready. Take me home." He closed his eyes and took his last breath.

"IF YOU DON'T MIND, I'd rather not get in the car," Bronson leaned back on the Mercedes, brought the coffee cup up to his lips, and smelled it. "You don't mind if we just stay out here, do you?"

"No, of course not. It's just that we'd have more privacy inside the car." Durango left the front door opened. "Is something wrong with your coffee? I noticed you're not drinking it."

"No, absolutely nothing wrong. I have a ritual I follow. I enjoy its aroma for several minutes before I enjoy its taste." He brought it up to his nose and smelled it again. "Ahhh." He lowered the cup. "You were going to tell me if you fathered Lorraine's child."

"Why is that so important to you?"

"Lorraine would have wanted me to follow up on that. Make sure her baby is well taken care of."

Durango took a deep breath. "You're right. Lorraine did get pregnant. This was shortly before she changed careers, from escort to nanny."

"Why would Jenkins hire her with the history she had?"

Durango eyed Bronson's coffee. Bronson once again brought it to his nose and smelled it.

"Jenkins knew Lorraine was my girlfriend. I told him Lorraine would be great for the job. He took my word for it, never checked her out. And as it turned out, she did a fantastic job. Even up to now, Jenkins doesn't know about Lorraine's past."

"Where's the baby?"

"Lorraine said she wasn't worthy to raise a child. She wanted to cleanse herself and prove she could be a good person, but until then, she didn't want anything to do with raising our child. I wanted to get married and raise our baby. Lorraine said, 'No.' She had an abortion. We were never the same after that. We still loved each other, but that special spark vanished."

Bronson drew a deep slow breath. Durango told a pretty convincing story, but so had Mrs. Jenkins. He thought of Daniel Jr., so much like Lorraine but with Jenkins' build and features. "Is there anythin' you wouldn't say or do to protect Jenkins?"

Durango eyed the still untouched coffee then looked into Bronson's eyes of steel.

A loud crash resonated from inside Ellen's house, followed by a woman's piercing scream.

Durango bolted toward the house, Bronson close behind him.

NINETY

"My whole life has been nothing but a lie." Daniel Jr. continued to stand by the bathroom door, glaring at the woman he had been led to believe was his Mother.

Mrs. Jenkins took a hesitant step toward him. "Daniel, I'm sorry. I didn't want you to hear it like this. If I'd known you were in the bathroom—"

"Doesn't matter, does it? It doesn't change anything. Dad killed Nanny." Daniel's eyes widened as the words sank in. He placed his opened hand on his forehead. "He killed her." He bolted toward the bedroom door, threw it open, and ran down the hallway.

Behind him, Mrs. Jenkins smiled.

Daniel stood shaking in the entryway leading to the living room. The more he watched his father, the faster his breathing became. His lips trembled and his fists shook.

Jenkins Sr. stood among a group of people, laughing and talking with them.

Daniel took a baby step forward and then another step until he found himself running toward his father. His hands formed fists and he held them in front of his chest, a prize fighter entering the arena.

Jenkins saw him coming and his eyebrows furrowed. He stepped around some people. "Excuse me."

People cleared a path between the two.

"Son, what's wrong?"

"You killed my mother." He spat the words out, loud and clear.

Jenkins half-smiled, half frowned. "What are you talking about?" He pointed to the entryway where Mrs. Jenkins stood, her arms crossed, her eyes sparkling with amusement. "She's right there."

"Not her. My real mother, Nanny, Lorraine Bronson."

Jenkins gasped and bit his lip. He straightened up, puffing himself up like a proud peacock.

"It's no use lying anymore," Mrs. Jenkins said from the doorway. "Your little game is over. He knows the truth."

Jenkins opened his mouth, but nothing came out.

"You killed my mother." Daniel's face contorted into an ugly grimace and continued his advance toward his father. "You killed her." He pounded his father's chest.

"Daniel, I didn't. She—"

"You lie." He threw him a punch that sent Jenkins crashing down to the floor.

Someone screamed.

Mike, Cannady, and Randig, who had been on their way out, turned to stop the fight.

The front door opened and Durango stepped in. In a matter of seconds, he assessed the situation and grabbed the woman nearest to him. As he did, he reached into his pocket, pulled out a revolver, and held it to the woman's temple.

She screamed and panic broke out in the room. People scattered in all directions in an attempt to get away from Durango.

Randig and Cannady drew their weapons and pointed them at Durango. "Drop it. Now." Randig's authoritative voice clearly told Durango he was in control, not the other way around.

Bronson stepped in and Durango waved him away from

him. "This is your fault. You wouldn't let go until you found the truth. Now it's too late for me. I ruined my life, but I want to set the record straight so no more lives are wasted. The congressman always trusted me and it's time I earn that trust."

Bronson nodded. "We're listening."

"The great congressman's wife gave me real good sex."

"Shut up, you fool." Mrs. Jenkins eyes narrowed and her lips trembled.

"In return, I killed Lorraine for her." Durango kept the revolver on the woman he held captive. "You were next, Bronson. I was supposed to kill you tonight, but you already knew that. That's why you wouldn't drink that coffee."

"I said shut up." Mrs. Jenkins bolted toward him, her fingers curved like claws.

Mike grabbed her and held her back.

She squirmed. "Shut up. Shut up. Shut up."

Bronson took a step toward Durango, but he caught the movement and inched the revolver closer to the woman's forehead.

Bronson raised his hands. "This is between you and me. She has nothing to do with it. Let her go."

"Sure. Anything you say." Durango threw her toward Bronson, swung the revolver, aimed, and fired.

At the same time, Randig released a round, and Durango tumbled to the floor.

"You okay?" Bronson held the woman Durango had held captive.

She nodded and her eyes filled with tears.

Bronson released her and knelt down. He felt Durango's neck for a pulse. He shook his head and glanced at Mrs. Jenkins. She lay on the floor, blood trickling out of her right shoulder from where Durango had shot her.

Cannady checked on Mrs. Jenkins' vitals. "She's okay, but we need to call 911."

Mike reached for the cell and made the call.

It took a couple of men to hold Daniel Jr., who fought to get free.

Jenkins Sr., still on the floor, halfway sat up, his eyes bigger than a full moon. He first glanced at his son, then at Durango's body, and finally at his wife. "Is that true? You set up Lorraine's and Bronson's deaths?"

In spite of her injury, Mrs. Jenkins squirmed her way to a sitting position and glared at her husband.

"Why did you do that?"

"They were getting in the way. After all I've gone through, I deserve to be First Lady. I earned that privilege. Then watching you here at the funeral, I changed my mind." Venom spat out of Mrs. Jenkins' eyes. "I've always believed that all that's important to you is your lousy ambition. You want to be President and for that you're willing to sacrifice everything, including our marriage. I saw the pain in your eyes when you saw Lorraine's body. Why couldn't you think Daniel was ours? You had no right to ask me to do that. And for what reason? So you can keep that Mr. Clean image alive." She breathed hard through her mouth several times and held her arm. "Your career is ruined and I'm the one who brought you down. So how do you feel now?"

In the not too far distance, sirens wailed, announcing their emergency. Within minutes, Ellen's house swarmed with police, the paramedics, and the press.

Bronson wrapped his arm around Daniel Jr. and led him back to the privacy of the bedroom. Both Ellen and Carol stayed with him while Bronson talked to the police.

NINETY-ONE

DANIEL JENKINS SR. clung to the shadow of the once-great man he had been. He swore he would create a new start, but often the public's unforgiving nature builds a wall too high to climb. Jenkins had become the main source of every comic's routine, especially late night TV hosts. Depression strangled Jenkins.

After a three days' stay in different motel rooms, Mike and Ellen felt ready to return home. "You sure you want me to move back with you?" Mike leaned on the dresser as he watched Ellen organize her clothes. It had taken him less than five minutes to pack and his suitcase showed it. "I'll be fine here in the motel."

Ellen finished rolling her blouses and placed them in neat rows in the suitcase. "We're both mature adults, and we need to find out if we—if I—can get past this. The next few days will be crucial, and we need to face them together."

Back at the camper, Bronson once again donned the black suit he had worn for Lorraine's funeral. This time he wore it for Wellington.

He and Carol sat toward the back of the very well attended service. The police hadn't released Amanda but Bronson would be willing to bet she wouldn't have wanted to come. She would rather miss her father's funeral than face the public's eye.

Bronson looked at the sea of faces. Some he recognized, but only because they were VIPs. From where Bronson sat, he had a clear view of the casket. Bronson imagined that Wellington and Lorraine stood side-by-side in Heaven. The image brought him a half-smile and a half-tear.

When the service concluded, Bronson grasped Carol's hand and led her out.

"Mr. Bronson?" Someone called from behind.

Bronson stopped and pivoted to face a woman in her mid-fifties. She wore a simple black dress and a plain gold chain. Bronson thought he recognized her, but couldn't place her.

"I'm Julia Nenji."

Bronson shook her hand, introduced Carol, and searched his mind. He had seen her before. Where? An image flickered in his mind and he remembered. At Wellington's. "You look different out of your uniform."

She smiled. "You do remember me. I didn't think you would. We never talked."

"My loss."

Julia looked at Carol. "Is he always this charming?"

"Sometimes he's more."

Bronson felt the blood rush to his face. He had never learned how to accept compliments.

"Lucky you." Julia opened her purse and pulled out a sealed envelope. "I was with Mr. Wellington when he passed away. His last thoughts were of you. He wanted to make sure I personally delivered this to you." She handed Bronson the envelope. "He really took to you, just as he did Lorraine."

Bronson reached for the envelope and stuffed it in his jacket pocket. They chatted for a few minutes longer before she joined the rest of the household staff. Bronson and Carol left the funeral.

Once inside the car, Carol pointed to Bronson's jacket pocket. "What's that about?"

"Ohh, you are a curious one, aren't you?" He reached into his pocket and took out a handkerchief to wipe his glasses.

Carol playfully hit him in his arm. "Harry Bronson, you open up that envelope right now."

"Not only are you curious, you're nosey—not to mention bossy." He winked and smiled.

"Harry Bronson."

That was her warning tone. Bronson smiled. Truth be known, he felt every bit as curious as Carol, and Carol knew it. He pulled out the envelope and opened it. He cleared his throat and read it aloud.

Bronson,

Did you know Lorraine had a tendency to be very stubborn? Reason I mentioned it is because you're exactly the same. In a way, I found that endearing but also frustrating.

That is in reference to the credit card I gave you and you still haven't really used. Okay, I can understand why you didn't want to charge to find your sister's killer.

So I'm hiring you for another job. I want you to find Lorraine's child. To that purpose, I put $300,000 in the bank to pay all of the monthly charges I'm hoping you make.

If you don't use the card, the money will sit in the bank until it eventually turns over to the state as unclaimed property. So use the card. Take your wife on a cruise, eat outrageously priced—but oh, so delicious—meals.

Enjoy the money, no strings attached, but find Lorraine's child. When you do, I have set another $300,000 (same bank, different account) aside.

You, as the guardian, will have complete control of that money.

Use it to pay for the teen's education or get him/her a car. Use it anyway you see fit.

In the event there's no such child, set up a scholarship account for deserving teens.

It has been a pleasure working with you.
Mark Wellington III

NINETY-TWO

BRONSON AND CAROL agreed to do a Bed and Breakfast tour of the area. Mike and Ellen would join them. The expenses would be charged to the credit card. The remaining money would supplement the Bronson's retirement fund.

Daniel Jr. returned to school. Bronson and Carol—and hopefully Mike—would come down for graduation and stay at Ellen's. Daniel Jr. planned to spend the summer between high school and college with Bronson. "But Lizzy will be with us a lot," Daniel wrapped his arm around her. Bronson and Carol both thought Lizzy would one day make a great addition to the family.

"This may not come as a shock to either of you," Daniel said, "but I hope to go into politics and clear the Jenkins' name of the sting of gossip. I want the world to know there can be good, clean politicians whose main concern is what the public wants and needs."

"Oh Lordy," Carol said. "That's what we need, a nephew in politics."

LIKE MIKE, BRONSON finished packing way before Carol and Ellen did. Bronson watched Carol pack, unpack, and repack. He shook his head. She never failed to amaze him.

She opened the medicine cabinet and took out the jars and gadgets she thought she'd need. She stood staring at the contents and caught Bronson studying her. "Shoo, scat. Go away. You're making me nervous, and I'll forget to pack something important."

That's what Bronson had been hoping to hear. "I'm going to grab me a cup of coffee at the local bakery."

"One teaspoon of sugar."

"Yes, Ma'am." He saluted her.

She stuck out her tongue at him and returned to packing.

Mike, who had a similar conversation with Ellen, decided to join him. Once in the car, Mike looked at Bronson. "Where to?"

"How about that bakery beside the gas station?"

"Is that before or after we do whatever you're planning on doing?"

Bronson flashed him the wide-eyed innocent look. "Whatever makes you think I have an alternate agenda?"

"Can't drive if you don't tell me where to go."

"Do you remember how to get to Miller's secret art studio?"

"Yeeeah, why?"

"Devono's expectin' Lorraine's paintin'. I've got to deliver."

Mike rubbed the bridge of his nose. "We'll be breaking and entering—again. Then even though the painting is considered still missing, we'll be stealing. You've got to draw the line somewhere."

"I'm one step ahead of you. I've already drawn the line. Now let's go before the girls start wonderin' what we're up to."

Mike frowned and drove off.

ALMOST AN HOUR later, Bronson and Mike stood—they refused to sit down—in Devono's office, the painting between them.

Devono smiled. "Don't know much—actually nothing—about art, but those sure look nice. Can't tell the difference between the original and the forgeries. You say the original is the one in the fancy frame?"

"Yep."

"I knew you'd come through." Devono indicated Mike. "It surprises me that you would involve your ex-partner at the scene of a crime."

"He's here as a witness."

Devono leaned back on his over-stuffed chair behind his desk. "Explain what you mean."

"We're through. I'm not doing anythin' else for you."

"Don't seem to me you have much choice."

"Sure I do. One, I'm not from here. Soon, I'll be gone." Bronson raised his fingers to emphasize the numbers. "Two, and more important, I know things about you that you wouldn't want me to tell the police."

"Are you blackmailing me?" Devono's eyes sparkled with amusement.

"Call it what you want. We are through." He turned and walked out. Mike followed him.

Once in the car, Bronson took a deep breath. "Now for a good cup of coffee."

Mike frowned and drove off.

Bronson opened his cell and punched some numbers. "Detective Joe Randig, please."

Bronson waited a few seconds while Randig came to the phone. Mike cast him a whimsical look.

"Detective Randig, Bronson here. I have an address for you."

"Who's address?"

"Remember the artist who was murdered a couple of days ago?"

"You're talking about Larry S. Miller?" Randig said.

"That's the one. He had another art studio that he kept secret. That's the address that I'm givin' you."

"And how do you know this? Oh, never mind. I don't want to know. But tell me why I need to go to that art studio."

"I'm sure if you look through the large pile of paintings scattered throughout the room, you'll find all of the missin' paintings you're lookin' for. When you get there, look for the paintings with fancy frames. Behind those paintings, you'll find the original missin' pieces and all forgeries."

"Let me grab a pen." Seconds later, Randig was back on the phone. "Give me that address."

Bronson did. "I have one more suggestion."

"That is?"

"I remember you tellin' me that you wished you could get Devono. All you needed was one small thing to pin on him."

"I did say that. Why?"

"If you hurry to his office, he's in possession of one of the stolen pieces."

"Which one is that?" Randig's tone sounded guarded.

"François La Carcé's *Mother Nature's Anger*."

"And how did he get hold of that piece?"

Bronson remained quiet.

"I see," Randig said. "Doesn't really matter, does it? The important thing is we'll get him with the goods. And speaking of getting him, the lawyer spilled his guts and handed us the twins. Both are looking at a very long jail sentence."

"That's good news."

"I agree and the credit goes to you. Thanks for what you've done. Working with you has been…different. Take care of yourself and stay out of my jurisdiction."

"Plan to." Bronson disconnected and smiled at Mike. "Let's get us a good cup of coffee."

* * * * *

ABOUT THE AUTHOR

HIGHLY ACCLAIMED AUTHOR L. C. Hayden is the creator of the popular Harry Bronson series. Five Star released the previous book in the series, *When Death Intervenes*, on April 2010 as a hardback and in 2012, Harlequin released the paperback edition. Prior to that, *Why Casey Had to Die*, became an Agatha Award Finalist for Best Novel and a Pennsylvania Top 40 Pick. Its editions include hardcover, paperback, audio, e-book, and large print.

Casey followed *What Others Know*, a Left Coast Crime nominee for the prestigious best mystery award. Hayden's other mysteries are *Where Secrets Lie*, *When Colette Died*, and *Who's Susan?* The books have made the Barnes & Noble Top Ten Bestseller List and have been featured on Oprah's Online Reading Café.

Her non-mysteries include *Angels Around Us*, which rose to the Kindle Angels # 1 Best Seller List. This book along with *When Angels Touch You* are spiritually uplifting books that deal with miracles and angels. *The Drums of Geruld Hurd*, a horror novel, promises all the punch of a first-class horror story and the sensitivity of a romance.

Hayden's latest non-mystery release, *Bell Shaped Flowers*, is a young adult inspirational novelette along the lines of Hallmark Hall of Fame.

Besides being an accomplished author, Hayden is a popular speaker who is often in demand. She has done workshop and school presentations, has spoken to clubs and organizations, and was recently hired by several major cruise lines to speak about writing while cruising all over the world. From October 2006 to October 2007, Hayden hosted Mystery Writers of America's only talk show, *Murder Must Air*.

REQUEST YOUR FREE BOOKS!

2 FREE NOVELS
PLUS 2 FREE GIFTS!

Your Partner in Crime

YES! Please send me 2 FREE novels from the Worldwide Library® series and my 2 FREE gifts (gifts are worth about $10). After receiving them, if I don't wish to receive any more books, I can return the shipping statement marked "cancel." If I don't cancel, I will receive 4 brand-new novels every month and be billed just $5.49 per book in the U.S. or $6.24 per book in Canada. That's a savings of at least 31% off the cover price. It's quite a bargain! Shipping and handling is just 50¢ per book in the U.S. and 75¢ per book in Canada.* I understand that accepting the 2 free books and gifts places me under no obligation to buy anything. I can always return a shipment and cancel at any time. Even if I never buy another book, the two free books and gifts are mine to keep forever.

414/424 WDN F4WY

Name	(PLEASE PRINT)

Address		Apt. #

City	State/Prov.	Zip/Postal Code

Signature (if under 18, a parent or guardian must sign)

Mail to the **Harlequin®** Reader Service:
IN U.S.A.: P.O. Box 1867, Buffalo, NY 14240-1867
IN CANADA: P.O. Box 609, Fort Erie, Ontario L2A 5X3

Want to try two free books from another line?
Call 1-800-873-8635 or visit www.ReaderService.com.

* Terms and prices subject to change without notice. Prices do not include applicable taxes. Sales tax applicable in N.Y. Canadian residents will be charged applicable taxes. Offer not valid in Quebec. This offer is limited to one order per household. Not valid for current subscribers to the Worldwide Library series. All orders subject to credit approval. Credit or debit balances in a customer's account(s) may be offset by any other outstanding balance owed by or to the customer. Please allow 4 to 6 weeks for delivery. Offer available while quantities last.

Your Privacy—The Harlequin® Reader Service is committed to protecting your privacy. Our Privacy Policy is available online at www.ReaderService.com or upon request from the Harlequin Reader Service.

We make a portion of our mailing list available to reputable third parties that offer products we believe may interest you. If you prefer that we not exchange your name with third parties, or if you wish to clarify or modify your communication preferences, please visit us at www.ReaderService.com/consumerchoice or write to us at Harlequin Reader Service Preference Service, P.O. Box 9062, Buffalo, NY 14269. Include your complete name and address.

WWL13R

ReaderService.com

Manage your account online!

- Review your order history
- Manage your payments
- Update your address

---

*We've designed
the Harlequin® Reader Service
website just for you.*

Enjoy all the features!

- Reader excerpts from any series
- Respond to mailings and special monthly offers
- Discover new series available to you
- Browse the Bonus Bucks catalog
- Share your feedback

Visit us at:
ReaderService.com

RS13